TEXAS KISSING

HELENA NEWBURY

Third Edition

© Copyright Helena Newbury 2015

The right of Helena Newbury to be identified as the author of this work has been asserted by her in accordance with the Copyright, Design and Patents Act 1988

This book is entirely a work of fiction. All characters, companies, organizations, products and events in this book, other than those clearly in the public domain, are fictitious or are used fictitiously and any resemblance to any real persons, living or dead, events, companies, organizations or products is purely coincidental.

Front cover photo: 4x6 / iStockPhoto
Rear cover photo: Phil Marley

Cover design by Mayhem Cover Creations

This book contains adult scenes

ISBN: 1516812603

ISBN-13: 978-1516812608

ACKNOWLEDGEMENTS

Thank you to:

My fantastic street team!

My editor

And to all my readers :)

Texas Kissing

ONE

Lily

I USE BLACKOUT DRAPES but Texas morning sun *don't give a damn*. It crept around the edges and through the pinprick holes where the material had worn thin and lit up my sleeping face like a laser. When I blearily opened my eyes, it was with my hands up over them, trying to push away the morning like it was a dog licking my face.

It was going to be one of those days.

I figured I might as well get it over with, so I knelt up on my bed and lifted the drapes. I tentatively opened my eyes just enough to glimpse a massive Texas sky dusted with marshmallow clouds, the sun already hot on my face through the rear window.

I should explain *rear window*. My home is a Greyhound bus.

I needed a project, when I arrived in Texas. Buying the bus and converting it was perfect—complicated enough that I could immerse myself in it for weeks and forget what I'd left behind.

My bed is where the last four rows of seats would

have been. A single bed, because that's all I need.

Walk forward through a curtain and you get to the kitchen. I ripped out all the seats and added a counter, stove and sink. Water and power comes from the farm I'm parked on—the dried-up creek bed wasn't any use to anyone, so the farmer's happy to let me park there for a few hundred dollars a month.

Downstairs, I expanded the bus's bathroom. You know the luggage bays under the bus where you stuff your suitcase? That's where my tub and shower are.

Why a bus? Because it's always ready to move.

My name is Lily, and I'm on the run.

***

People say that, when you move somewhere new, it takes a couple of days to acclimatize to the weather. It's been two years and I'm still waiting. In winter, I long for snow and the slippery-smooth feel of a freshly-broken-off icicle. In fall and spring I hanker after those cool, comfortable days where the rain's just cleared the air and everything feels fresh and new. And in summer, like it is now...I just want to be in civilization, where the outdoors is tamed—something to be enjoyed from behind darkened glass in the cool breeze of air conditioning.

I miss New York.

I left the drapes closed (have you any idea *how many* drapes you have to make for an entire bus?) and padded in my nightshirt downstairs to the bathroom. It was way too hot for a nightshirt, even with the bus's a/c, but I'm not one of those women who's comfortable walking around in her underwear, even when there's no one to see.

I've rigged up a system of mirrors to bring sunlight down from the roof of the bus to the bathroom, so it feels almost like showering outdoors. I washed my hair, drawing conditioner through the ends so that—hopefully—it would freak out slightly less when the sun hit it. You would have thought raven-black, Italian-American hair would feel like it's in its element in Texas, but not mine. Back in New York, I think I spoiled it with fancy salons and now it sulkily refuses to cooperate.

Ditto my skin. My ancestors, I'm told, came from some village in Sicily, so I know that in theory I can tan with the best of them. But my skin's as pale as my name—Lily—suggests because....

Well, because I spend a lot of time indoors.

Part of that has to do with having *too much* skin. Too much flesh. I was never the slender, foxy girl, bouncing around New York from party to party. That's the movie star role. I'm more like the comedy sidekick, the one who has to struggle into her plus-size jeans and is there to make the main character look good.

That was always okay with me; I knew my place.

But that slender, foxy girl I was best friends with? She's dead. And I'm not anyone's comedy sidekick, because I don't dare become friends with anyone anymore.

***

When I'd finished patting the water from my body with a faded towel, I dressed in a blouse and jeans and got ready to go out. *Not* my favorite thing in the world. With grocery deliveries and an internet connection, I can go a week without leaving the bus and that's exactly how I like it. But there was business to attend to.

I reached under my bed and pulled a lever and the whole thing folded up on springs. Beneath it is my work area.

On the underside of the bed, in little plastic pouches, were over thirty fake passports and driver's licenses, all in various stages of completion. More pouches held my raw materials—the special paper and bindings, the holograms and electronic chips that are supposed to be impossible to fake.

I picked up the bag containing this month's delivery: five of my special "All in One" packs (passport, driver's license, social security card—buy together and save!) and I was ready.

Almost ready. Also attached to the underside of the bed, where I can grab it quickly in the night, is my gun, a cute little snub-nosed thing that fits in my purse. It has mother-of-pearl grips and looks like a toy, and it'll happily chew up anyone I turn it on. In two years, I'd never had to use it. But I was ready to.

***

I hate crowds. Not in a social phobia sort of a way. I just get kind of antsy and breathless and irrationally angry and there's never enough air....

Okay, maybe I'm on the social phobia *spectrum*.

Whatever, I don't like crowds. Or the hooting, crowing war cries Texan men feel it's necessary to give when they're doing anything exciting. Or animals, which are big and unpredictable.

So a rodeo? Not my thing.

Gold Lake is a pretty small town and really doesn't need a sports arena anything like as big as the one it has—I suspect some greasing of palms went on somewhere to get it built—but now that it's here, the rodeos, Monster Truck shows and other events bring in big crowds. For the whole two years I'd been in town, I'd studiously avoided going anywhere near it.

But for some reason, that was where Francisco wanted to meet and I wanted to keep him happy. I'd been supplying passports to the Mexican cartel since I arrived in Texas and they'd become my biggest customer.

I paid and went in...and then realized my mistake. The message had said they were in Block Q. I'd come in through the wrong entrance and I was way on the other side of the arena. I'd have to thread my way between about a million people to get to them. I felt my skin crawling at the thought of all those bodies pressed against me. Plus, I'd be late. And I *hate* being late.

Then I spotted the stairs heading down under the arena. Some sort of backstage area—I could cut through and emerge on the other side.

I hurried down the stairs. It was dark down there and pleasantly cool. I passed storerooms and dressing areas and then the floor turned to bare concrete, dusted with hay. And then—

Oh crap. I'd reached a dead end. There was a wooden fence and, beyond it, an open area with straw on the floor, so big that the edges disappeared into the darkness to my left and right. Some sort of holding area for horses or something, although it seemed to be empty at the moment.

And there, on the far side was the exit. I could see

the sunlight blazing in and hear the crowd roaring. I could cut across and be at my meeting in a few minutes.

I climbed inelegantly up the fence, swung my leg over and clambered down the other side. Then I started to trudge through the straw. It was further than it had looked to the other side.

My first sign that something was wrong was a snorting noise, like someone was trying to blow an obstruction out of their nose. It was much, much louder than it had any right to be. I spun around, trying to place it, but could see nothing.

Then two gleaming white horns emerged from the darkness.

Oh shit.

I'm 5'5". The bull's shoulders came to the top of my head. It was only walking at the moment, but each step was a pissed-off stamp. It was eying me with a look that said, *what the fuck are you doing in my home?*

I glanced around. I was roughly in the middle of the area, too far from either fence to get there in time.

Maybe if I keep still. Don't antagonize it.

The bull pawed at the ground, sending straw flying. *Shit! That's bad, right?*

It charged.

I froze for a split-second, by which time the bull had picked up a terrifying amount of speed. When I started running, the ground was shaking with the thunder of its hooves. I knew I wasn't supposed to look back but I did—and saw the thing had its head down, its horns pointed right at me. It was easily going to outrun me, well before I hit the fence. And then I was going to be—my stomach lurched. *Gored.*

I raced for the fence, but with my body I'm not exactly nimble. The bull snorted and the sound was horribly close. I couldn't stand the thought of it hitting me in the back, of not knowing when it would happen, so I spun around, still stumbling backward. The bull was ten feet away, eight, six—

A man crashed into the bull from the side and gripped its horns. Any normal man would have been tossed aside, or simply flapped around like a balloon attached to a freight train.

But this wasn't a normal man. His hulking body actually made the bull look small. He hauled on the bull's horns, steering it away from me. The two of them missed me by inches and came skidding to a halt a few feet away.

"Now *you*," the man told the bull, "cool your damn heels!"

The bull glared at him and snorted. I caught my breath, expecting it to charge him. But, as the two of them faced off, the bull seemed to lose confidence. And no wonder—the guy was *massive*. He looked as if he was ready to wrestle the thing to the ground, if he had to.

"Go on!" the guy told it. "*Get!*" With his accent, it sounded more like *git!*

The bull snorted a final time...and sulkily plodded away.

The man turned to face me and I looked up...up...*up* into his face. A black cowboy hat threw a shadow over his hair, but I could just make out that the curls were very dark brown, not black. His eyes were the same clear blue as the Texas sky, stunningly bright against his tanned face. He was breaking into a broad grin and those lips above that roughly-stubbled jaw looked...dangerously enticing. *Oh Christ, he's gorgeous.*

"Well," he said. "Lookee what we have here." His accent was as broad as a prairie and as hard and unyielding as a cliff. It seemed to make my whole body vibrate and sing, as if I'd been crafted specifically to react to it.

I just...*stared* at him. There was a lot to stare at. He was a full head taller than me, well over six feet. And he was wide enough that I could barely see the retreating bull behind him—he blocked out the world. But it was all muscle. His pecs were like tanned, curving footballs, his abs a series of hard, smooth-edged ridges. And all of it was the same golden-brown tan.

I could see all this because he was—*ulp*—stripped to the waist. Black cowboy boots, tight jeans with a broad leather belt and then...just all this *man,* tanned and hard. My brain kept trying to process it but the sheer *maleness* of him kept overpowering it. He was too big, too close. Trying to study him from that distance was as impossible as studying a hurricane close up.

And yet...I didn't move back. Couldn't move back, even though he was so big and so close. You know that feeling you get when a guy invades your space and you get antsy and uncomfortable and you want to step back?

This was the opposite of that.

I was caught in his gravity, somehow, actually *affected* by his nearness. His presence was moving things inside me, sending energy twisting and spiraling down to my groin.

"They call me Bull," said the man. Damn, that

voice! Like gold-flecked molasses invading my brain. "And who, lovely lady, are *you?*"

TWO

Bull

Three goddamn minutes earlier

I WAS TALKING TO A HORSE. Don't look at me like that. You're *goddamn straight* I talk to horses, especially the ones I'm going to ride. If you're going to put on a show with a partner, and that partner is going to spend most of it doing its best to kill you, wouldn't you want to develop a rapport?

Besides, they make a lot more sense than people, most of the time. Especially the females.

When I heard Max snort I turned around, puzzled. I'd been around that bull for the best part of a year and he only got mad when there was a stranger around. But there was no one backstage except me, Max and the bronco I was talking to.

I hopped the fence and wandered across the enclosure towards Max. That's when I saw her. She was standing dead still in Max's area, her white blouse all lit up from the overhead lights. Her skin was creamily, richly white and it was set off by her long black hair. It hung right down her back, wavy and thick and glossy. The sort of hair you want to plunge your fingers into and wrap around your hands as you bring it up to your face. Somehow, I knew it was going to smell good.

Her skin was so pale and her hair so dark, and that white blouse she was wearing was glowing so much from the overhead lights, that she would have looked like a ghost...except that, as my eyes tracked down, I could see she was deliciously solid. Tight blue jeans hugged curving hips—ones that made me want to spin her around, *now,* to get a look at the incredible ass they promised. She wasn't like most of the girls who hung around the rodeo, their shirts peeking open to show stomachs as taut as trampolines. She looked gorgeously soft and feminine, and that was before my eyes even got to her tits.

Oh, holy mother of Jesus, her tits.

Pressing out the front of her blouse were two full cantaloupes of womanly delight. When God sculpted her, he'd blessed her with generous scoops, firm and weighty, the sort you immediately want to stroke your hands up under and lift and just enjoy for a moment before you even touch the nipples. I didn't even have her clothes off yet and I could already imagine how they'd feel under my palms. God*damn!*

This girl *had* to be mine.

And then the sound of Max pawing at the ground woke me from my little trance. Aw, hell.

I raced over there, trying my damndest not to get distracted by the way her breasts bounced as she ran. She hadn't seen me yet, too focused on fleeing. But she wasn't going to reach the fence in time. It was all over, unless—

I pulled Max away from her and hustled him out of there. Then I slowly turned around, savoring the moment. When it comes to getting a girl's panties off, you can keep your billionaire yachts and your fancy champagne because there ain't nothing better than saving her life.

I couldn't stop myself taking a deep breath in when I saw her. I figured she was a couple of years younger than me: twenty-three, or so and *damn*, she was even better up close. She had big, dark brown eyes you could just fall right into, a slender, elegant nose that made me want to kiss my way down it and big, sensuous lips. That mouth was made for long, hungry kisses...or even filthier things.

"Well," I said "Lookee what we have here." And I gave her the Bull grin, which is certified to make any girl giggle and melt. I was already thinking about the table where we put the saddles and reins for the shows. It was just the right height to fuck her on, with those creamy thighs wrapped around my waist. A couple of minutes, a little of the old Bull charm and—

But she just stood there, open-mouthed.

"They call me Bull," I said, a little thrown. I stuck my thumbs into my belt as I said it. "And who, lovely lady, are *you?*"

She didn't flush or simper or throw her arms around me. She just sort of gaped at me. *Maybe she's foreign. That'd explain it.*

She seemed to be checking out my body, which I was used to, but it wasn't accompanied by any of the normal flirting or smiles. I felt like I was trying to play tennis with myself. Eventually, she sort of shook her head as if to clear it and said, "I have to go."

And then she turned and started to walk away.

What? Did she not understand we were meant to be having sex, now? I let her get about six paces before I reacted, partly because I was so shocked and partly because I got distracted by my first glimpse of her gorgeous, curvy rump.

"Now hold on a minute!" I said, jogging after her and catching her just as she reached the fence. "Didn't anyone ever teach you to say thank you?" *You know, maybe on your knees, shaking all that dark hair back over your shoulders as you...*

Except...that wasn't the only thing I was thinking. It was the *main* thing I was thinking but, underneath it, something else was disturbing the dark depths, something I wasn't used to. I felt a little...*hurt,* that she'd walk off so easily. That I didn't seem to matter to her at all. It bothered me. And that made no sense. Plenty of women fuck me, but I don't much care if they *like* me.

She turned around. "Oh. Sorry. Thank you." It sounded genuine but she didn't seem to want to look at me and, when she did, she was blinking as if confused. The combination of those deep brown eyes and her long lashes raised something like a mini-tornado inside my head, scattering my thoughts. She was goddamn beautiful. *Gorgeous.* And between those eyes, those lips, those tits—damn, she was the most *feminine* woman I'd ever met. I almost got tongue-tied.

Almost. I mean, this is *me.*

"I saved your damn life," I said, folding my arms. "You owe me a drink. Lucky Pete's, at eight."

She shook her head, looking at her feet. "I don't go to bars."

Who doesn't go to *bars?!*

"Eight," I said firmly, and just stared her down. The Bull stare has been known to make women spontaneously drop their panties.

But she didn't melt like she was supposed to. She sighed, almost like she was annoyed. And her eyes were going everywhere except on my face, as if she was afraid to look at me. But when we did lock eyes, I caught just a glimpse of the need inside her and *goddamn,* it was bubbling hot like lava.

Finally, she nodded. "Eight," she muttered and turned away again. This time, I let her leave. I watched her climb the fence, which was a whole epic movie of denim stretching tight over perfect, rounded ass and breasts bobbing under her tight blouse. My cock had been hard for her ever since I'd first seen her. Now it was swelling almost painfully against my thigh. *Damn!*

"What's your name?" I called after her as she headed for the stairs.

She looked back at me, just a quick glance—but when our eyes met, they locked and neither of us could look away. She was wide-eyed and almost panting. *Helpless.* "Lily," she mumbled. And then she was gone, almost running up the stairs.

I swept my hat off my head and stared at the spot where I'd last seen her. I'm very seldom lost for words, but that was one of those times. "Well, goddamn," I said at last.

THREE

Lily

I BARRELED UP OUT OF THE STAIRWELL and hurried over to Francisco. My mind was whirling with what had just happened. I felt almost drunk with it, overwhelmed with sensation, and that's a bad way to go into this kind of a meeting. I let the sun blast the memories from my mind and tried to focus. *Later.* I'd think about the whole thing later.

By now, the rodeo was getting started. There was a lot of shouting from an over-enthusiastic announcer and cowboys on horseback were rounding up cows. I surreptitiously checked, but none of the cowboys were Bull.

I slumped down in the empty seat beside Francisco. He took one look at me and said, straight-faced, "You look hot."

If I was some svelte beauty, it might have been flirting. But he was right—I *did* look hot. The run through the arena and up all those steps had left me red-faced and sweating, my hair sticking to my forehead. And...okay, yes, getting up close and personal with Bull had reduced me to a hot mess, too.

I gave Francisco a glower, grabbed the soda out of his hand and took three big glugs. "There," I panted. "Better now."

It's a mark of how well we get on that I dared to do something like that. The Gallegos put the fear of God into most people and Francisco answers directly to Isabella, the head of the whole cartel. But after two years, I counted him as a friend. We'd even been out for drinks a few times—I mean, not in *that* way: he's pushing fifty. But he was friendly and paid on time and didn't give me a lot of sexist crap about being a woman, so I liked him. Plus, meeting with him was one of the few bits of actual social contact I had.

He grabbed the soda back off me and blinked at me from behind his huge, gold-rimmed sunglasses. "You got the stuff?"

I slapped the package of fake IDs onto his lap, concealed within the latest *Sports Illustrated*. It was part of our routine that I picked up an issue for him each time we met.

He didn't even bother to check them, just passed me a *Vogue* with my money inside. That was kind of a running thing, too, because he'd done it the first time we'd ever traded, having heard on our phone calls that I was a woman. He'd kept it up ever since, despite the fact that I'm about as far from a fashion model as it's possible to be and the last time I'd bought any new clothes was...yep, I literally can't remember. No one who does business with me cares what I look like and no one I see socially—

Well, I don't see anyone socially.

The crowd whooped and cheered because some cowboy had just roped a horse. I craned my neck to look...but it still wasn't Bull. And then I caught myself and flushed, embarrassed that I'd looked.

"You stayin'?" asked Francisco. "They got chuck wagon racing and chute dogging coming up."

Part of me was tempted. Somewhere in that mess of sweat and rope and action there was a hulking cowboy with the bluest eyes I'd ever seen. A cowboy who, against all logic, had actually asked me out for a drink...

I stood up and shook my head. "Nope," I said. "You knock yourself out. I got air conditioning and artificial light to get back to."

He shook his head and gave me a long-suffering look. "There's a whole world out here you're missing out on."

"Yeah," I told him. "But it's not my world."

FOUR

Lily

WHEN YOU DO SOMETHING ENOUGH, it becomes magnified in your mind until you know every detail. I know every swirl and loop of the stenciled paper on a passport just like you know every pothole on your commute to work.

Which is bad. Because, as I sat there at my desk, working away, it meant that my mind was free to think.

I squirmed inside when I remembered how I'd reacted to him. It was as if all the normal parts of my brain, the ones that let me escape New York and customize the bus and build a little forger empire here in Texas, all suddenly shut down. All I'd been left with was some primal, animal brain that I hadn't even known was lurking underneath. And *it,* faced with Bull, had been reduced to a puddle of hormones. I'd stood there slack-jawed and helpless.

I've always been proud of my independence. When you're on the run, being *a woman on her own* isn't any kind of worthy feminist crusade, it's simple survival fact. I didn't need a man because I didn't need *anyone.* And yet I'd just stayed there gaping up at him as that arrogant, cocky bastard had—somehow—talked me into a date. A *date?* I didn't go on *dates!*

I couldn't go on dates.

I'd made a decision, back in New York. A very simple decision which had kept people around me safe ever since. The decision had been that, live or die, I was on my own. No friends. No boyfriends. No connections of any kind.

No one my uncle could hurt.

And then, just because he was all—all—*muscley* and *male,* I'd somehow forgotten all that and turned into a weak-kneed idiot.

I'd looked him up on Facebook—it's not hard to find a six foot-something rodeo rider nicknamed "Bull" in a small town. His last name was Rollins, but there was no mention of his real name—he always called himself *Bull. Asshole.* And when he wasn't working with horses on a local ranch, he was a rodeo rider, getting paid to be thrown around by wild broncos. What kind of idiot would choose that for a career?

I was fairly sure he wanted to fuck me and that surprised me as much as it annoyed me. Surprise because—well, this is *me,* curvy and big, and with precious little in the way of feminine wiles even *before* I spent two years living as a hermit on a bus. And annoyed because his Facebook page was a non-stop stream of photos of him in bars—each time, with a different woman. It was a barely-disguised list of his conquests, the modern equivalent of notches on his bedpost. *Me and Charlene, last night. Me and Kara, last night.* If he slept with me, it would be *me and Lily, last night,* and then, just one mouse-scroll further down the page, would be the next one. Women, to him, seemed to be disposable playthings. He was just another cocky, irritating alpha male.

But the more I thought about it, the more the hot anger seemed to seep down through me and sort of...change.

Bastard. Arrogant bastard. I bet he wanted to fuck me right there, in the basement of the arena, with all those animals around. Down in the hay. Or on a table or something, pulling my jeans off and him shoving down his pants and grunting as he shoved his—

I was uncomfortably aware of how, the more annoyed I got, the more I found I was pressing my thighs together. I tried to focus on my work—I was cutting plastic with a craft knife, a precision job.

It's just because it's been a while. And by *a while* I meant over two years, since well before I'd left New York. I mean, I hadn't been completely idle—I had my vibrator and my imagination, but—

But suddenly, that didn't seem like any kind of replacement for a hard, muscled body, so heavy on top of mine, his knees spreading my thighs....

The blade of the craft knife snapped, the tip of it pinging across the room. I'd been pressing too hard.

This is ridiculous. I should have been concentrating on real things that mattered, like the passports for Luka, the Russian arms dealer, and the next batch for the Mexican cartel, and those couple for the weed farmers in Canada. You know, normal stuff.

Rules were rules. Of course I wouldn't go on the stupid date. I'd avoid ever going back to the arena. I'd never see him again. In a few days, I'd have forgotten all about him and everything would go back to normal. Everything would just carry on, just the same as it always had.

I found myself staring at my single bed.

And I started to get ready to go out.

FIVE

Lily

I'D NEVER BEEN TO LUCKY PETE'S, but that didn't mean I went in cold. I've met with Colombian drug lords in old train yards and Japanese mafia in theme parks. I *never* go in cold. I'd pieced together the interior of the place from photos on the web and knew all my exits in case of disaster. I debated whether to take my gun but eventually decided it was inappropriate for a date. So I took a Taser instead.

Imagine every cheesy Wild West saloon bar you've seen in a movie, recreated on a low budget and then filled with too many people who've had too much beer. The highlight of the place was the mechanical bull and the animatronic prospector (complete with pickaxe and long white beard) who stuck his head out of a barrel every few minutes and asked if anyone had seen his mule. That line probably got pretty tired, after you'd heard it four hundred times. I'd only been there ten minutes and I was ready to bury the pickaxe in the puppet's head.

Where the hell was Bull? It was five past eight. Was this normal? Were guys always late for dates?

I was uncomfortably aware that I didn't have a whole lot of experience to go on. My teenage years hadn't been exactly normal.

I hadn't known what to wear, so I'd put on a fresh blouse along with my jeans, added a little make-up and left it at that. Now, looking around at the other girls, I realized that maybe I should have spent less time checking the exits and more time looking at what people were wearing. Everyone else was in little skirts or shorts and strappy tops, with either towering heels or some quirky take on cowboy boots. I was showing about ten percent of the skin all the other girls were, and theirs was beautifully sun-kissed and smoothly tan.

I *still* couldn't see him anywhere. I stalked over to the bar and asked for a beer. At least I could enjoy the one benefit of being out on the town. I don't drink in the bus. I figure that if I start drinking out there on my own, things could get out of control very fast. And I'm kind of obsessive about staying in control.

When my beer came, I tipped the barmaid and said, in a low, slightly embarrassed voice, "I'm looking for Bull."

She rolled her eyes.

"Not like that," I said quickly, feeling my cheeks flush. "I'm just having a drink with him."

She nodded towards a corner. "Join the line."

I'd pretty much ignored the gaggle of girls over on that side of the bar because they seemed to be the loudest, most irritating bunch in the place. But now that I craned my neck, I could just see, amongst all the bare shoulders and perfectly-coiffed hair, a black cowboy hat. He was sitting down, hidden by his crowd of admirers. *Well, of course he was.*

I edged closer to the crowd. The girls had formed a solid wall of perfect, slender shoulders and trim little waists. Most of them were taller than me and even the ones who weren't were lifted by towering heels.

He wasn't even going to be able to see me.

Maybe that's for the best. This whole thing had been crazy anyway. I knew I couldn't start anything with him, so what the hell was I doing there? *I'm fulfilling an obligation. He* did *save my life.*

That's what I told myself.

I edged my way through the crowd. A few of the girls turned and eyed me with disgust. They didn't have to call me names: the disbelieving snorts were enough.

I'd been a hermit so long, I'd sort of forgotten what bitches women could be. I kept going, my face heating up. Then, as I broke through to the front of the crowd, I stopped and stared.

Bull's chair was tilted back on two legs so that he could lean against the wall. He wasn't topless now, of course, but the white shirt couldn't hide the breadth of his chest or the thickness of his forearms. His long, denim-clad legs were stretched out, his boots resting on another chair, and two girls had perched their dainty behinds there, one on his calves and one just above his knees, as they giggled away at him. A third was just arriving with a fresh beer for him. A fourth was beside him, massaging his shoulders.

Now I began to see where all his arrogance came from. God, they just threw themselves at him! And why? Just because he was muscley and confident and had an enormous—

He looked up, saw me and grinned as if he was genuinely pleased to see me. And my idiot body reacted. My lungs point-blank refused to move any air and, as his eyes flicked down over my breasts and thighs, a wave of heat rolled down in their wake like thunder following lightning.

"Lily," he said in that slow Texas drawl. He tipped his hat back just a little. "Come sit down."

And he glanced down at the one remaining space—his groin.

Ego. That's what I'd been about to think. He had an enormous ego.

"Careful," one girl muttered. "You might crush him."

I hadn't had any intention of sitting in his goddamn lap anyway, but that did it. I turned and pushed my way back through the crowd, head down. I'd done my part. I'd showed up. Fuck him and the horse-sized ego he rode in on, if he thought I was going to join his fan group and—

A hand grabbed my arm just as I reached the door. A *big* hand. The heat of it soaked through my thin blouse and throbbed into my skin.

Bull hauled me around to face him. I didn't resist. "Now, that ain't very sporting," he told me. "You just got here."

I glanced towards the crowd, confused. Why had he come after me? "Seems like you've got all the attention you need."

He glanced over at the girls who were now staring at us, frowning. "I don't care about them," he said with an easy shrug. He squeezed my arm and I went squidgy inside. It was something to do with the strength of those fingers and the heat of his hand, soaking right into me.

I took another look at the girls. They were frowning and pouting, now. At *me*.

"I didn't come here to get between you and your groupies," I said.

He laughed—a big bass laugh that made heads turn. The sort of laugh you can only do when you're completely unconcerned what anyone thinks—the sort it'd be impossible for me to do. He glanced over at the girls again and gave them a wave. They started to glare at him, too. I think I actually saw one stamp her foot.

He really didn't give a shit what they thought, I realized. What *anyone* thought. He'd had fun with them and then—for some reason—he'd wanted to toy with me and so he'd dumped the whole lot of them.

And then, no doubt, the next girl would come along and he'd walk off with *her*.

"I'm outta here," I told him, and turned to go.

He still had his hand on my arm. He didn't grip me tight and pull me back, he just used his hand to guide me in an arc back towards him. "Hey, hey, *hey*," he said, his tone changing. When I reluctantly looked him in the eye, he was frowning. "What's the matter?"

The funny thing was, if I hadn't already pegged him as a cocky, womanizing bastard, I would have believed he actually cared.

"Nothing," I said. "This was a bad idea." And I took a step back.

And he took a step forward.

I looked up into those big blue eyes again. They really were like the Texas sky—when I looked into them, there was this impression of *size*, like I was in the middle of a desert, turning slowly to see the blueness that was all around me. It felt as if he was seeing me from every angle, even the bits of me I tried to hide.

It didn't *feel* like he saw me as just another girl, when he did that.

"Stop it," I muttered. I only realized afterwards that I'd said it out loud.

He let go of my arm, but didn't move away. "Stop what?" he asked. He wasn't smiling anymore but he didn't look angry, either. He looked almost concerned. "Why are you so damn keen on running out on me?"

I swallowed and forced myself to lift my chin. I wasn't going to look like I was scared of this. I mean, I *wasn't* scared of this. *Goddamnit!*

I grabbed the back of a chair, pulled it out from under the table and sat down.

Immediately, he relaxed. That lazy smile came back. He dropped into the chair opposite me, leaning back with his arm resting on the back. For just a second there he'd seemed really worried that I'd leave. *Why does he care?* It wasn't like he was short of women.

I glanced over again at the crowd of girls. Most of them were standing with their arms crossed, stares of pure death aimed right at me. If I ventured over there again, I was pretty sure I was going to get bludgeoned to death by ten pairs of heels. *That's ridiculous. They think I've stolen their man? Me?!*

Bull grinned at me across the table—laidback and easy, not a care in the world. The polar opposite of myself. He didn't seem to be in any hurry to make conversation. He was happy to just look at me and, the more he looked at me, the more antsy I got. I could feel his eyes sliding over every part of me: my cheeks, my neck, down my collarbone to my breasts. Down over my stomach to the little bit of leg he could see around the table. I could understand him drooling over one of those girls in the crowd, but a big girl like me?

He was looking at me as if I was something special, which made no sense at all.

And *God* he was hot. The hard line of his jaw. Those full lips that suggested rough, powerful kisses. The sheer size of him—he looked as if he could carry a horse across those shoulders, and the way his pecs pushed out the front of his shirt...

You know it's impossible. Just have a drink with him and go.

"Why do they call you 'Bull,' anyway?" I blurted, just to break the silence.

His grin got even wider. He leaned back further in his chair, almost lying on it, and humped his hips skyward. "I'd be happy to show you."

Before I could stop myself, I was looking at the thick bulge in the denim, a bulge that extended well down his thigh. The more I stared, the more the heat gathered inside me, rolling down through me and turning to sticky wetness as it hit my groin. I tried to tell myself, *that's ridiculous. It must be padded. No guy is—*

I'm staring at his groin. How did I fall for that?

I tore my eyes away, face flushed, and heard him laugh. I felt the anger bubble up inside me. *What the hell am I doing here?* Let the local girls fawn over the alpha male. I didn't need the cocky son of a bitch.

I was just fine on my own. And I didn't have any choice in the matter, anyway.

What I should have done was to get up and walk

out. What I actually did was to clear my throat and say, in a cool, crisp voice, "Aren't bulls often castrated?"

SIX

Bull

Ha ha ha, ha ha ha ha wait WHAT?!

I sat up in my chair and pressed my legs together. No guy wants to hear that word.

"Especially the randy ones," said Lily.

I just sat there open-mouthed for a few seconds. And a few seconds is a long time for me to be dumbstruck. I *always* have a line.

Except, apparently, with her.

I could feel the eyes of the girls I'd abandoned on me. They were too far away to have heard her put-down, but they'd certainly have seen my reaction. Normally, that would have bothered me. But all I cared about, right at that moment, was looking back into those big, dark brown eyes. All I wanted was more of her, this mystery woman with the curves to die for and her way of pulling the rug right out from under me.

When she'd suddenly walked away from me, I'd jumped up so fast I'd dumped one girl clean off my leg and onto the floor. When she'd nearly walked off the second time, my heart had been in my throat. Now I'd finally gotten her sitting down and got her looking at my cock and, instead of melting like any reasonable girl would, she was knocking my lines back at me.

Why was she not playing the game? Was it possible she didn't know how it was played?

No. That was stupid. *Just look at her!* A girl as gorgeous as her couldn't be some innocent.

Then I figured it out: *she must be deliberately teasing me. It must be a city girl thing.*

Now it all made sense! I'd figured out she was a New Yorker from her accent. She was an evil genius man-eater from the land of cocktails and designer shoes and she'd traveled to small town Texas to find herself a stud and now she was toying with me. Yeah, that was it. She probably went through a man a week.

Well, fine. I had no problem with a girl with a healthy sexual appetite. But she'd picked the wrong guy to toy with. I was mad at her, but the anger was wrapped around a hot core of lust. I wanted her more than any girl I could remember.

If she'd come here to find a stud, she was going to damn well get one.

You mess with the Bull, you get the...well, the horn.

I leaned forward. "Yeah, people do that," I said. "If they need a steer, because they can't handle a bull."

"Oh, you think I couldn't handle you?"

"I'm sure you couldn't handle me."

"Oh, really?"

"Not all of me?"

She raised an eyebrow. "Not *all* of you?"

The madder I got, the hotter for her I got. And the hotter for her I got, the calmer and cooler she seemed to be. *Oh, goddamnit, I want to teach this girl a lesson.* I imagined her bent over in one of the stables, that full peach of an ass naked and perfect.

I leaned forward even more and my voice dropped to a low growl. "Why don't we find out?"

SEVEN

Lily

IT WAS THE FIRST real...*flirting,* if that's even what it was, that I'd done in two years and I'd gotten lost in it. I was angry at him for thinking—*assuming*—I'd want to fuck him.

Even if I did.

Very, very badly.

But that wasn't the point. I was mad at him and, at the same time...the way those big hands pressed into the tabletop, his forearms like a couple of tree trunks as he leaned forward; the sight of that big, muscled chest peeking out through the collar of his shirt....

It did something to me. Made me go a little weak on the inside and even spikier on the outside. As if I needed to keep knocking him back so that he couldn't get close enough to see what he was doing to me. Or, maybe, because I wanted him to get mad enough to just damn well muscle through the spikes and get...*inside* me.

Did I really just think that?!

And then he suggested we *find out* and the reality

of my situation rushed up to meet me. What the hell was I doing? I'd had less than half a beer, but I was flushed and panting, the blood pounding in my ears. I felt drunk...drunk on him.

Go home. Go home and get into a hot bath and probably jill off to the thought of him bending me over in some stable somewhere, my ass in the air and—

Stop thinking like that! I prayed that it wasn't showing on my face. Hopefully, I looked cool and calm. You develop a pretty good poker face, when you're dealing with arms dealers and drug cartels.

I pushed my chair back and stood up. Immediately, Bull's hand slapped down on top of mine, covering my much smaller one completely. He stood up, too. When I looked up, he was staring into my eyes. Daring me to stay.

Suddenly, a girl was beside us. She was all movement and energy: *look at me!* Her long, ash-blonde hair never seemed to stay still. Just as it settled, she'd toss her head or twist and it would start swishing and gleaming all over again. She kept shifting her weight from foot to foot, too, as if she couldn't bear to be still, and that made her firm little breasts bounce under her strappy top, the tops of them peeking out above the sequins like two perfectly-tanned oranges. "Just leaving?" she asked me.

"Yes," I said.

"No," said Bull.

The girl stared at me, then hooked a slender arm around Bull's neck. She grabbed his cowboy hat and put it on her own head. "I was just wondering," she told me in a voice that was syrup laced with arsenic, "because I was planning on riding the Bull."

I just stared at her. I'd known they fawned over

him...but *really?*

She gave a little snort of laughter at my expression and looked over my shoulder. I turned to see the mechanical bull. *Oh.* But when I turned back, the gleam in her eye told me that both meanings were very much intended.

Well, fine. This was a good thing. I was about to leave anyway. Right?

"Bull was going to give me a few tips," she drawled, snaking her hand across his chest and sliding it under his pec. "Weren't you?"

Bull was still staring at me, ignoring her. But the feel of those expert, delicate hands caressing his chest was definitely having an effect. I saw him shift slightly. *His cock is probably getting hard.* And then suddenly I was thinking of his cock again.

What if that bulge wasn't padded?

The girl looked at me, arching a perfect eyebrow as if to say, "Well?"

She's welcome to him. She can ride that thing and whoop and giggle and then he can rut her like an animal and they'll both love it. That's what my brain was thinking. But my stomach had tightened right up as if—

As if I didn't want some other girl to have him.

I shook my head as if to clear it. *That's nuts.* I opened my mouth to speak—

And found myself looking into Bull's clear blue eyes again. He was willing me, *willing me* to tell her *no.*

But I knew the rules. No boyfriends. No connections. No one my uncle could use to hurt me.

"The Bull's all yours," I told her.

She grinned a toothy smile of victory and grabbed

Bull by the hand, dragging him off to the mechanical bull. *There.* I'd totally solved that problem.

She climbed up onto the bull. Like me, she was wearing jeans, but in her case the denim was so tight it looked as though someone had spray-painted her legs blue and then glued on a couple of rivets. Her friends—the crowd of girls I'd run into before—came over to watch, crowding me out.

The girl said "Five," to a gum-chewing cowboy behind a control panel and the thing started up—slowly, at first. As I'd predicted, there was whooping. And twisting. And arching her back and—goddamnit, she was just showing off for him, thrusting out her boobs. Then she took off the hat and waved it in the air just to demonstrate that she only needed one hand to hang on.

Bull stood off to one side. "Follow it with your hips," he told her. "You gotta know where it's going to go next." He glanced over at me. "Don't let it get away from you."

The girl was really putting on a show, lifting her ass off the saddle and grinding it in mid air. Sometimes, she'd glance at me. Sometimes, she'd check that Bull was still watching her and, if he'd looked towards me, she'd give an extra-loud whoop.

I leaned against the bar. I didn't want to give the girls the satisfaction of walking out, so I had to wait until the ride was over. I started fooling with the stuff on the bar—napkins, toothpicks, coasters—to make it look as if I was distracted and didn't care at all. I wanted everyone to be completely clear that the girl with the ash-blonde hair could take Bull by the hand and lead him out to the parking lot or to a motel or wherever the hell they wanted and ride *him* just like she was riding that bull, for all I cared.

I mean, he was just a cocky, arrogant idiot and I'd only had a drink with him because he saved my life, so why would it bother me anyway? Right? Right.

The bull came to a stop and the girl swung her leg over the beast and slid down, letting the momentum carry her right into Bull. She threw her arms out and opened her legs so that he had no choice but to catch her. Then she wrapped her limbs around him, grinding her groin against him. As he turned around, she gave me a victorious grin over his shoulder.

And suddenly, I was walking towards the bull.

EIGHT

Bull

KIRSTEN—or Kristen, or was it Krystal? It definitely started with a K—squirmed her pussy against me. But my gaze was fixed on Lily as she strode towards the bull. *What is she...she's not going to—*

She pushed through the crowd and stepped right up to the bull. At the last minute, she seemed to realize she had a napkin in her hand and shoved it into her pocket. "I'll give it a try," she said, looking me right in the eye.

I swallowed. My mouth had suddenly gone dry. "You sure?" I didn't want to see her get hurt.

She didn't answer, just jumped up onto the bull. Or tried to. It's higher than it looks and the soft, squishy safety mats on the floor don't help. A few of the girls tittered as she tried to hook her leg over. I turned and glared at them and they went instantly silent.

Lily got herself in position and sat up in the saddle. Her face had gone pale—it probably looked a long way down, now she was up there.

"What number do you want?" asked Pete, whose job it was to run the thing.

I saw Lily look at the girl in my arms. I'd completely forgotten I was still holding her. I opened my arms and Kirsten or Kristen or whoever the hell she was slithered down and stepped back, glowering.

"Five," said Lily.

I stepped forward, gently nudging Kirsten out of the way. "Three," I corrected.

Kirsten glanced at me. "Yeah, that'd be better for a beginner." She smirked. "I've had a lot of practice."

Lily looked her right in the eye. "I don't doubt it."

I saw Kirsten's smile collapse. *Damn*, this girl had a mouth on her.

"Five," said Lily again, firmly. *Aw, hell.* She was stubborn as a mule, too. Pete shrugged and hit the button and the bull started to move.

NINE

Lily

How hard can it be? All I had to do was hang on and—

The bull started to dip and sway under me. I discovered there was a surprising lack of things to hang onto. Everything was smooth and slippery. It was almost as if someone had designed it to throw people off. *What kind of fun is that?!*

The bull turned, still moving as slowly as a kids' ride, and I saw the crowd of girls smirking at me. Waiting for me to fall. *What the hell am I doing up here, again?* The bull suddenly lurched to the other side and I slid. *Whoah shit.*

When the girl with the ash-blonde hair had ridden it, she'd been all light and airy and sitting up in the saddle, waving Bull's hat. I was...not like that. I was glued in place, clinging on with both hands to whatever I could find. And, as it started to move faster, things started to sway beneath my blouse. I'd come dressed for a drink, not an aerobics session. It was okay when you were a slim, willowy thing, but when *I* started being thrown around—I could feel my boobs beginning to bounce and wished I'd buttoned up my blouse a little higher. I heard a round of low chuckles rise from the girls and felt my face go red.

But when I found Bull in the crowd, he was looking at me in a very different way. His eyes were locked on me—not just on my face but drinking in my entire body, watching as I lurched and flailed and tried to hang on. He wasn't laughing at me. His gaze was burning into me, devouring every inch of me in way that made my groin tighten.

The bull sped up again—*that's got to be the top speed, please let that be the top speed*—and I tilted way over to one side, my jeans sliding on the smooth surface—

Suddenly, Bull was beside me. "Use your legs," I heard him say. "Press your thighs around it. Just like riding a horse."

I snapped my head around to stare at him, unsure if it was another one of his lines. But he just nodded at me.

"I never rode a horse," I muttered.

He blinked at me disbelievingly.

I gripped the bull with my thighs. That made everything feel...different. I didn't slip around so much but, because I was now locked in place, every jerk and turn of the beast was transferred right into my body, whipping me around.

"You gotta ride it," Bull told me. "Shift your weight around."

"*She's got plenty of that,*" muttered a red-haired girl to her friends.

Bull spun to face them "Why don't you *SHUT THE FUCK UP,* Becky?"

Becky went pale, her mouth still open. The giggles died on her friends' lips.

I'd gone even redder than before, humiliation threatening to overwhelm me. There'd been girls like that in New York, too. One of the few things I *didn't* miss. But in New York, no one had ever stuck up for me.

I started to shift my weight, following the bull as it moved. My ass started to lift out of the saddle just a little, in a clumsy parody of the girl who'd gone before me. I knew I probably looked ridiculous, with my oversize ass and my boobs bouncing around, but I was starting to get it—

And then, quite suddenly, the bull spun to the side and I was tipping sideways. I just had time to register my legs losing their grip and then I was falling headfirst towards the ground.

TEN

Bull

SHE LOOKED INCREDIBLE. Those luscious breasts were damn near escaping, bouncing up into the open neck of her blouse so that I could see almost all of the creamy flesh, right down to her bra. And when she started getting up out of the saddle I could see that gorgeous ass, all curves and bountiful promise, bouncing up and down just like it would on top of me, if I had my way. And she was brave as hell. She didn't know a damn thing about riding a bull but she'd gotten up there and done it anyway.

Brave and beautiful. *Goddamn.* She was like that warrior queen with the spikes on her chariot who led the Romans. *Lady Godiva,* that was it.

And then she was falling and I was lunging forward, catching her just in time.

I pulled her to my chest—*just to make sure I had a good hold on her.* Those fantastic breasts squashed against my chest and I almost growled. Okay, I'd probably pulled her slightly closer than necessary. And the hand on her ass, lightly squeezing her rump, probably wasn't strictly needed. But safety first.

She looked up at me, her eyes big and panicked...but then they narrowed in a look I recognized. I could feel the heat of her body throbbing into mine. As I straightened up, her thighs wrapped around me and the softness between her legs pushed tight against my groin. I was suddenly harder than I'd ever felt.

Her lips were just slightly parted. We stared at each other....

And then she was jumping down and—

Running for the door?

Oh, hell no. Not happening.

I raced after her, bursting out into the evening heat. She spun around when she heard me and stumbled to a stop. The doors slammed behind me, quieting the blare of the jukebox. The only sound was the cicadas and the occasional rustle of the breeze in the trees.

I could tell she was about to run again. Well, the hell with that. I jumped forward and grabbed her wrist, then yanked her back towards me. She gave a little cry of surprise and staggered forward. I put both hands on her waist and pushed her up against the wall of the bar. "Goddamn it, woman! What the hell is the matter with you?"

She squirmed in my hands. "It's not—I can't—"

"You can't *what?*"

"I don't do this."

"Do what? Date? Fuck? *Kiss?!*"

Her breath was coming in shudders, now. I frowned and released my grip on her. Suddenly, my theory about her being some man-eating New Yorker looking for fun didn't feel right. Which only left—

Was it really possible that she *was* some innocent? With a face and a body like hers? What the hell had she been doing—hiding under a rock?

And it wasn't as simple as her not liking me. She kept looking at me and then looking away. Every time she met my eyes, I could see the raw need in her; every time she looked away, she looked terrified. She was into me...but some fear she had was winning out. I was pretty sure it wasn't me she was scared of. Who, then?

"Are you married?" I asked.

She blinked. "What? No!"

"Then what the hell is your problem?" I moved my head in closer and lowered my voice. "Lily, I want you. I want to bang seven shades of hell out of you. I want to hear you screaming my name until your goddamn throat is raw. And I'm pretty sure you want me, too, so why do you keep running away?"

She shook her head. "I can't be with you."

I frowned. "Why?"

"I can't be with anyone."

I sighed in exasperation. "Why? You promised your body to Jesus? Give me a straight answer!"

She was silent and, for a second, I thought she was going to do just that. But when she met my eyes again, I could see something there...something awful.

She *was* an innocent. An innocent who'd seen some seriously bad shit.

Then, before I could say something, she'd pushed me back and was running away down the street.

Goddamnit! I felt like pulling off my hat and throwing it in the dirt, but then I remembered Kirsten was still wearing it. I stalked back into the bar, horny and frustrated and in need of liquid solace.

Instantly, Kirsten was by my side, pressing her body to mine from ankle to shoulder, her ash-blonde hair brushing silkily against my neck. "City girls," she said disparagingly.

I looked down at her lithe body and all the pleasures it offered...then grabbed my hat off her head and pushed her away. For some reason, I wasn't in the mood anymore.

ELEVEN

Lily

I MADE IT TO THE CORNER before the tears started. That was the important thing—I didn't want him to see. Once I was around the corner, I slowed down, sniffing and swallowing and trying to hold on long enough to—

There. My little red Toyota, just about the dullest, least conspicuous car you can buy. Exactly what you want, when you're trying to keep a low profile. And exactly the safe place I needed, right now. I needed to calm the fuck down, if I didn't want all the memories to start welling up.

I slumped into the driver's seat but didn't start the engine. I sat there with my face in my hands, the hot tears filling my eyes. *How could I have been so stupid?*

I'd nearly kissed him. When he'd gathered me up into his arms, it had been like every teenage dream I'd ever had. A big strong man, ready to save me from whatever the world threw at me. It had felt so *good*.

Except no one can save me. There's no escape from

the sort of prison I'm in and, if I got involved with him, I could get him killed. Just like—

No.

I squeezed my eyes shut tight, willing it not to happen. But the memories were already stirring, monsters awakening from their sleep.

Two Years Earlier

Other kids drew their mom and dad as stick figures with sunburst hair and big, happy smiles. My teachers used to ask me why mine were different each time I drew them: sometimes princesses and sometimes astronauts and sometimes with useful tentacles. I explained that I didn't know what my mom and dad looked like because they'd gone to the angels when I was just a baby.

So they told me I should draw my Uncle Erico, instead. The man who'd raised me since they died.

You think you know where this story is going, but you don't. Uncle Erico never touched me. His was a different sort of evil.

I understood from an early age that my family was Italian-American. But I didn't understand, at first, the things people said about us. I heard the word *Don* and didn't know what it meant. I heard *family* used a lot, and couldn't comprehend why that would be a bad thing. Didn't everyone have a family?

I especially didn't understand the way people sometimes shied away, when they saw us coming, or the way mothers wouldn't let other children play with me. I didn't understand why our surname—

Fiorentini—was spoken with such fear. I didn't understand what they could possibly be scared of, because we seemed so normal.

There was Uncle Erico, who acted as my dad but who didn't really seem like one of the caring dads I saw on TV. He never seemed to have time to drop me off at music lessons or pick me up after swimming. But he did have an endless supply of friends, some of them distantly related, who scurried to do his every bidding. And I didn't have a mom, but my uncle did have a string of ladies who lived with us for a while. They were always blonde, with big, complicated hairstyles that needed a lot of preparation, and they thought I was cute and did my nails until Uncle Erico shouted that he *didn't want Tessa growing up like you.*

Oh—Tessa. That's my real name.

I always wished the ladies would hang around because then maybe one of them would sort of morph into a mom who would teach me to bake and shop for prom dresses with me and do all that mom stuff. But inevitably, after a few months, the arguments would get louder and louder and then there'd be the sound of something shattering, suitcases would be hurled out of the front door and a tearful, cursing woman would stagger down the driveway to a cab.

I always used to side with Uncle Erico, of course. I mean, he was family and everyone was always telling me how important that was. He was the only family I had, and he'd kindly taken me in after the car crash that killed mom and dad. And he gave me so much—a nice room and a fancy house in New York with its own pool, and a cook who made all our meals. I owed him.

I heard plenty, growing up in that house. People

get used to kids—they forget they're there and say things they shouldn't. I heard about people who needed to be taught a lesson or take a holiday or simply disappear. I knew the real meaning of all those phrases by the time I was eight.

I heard the word *loyalty* a lot, too. Especially when I started to leave the house by myself. But I didn't really understand until, when I was sixteen, a female FBI agent befriended me in Starbucks. I didn't know she was FBI, of course. I thought she was just a fellow artist, who'd seen my half-assed doodles in my sketchbook and thought they were cool. I only found out the fourth time we met, when she asked me if I had any idea what Uncle Erico did.

I went home that night and sought my uncle out in his study. He was practicing his golf putts, knocking balls into a can. When I told him about the woman—Lisa—he sat down and laid the putter across his lap, gripping it with both hands. He isn't an especially tall man or especially wide but, somehow, facing up to him in that room, watching him grip that golf putter harder and harder, he seemed seventeen stories high.

When I'd finished, he threw down the putter and told me I'd done the right thing in telling him. I nodded, staring at the putter. He'd bent it so hard across his knee that it was twisted out of shape. I think that was the first time I was truly afraid of him.

Then he told me I would never leave the house alone again. And I never did. One of his most trusted men, a guy named Antonio—became largely responsible for me. He'd either drive me places or organize someone else to do it. He knew where I was at every second of every day. The other kids at the exclusive private school I attended thought I'd been given a bodyguard. The truth was, he was my jailer. I was too valuable, too dangerous for my uncle to ever let me go.

Antonio was about ten years older than me with blond hair and a sour face that only got sourer as the years passed. He resented the fact he had to "nursemaid the brat," as he put it when he thought I couldn't hear. I knew he'd hurt people. When he wasn't watching me, he'd sometimes go off on an errand for my uncle and return with a satisfied smile, as if that was the sort of work he really enjoyed. Sometimes, there'd be tiny flecks of blood on his shirt collar, almost invisible unless you were looking for them.

When I turned eighteen, my plans of going to Caltech were scorned. I was told I'd go to New York State, dropped off each morning outside the doors and collected again outside the same doors when my last class finished. Study dates, revision meets—all fine, as long as I could persuade people to come to my house. I rarely could, so I studied alone.

By the time I was in my junior year, my eyes had fully opened. I saw that I was trapped in a gilded cage. I saw how it was going to be, how my uncle was lining up good, clean suitors for me, men who weren't actually related but might as well have been—men who worked for him, men he could trust. The honors degree in computer science I was working so hard for would be irrelevant—a curiosity, just like my hobby of sketching. I'd be a trophy wife.

The first time I realized it, I was physically sick. I knew I had to escape.

I had a best friend, Annette, who I'd known ever since I was a kid. A pretty girl with long, dark frizzy hair and an infectious smile. We'd gone to school together and then, when I'd been forced to attend New York State, she'd applied there as well, claiming it just happened to be the best choice for her, too. She was too close to the family for Uncle Erico to suspect anything.

So we plotted.

I had money saved—Uncle Erico gave me a generous allowance and I didn't see the point in spending money on fancy clothes when I wasn't going to be allowed to go to parties anyway. My only indulgence was coding and hacking, chatting away to hackers in Beirut and London and LA long into the night. And that's cheap, as hobbies go.

Annette had bought a car for me—an old, clapped-out thing most scrap yards would reject, but it would get me into the next state. I'd be dropped off at her house by Antonio, supposedly for an evening of giggling about boys.

We'd sneak out through the window above the garage, pick up the car from where she'd parked it down the street and I'd be gone. I'd been stashing clothes and possessions for months, smuggling a skirt or a top to college in my backpack each day and giving it to her to pack for me. We thought we were so fucking clever.

We were so fucking stupid.

I showed up at her house, said hi to her parents and ran upstairs to her room. We hugged, double-checked the plan, then slipped out of the window. It took us thirty seconds to reach the car. *This is it! It's happening! I'm free!*

I opened the door and the interior light came on. Antonio turned to me from the driver's seat and smiled a smile that had absolutely no warmth. A smile that said he was finally going to get his revenge on me for all those years spent nursemaiding me.

"Get in the car," he told us. "Both of you."

He drove us back to my house. Annette was shaking and sobbing in the back seat, but there was nothing I could do. When she tried to dial her parents on her cell phone, Antonio snatched it out of her hand. And because we'd oh-so-carefully instructed her parents not to disturb us—we had *boys* to giggle about—no one would miss us for hours.

When Antonio pulled up outside our house, three of my uncle's men were waiting to hustle us out of the car and into the living room. Standing in the middle of the room was my uncle, his face dark with fury. I realized the blinds were all drawn and the TV was turned up loud. That's when I started to get really, really scared.

There was a kitchen chair next to my uncle and the men pushed Annette down into it. One of the men stood on either side of her with their hands on her shoulders, to keep her in place. I was pushed into an easy chair across the room from her.

"How *dare* you?" Uncle Erico spat. "How fucking *dare* you?"

Annette and I stared at each other, eyes huge. She looked like I felt: pale and shaky, ready to throw up from fear.

"I'm really, really sorry," I said. "I'm really, really sorry." I kept saying it, repeating it like a litany.

"You want to get involved with our family?" Uncle Erico asked Annette. I'd never heard his voice so cold. "Congratulations, you're fucking involved."

"I wouldn't have talked to anyone!" I yelled. "I

wouldn't have gone to the FBI! *Ever!* I just wanted to get out!"

Uncle Erico snapped his head around to look at me. "You will never, *ever* leave your family behind," he told me. Then he squeezed Annette's cheeks until her jaw was forced to open.

And he popped the first pill inside.

Antonio had a cardboard pill carton and was systematically popping pills out of the foil and making a pile in his hand. I read the carton and the name printed on the side and felt sick. Annette's mother's sleeping pills.

Uncle Erico shoved another pill into Annette's mouth. Another. Another. Annette was sobbing, mascara running down her face. She was too scared to spit the pills back out and I could see them rolling around her dry mouth.

"Please," I sobbed. "Please stop."

"You need to learn, Tessa," my uncle snapped. "This is what happens when you get involved with outsiders."

My uncle took a bottle of water and upended it into Annette's mouth. She thrashed and struggled but, with two men holding her down, she had no hope. I saw her throat bulge and swallow.

And Antonio handed Uncle Erico the next mouthful of pills.

"*Stop!*" I yelled hysterically, tears coursing down my cheeks. I still thought, at that point, that it was just going to be a warning, that he'd stop before he'd done more than knock her out for a while. "Please! I'll stay. I promise, I'll stay. I'll never leave."

Uncle Erico looked over his shoulder at me. "You're goddamn right you won't," he whispered. And stuffed another six pills into my best friend's mouth.

Annette was kicking and thrashing, now. She knew what was being done to her and she knew she was powerless to stop it happening. It must have been like drowning in slow motion, feeling pill after pill slide down her throat, knowing what they'd do to her. I can't imagine anything worse, except maybe watching it happen.

Uncle Erico kept going until the pills were all gone. His men kept holding Annette down until they took effect. That was the worst part—sitting there, staring at each other, feeling the seconds tick away, knowing that if she could only stumble to a toilet and make herself sick, she might still be okay. A couple of times, she whipped a hand up to her mouth and tried to shove fingers down her throat, but my uncle's men always caught her in time, gently but firmly holding her wrists.

I saw her head start to nod and her eyelids slide down. She fought it as long as she could, sobbing for mercy, pleading with them. And, when that didn't work, pleading with *me*.

And finally, just before she went to sleep, she half-opened her eyes and looked right at me. A look that I'll never forget, one of pure hatred and anger and shattered loyalty. Her eyes asked me, *why?!*

And then I watched her die.

Uncle Erico explained what would happen if I ever tried anything like this again. Anyone who helped me would get the same treatment.

He made me help his men carry Annette out to some woods near her house and lay her body on the ground, along with the empty sleeping pills box from her mother's medicine cabinet. Antonio must have sneaked in and stolen them earlier that day, when Annette's parents were at work. My uncle had known about our plan the whole goddamn time.

I had to sneak back into Annette's house and then come happily down the stairs and tell her parents that Annette had dozed off upstairs and that they probably shouldn't wake her. Then I went home and cried my heart out.

The next morning, Annette's parents found that she wasn't home and that her bed hadn't been slept in. The police were called. I was summoned.

I'm sorry, I told them. *Annette asked me to cover for her. She slipped out the window—said she needed some time alone. No, I don't know where she went. I'm sorry I lied.*

Then Annette's mother discovered the missing sleeping pills and the search turned frantic. They found her body in the woods, cold and alone and without a friend in the world.

I had to pretend she'd been depressed. I had to stand there and take it as her mother sobbed and screamed and cursed at me, demanding to know how I could be such a terrible friend. There was free counseling at our college for her friends and our parents were told to put us all on suicide watch.

No problem, Uncle Erico told the college. *I'll keep a real close eye on her.* He even came to the funeral, clasping Annette's mother's hand and telling her how awful it all was. She blamed herself, of course, because they'd been her sleeping pills.

I couldn't even look her in the eye. She'd been right—I was a terrible friend.

Uncle Erico thought he'd broken me. I did everything I was asked without complaint or hesitation. I went to college every day like a good girl and was driven home every night by Antonio. I never left the house without an escort.

But I hadn't given up. I'd simply made a decision. I was going to escape, but this time I wasn't going to bring anyone else into my problem. I was going to do it all on my own and, if I failed, I'd be the only one who suffered.

At college, I slept, dozing off in a quiet corner of the library. My grades plummeted. In my room at night, I returned to hacking and coding with a vengeance, learning everything I could. This time, I wasn't exploring aimlessly; this time, I had a purpose.

I was learning everything I could about government databases and forgery. I was going to create a new identity for myself.

I learned about where in China makes the best fake holograms and how to trick the DMV database into thinking you're an engineer running tests. I struck up relationships with people who could help me—hackers and forgers and low-paid clerks in government departments. I switched some of my college classes to arts so that I had an excuse to spend hundreds of dollars on plastics and paper. My uncle didn't care about that or my falling grades—when I was married off, I wouldn't need a college degree anyway.

It took me over a year of painstaking work to become an expert. I must have made and destroyed a few thousand fake passports and driver's licenses before I finally had a set that were perfect.

Then I gathered up my savings and, one morning, I simply walked out of a fire exit at college and disappeared.

I knew my uncle would be looking for me—he

couldn't risk just letting me go. It was about more than just the fear of me going to the FBI and testifying against him and the rest of the mob—I'd betrayed him by leaving and he'd never, ever forgive that.

The irony was that I was far too scared to go to the FBI. I couldn't face my uncle across a courtroom and recount what he'd done to Annette, or all the contract killings and extortions I'd heard about. I couldn't face all those months in hotel rooms and safehouses during the trial, wondering when someone sent by my uncle would get to me. Maybe if I'd had someone with me, someone to support me, but not on my own.

I could change my name but I couldn't change my face, so I stayed the hell away from cameras and looked for a way I could earn a living—something I could do from home, with minimal contact with people.

Fortunately, I'd accidentally taught myself a very marketable skill. I bought the bus and set up in Texas, convenient for meeting with the Mexicans. They were always in need of fake passports.

My fake IDs became known in the underworld as the best around and I made them for criminals from Russia to Japan...but never, ever for the Mafia.

And I never let myself get close to anyone again.

TWELVE

Lily

Now

I SAT THERE in the darkened car for a full half hour before I finally had myself under control. The drive home helped—it was familiar, relaxing. It helped me remember that I was thousands of miles away from New York. I didn't kid myself that I was safe: I'd never be safe, with my uncle out there looking for me. But I was as safe as I'd ever been.

As the memories receded, the anger started. It was almost a relief.

I hadn't had a full-on breakdown like that in months, and it was all because I'd forgotten the rules. I'd gotten lazy and careless and let myself believe that I could start some kind of *thing* with some guy. As if it was possible for me to be happy.

As if I deserved it.

I parked beside the bus and stomped inside, slamming the door behind me.

Or I would have done, if I hadn't lived on a goddamn bus. I had to hit the key fob remote and then stand outside, fuming, while the door did its agonizingly slow *pump...hiss* and folded open. And once I was in, I found that bus doors don't really slam, either, so I had to settle for mashing the button as hard as I could.

Now I was even more frustrated. With him. With me. Mainly with me.

I turned on the coffee pot. It was getting late but I needed to work. My stupid attempt at a night out had put me behind. What I do pays well and there's no need for me to take on as many jobs as I do, but staying busy keeps me from thinking about the past.

I fell into my seat and picked up where I'd left off. But working didn't vent my anger or quiet my brain. *Stupid!* I trimmed an edge that wasn't quite straight. *Idiot!* I checked the printing. *Moron!* I tested the hologram. *Stupid, idiotic, moron acting like a freaking teenage girl—*

I threw down the passport and stomped to the kitchen to get coffee, adding lots of milk so that I could drink it immediately. I stood there glowering at my own reflection in the darkened window, glugging the entire mug. I resisted the urge to hurl it at the floor.

It wasn't Bull. Or it wasn't *just* him. Yes, he'd been cocky and presumptuous and annoying as hell. But that was *him*—that was what he did, every day. Judging by what I'd seen at Lucky Pete's, his brand of dim-witted, over-muscled arrogance was exactly what the local girls wanted. I couldn't blame him for being *him*. The person acting out of character was me.

And *dim-witted* wasn't fair. The slow talking and

that broad accent were misleading—I'd seen the sharp intelligence in his eyes. He wasn't dumb...just stubborn as hell. *Simple,* in the good sense of the word. Uncomplicated.

Pretty much the polar opposite of me. One of the many reasons we'd never work.

Why the hell had I gone there in the first place? What had possessed me to sit with him and drink with him and—*Dear God!*—ride a freaking bull in front of him? I leaned against the counter, put my palms over my eyes, and groaned at the memory.

It was an infatuation. That's all it was. It was just because I'd been sleeping alone for so long. A simple maintenance problem that could be taken care of with a long bath and a vibrator. In the morning, I'd feel much better.

I decided that I'd finish off two more passports. They were Russian ones, for Luka, the arms dealer, and Russian ones were easy—it wouldn't take more than a few hours.

Luka. I'd met him a handful of times over the last few years. With his chiseled jaw and his sharp suits and that accent... Not my type, but he was gorgeous in his own way. I hadn't seen him in months—he was probably busy bedding one of his Russian blondes. Life seemed to be one long party, over in Moscow. *I bet he's never had to go on the run,* I thought miserably.

Yes. A few more hours of work and then I'd get in the tub. I'd hit my...ahem, *reset switch* and everything would be just fine.

When I sat down again, though, I found I couldn't concentrate. The caffeine hadn't really kicked in yet and the combination of tiredness and frustration had me frowning at the little bits of paper and rubbing my eyes. Even with my magnifying glass, I couldn't seem to align things quite straight. Nothing would stay in its proper place.

I rested my head on my forearms and gave a silent scream. I knew that this was coming from somewhere deeper down. This wasn't just about Lucky Pete's or a stupid bull—*either* bull. It was about the limitations I'd placed on my life, that night in New York when I'd made my decision. It was about the path I'd chosen to keep everyone else safe.

I had to convince myself that I didn't really like him. That it wouldn't work. That the whole thing was stupid. Because the alternative—that I wanted him and could never have him—that was too painful to think about.

I only intended to close my eyes for a few seconds. But sleep dived on me from a thousand feet, plunging me down into the depths.

Sleep is the time when the memories of New York sometimes stirred, uncoiling and lunging up at me as nightmares. But I'd cried all my guilt and pain out, for tonight. So something else took their place, something deeper, warmer and more primal.

As the caffeine finally kicked in, stirring up the day's memories to swim around me, I dreamed.

THIRTEEN

Lily

"Oh, Mary. You have such a lovely home," said Peggy-Sue.

I smiled at our little homestead. I'd always liked it here. Close enough to town that I could easily ride in to see friends or attend my quilting circle, yet far enough away that we were private. Green fields and a river and a couple of horses. Everything we needed. "Come inside," I told Peggy Sue. "I'll fix us some iced tea. And then you must help me package up the slates and chalk for the start of school tomorrow. Those children won't teach themselves."

Just as we sat down, though, the door crashed open. "Woman!" bawled Bull. "I'm going to root you like you're a mare in heat.

"Husband!" I squeaked. "We have company!"

"Oh my!" yelped Peggy-Sue.

Bull ignored us both. He picked me up and threw me over his shoulder, carrying me towards the bedroom. Then he kicked the door closed behind us and tossed me on the bed. My long skirts flew up around my hips revealing all sorts of complicated petticoats and bloomers. I wasn't quite sure how I was going to get them off.

Bull filled his fists with lace and cotton. With one heave of his powerful shoulders, I was bared.

I stared up at my husband, panting. He was shucking his pants down his thighs and brandishing himself in one hand, moving towards me. The hot press of his manhood parted my sex and—

FOURTEEN

Lily

"Heavens!" I said and opened my eyes.

Reality slowly oozed back. But my mind was still awash with a safe, snug little house and a big, strong....*husband?!*

My groin ached with the remembered stretch of that first penetration, his cock thickly hard. I could still feel the heat of him inside me.

I groaned and sat upright. I had a horrible feeling that—yep, I'd been drooling.

I stumbled to the mirror. I had a Department of Homeland Security hologram stuck to my forehead. The tamperproof kind, where it leaves a mess behind when you peel it off. *Great.*

What the *hell* had all that been about?

Me, in the old west? Why was I called *Mary?* Why was I a schoolmarm, in some kind of domestic bliss? That wasn't me!

All that was avoiding the main issue, though. I'd dreamt of him. I could feel my face reddening, hologram and all. I'd never dreamed about a guy before. I mean, movie stars occasionally but not a *real* guy. Not someone I knew.

And in the dream, I'd wanted him. Wanted him so hard that I'd let him take me even though it was inappropriate and bad timing and *wrong*.

I leaned against the kitchen counter and stared out at the night. This was getting completely out of control.

FIFTEEN

Antonio

ERICO WAS PLAYING GOLF. That meant he was in a shitty mood, but then he was in a shitty mood most days, since the rumors of the trial started. When he saw that I'd arrived, he slapped the guy he was playing against on the shoulder and told him to go ahead without him. We walked out of earshot and then stood pretending to watch as the guy teed off or teed up or whatever the fuck it is you do in golf.

"I got a job for you," said Erico. "I want you to find Tessa."

I blinked and fought the urge to say *what?* because that's one of the many things that annoys Erico. "How?" I said at last.

"I don't care how. Just find her. I got the FB-*fucking*-I crawling up my ass. The house is probably bugged. The trial isn't just a rumor, any more. I got word this morning—it's happening."

My chest tightened. If the Feds were really going to move against Erico, I was probably on the list, too. "I looked for her when she left," I reminded him gently. "We couldn't find her then."

"Well, try fucking harder. You want the Feds to find her first?"

I thought back to the little bitch's friend, the one we'd suicided. "No."

"Then get to work."

SIXTEEN

Bull

SHE WAS BEAUTIFUL—long legs, gorgeous dark eyes. Getting on top of her was going to be amazing.

I spoke right into her ear. "Now I know you don't know me," I told her. "But all your friends do. You ask any of them and they'll tell you. I'm real gentle, 'long as you behave yourself."

She gave me an uncertain look. Her eyes grew even bigger when she saw what I had in my hands.

"Don't you worry about the rope," I said. "That's only there if we need it. But we don't need it, do we? You're going to be real sweet with me, aren't you?" I ran my hand over her neck. "Don't be scared," I said. "I've done this with all your friends."

And I mounted her.

For a moment, I thought I'd judged it right because she was passive and willing under me. But then I was flying through the air, barely hanging onto my hat as I cleared the fence and landed, sprawling, in the hay.

"Well *goddamn,*" I said mildly. "I thought we had a

connection."

The horse put her nose through the fence and snorted disparagingly at me. I clambered to my feet to try again.

I know where I am, with animals. Always have. Animals are simple creatures and I don't say that in the sense of looking down at them. *I'm* a simple creature. That's why we get on so well.

Animals are driven by instincts and needs: food, shelter, safety. People, though—they're just a mess of contradictions and women are the worst of all. Trying to work out what a woman's going to do next is like trying to predict the path of a paper dart in a tornado.

Case in point: Lily.

One minute, she was into me, the next she was running. One minute she seemed to hate me, the next she was wrapped around me, soft and eager. She was the most frustrating woman I'd ever met...

...and yet I hadn't stopped thinking about her in three days.

I kicked the fence, being careful not to spook the horse. I still couldn't believe I'd pushed Kirsten away. Was I *nuts?* Kirsten, with her tight little body and that way she had of riding me, circling her hips like a goddamn belly dancer and gripping me between her thighs like I was a bronco trying to throw her off. We'd go like that for hours, out in the barn of her dad's huge ranch, both of us bathed in sweat and her hair gleaming in the evening sun. Just the thought of her cute, perky breasts was enough to get me hard.

Or it had been, until Lily. Now, Kirsten didn't interest me. I'd always loved that toned, tanned stomach with its little silver and diamond navel stud, displayed so proudly in crop tops and tied shirts. But now all I could think about was uncovering the creamy curves under Lily's clothes. I wanted to strip her, slowly and carefully, exposing her inch by inch until she was nude. And then I wanted to run my hands all over her, cupping her shoulders, rubbing up and down her spine, stroking the outside and then the inside of her thighs until I knew every damn part of her, until she trembled and moaned under my touch.

I sighed at the horse and pulled the rope taut between my hands. "Now, are you going to cooperate?"

The horse stared back at me. If it could have raised an eyebrow, it would have.

Lily sure as hell wouldn't cooperate. Part of me wanted to teach her a lesson—tie her and pull her over my knee and spank her ass until it glowed red and then roughly fuck her into submission. But she'd have to be into it, of course.

God, imagine if she was. The world stopped for fully five seconds as my mind turned over the possibilities.

No. She was way too innocent for that kinky shit. And right now, I'd take missionary position with the lights off, I was so hard for that girl.

I climbed up on the fence and put a comforting hand on the horse's jaw. "How about we start over?" I said. "I'm Bull. I'm going to ride you. We can do it the hard way or the easy way, but I'm going to break you, no matter what."

Dealing with horses really isn't that complicated. Gentleness and force—it's just a matter of using the right combination. Too gentle and you don't make any progress. Too strong and you'll scare them.

I stood there staring at the horse for a moment. It'd

been three days. Maybe it was time to try again with Lily...but this time, with a gentler approach.

I don't do *gentle*. Not with women. Some guys are all poetic: *starlight* this and *tranquil* that. I've never been much good with words.

But maybe it was time to start.

I pointed at the horse. "Don't you go nowhere," I warned. And pulled out my phone.

SEVENTEEN

Lily

I'D SPENT THREE DAYS making passports and determinedly not thinking about him. Then, that morning, the air conditioning had gone on the fritz, so I was busy fixing it. I do my own maintenance, not because I enjoy it or I like the challenge but because I can't have a maintenance guy poking around the bus and discovering tens of thousands of dollars worth of fake documents.

Because fixing the air conditioning meant digging into the bowels of the bus, from the inside, in July, *without a/c,* I'd taken most of my clothes off. I had the blinds drawn anyway to keep the worst of the sun out, so I figured it didn't matter.

That's why, when the phone rang, I was inside a claustrophobic crawl space, on all fours in my bra and panties, trying to keep the sweat out of my eyes while I tightened a loose hose. I listened to the ring tone and frowned, confused.

I have several phones on the go at any one time, "burners" I can use for business and periodically throw away. I color-code them with electrical tape.

Except this wasn't the green phone I used to call the Mexicans, or the red one I used to call the Japanese, or even the blue one I used to call the Russians. This was the plain, boring one without any tape on at all. The one I kept for my normal, non-business life.

The one that never rang.

I backed out of the crawl space and grabbed the phone, expecting it to be a telemarketer. "Hello?"

"Been thinking about you," said a deep Texas rumble. I almost dropped the phone. "How did you get this number?" I said when I'd recovered.

"Well now *there's* a story. I had to do a whole heap of calling around. Eventually, I got it from Greta, at the library. I figured you probably read."

"She shouldn't have given that out! That's confidential!"

"I threw myself on her mercy. I told her I wanted to woo you."

"*Woo* me? That's what you call it?"

"She's eighty-three, Lily. What did you want me to say, that I want to rip off your panties and fuck you until you bite my shoulder?"

The phone slipped out of my hand and I fumbled it three times before I got it to my ear again. "Why are you calling?" I asked, my face scarlet.

"I wondered if you wanted to drop by the stables?" he said. "See the horses?"

"I don't like horses," I said.

"Who doesn't like *horses?*"

I tried to put into words why I didn't like them, but it sounded stupid in my head. So I just said, "Me."

"So don't come for the horses."

"Why else would I come?"

Silence. A deep, hot, throbbing silence. I swallowed.

"What are you doing?" he asked. "What are you wearing?"

That goddamn voice—dust and sweat and whisky-raw heat. It twisted deep into my mind and made me go mushy inside.

I looked down at my bra and panties. I was still on all fours. "I'm baking cookies," I said. "Double-chocolate. And I'm in a summer dress."

"I *love* cookies," he said. "Bring some with you."

"Oh no, I've irretrievably burned them."

"I don't think you're baking at all."

"I have to go. I have work to do."

"You want to know what I think you're doing?" he asked.

"Not especially."

"I bet you're still in bed. Lying on your back."

I looked down at my tools and oil-covered hands. "Not even close."

"On your knees, then. No, wait—on all fours."

I swallowed. "No." *Goddamn, that voice.*

"I bet you're thinking about me." Each word was like dark, sweet molasses. "My hands on your hips."

"No."

"Rubbing you with my thumbs. Drawing your panties down your thighs...."

"I'm hanging up the phone now," I said, not hanging up the phone.

"Pushing your knees apart a little, so I can get my head between your thighs."

I stopped talking.

"Can you feel my breath on you right now, Lily? My

hot breath right on your pussy?"

I bit my lip.

"Are you getting wet for me? Ready for me? Are you touching yourself?"

I jumped to my feet. "Goodbye, Bull."

"Come to the stables," he rumbled. "The Hollister ranch."

"*Goodbye!*"

I ended the call and just stood there for a second. I was panting and flushed, my hair sticking to my forehead. Well, the air conditioning was broken. That's all it was.

Then I spotted it in the mirror—a big, dirty oil mark on the front of my panties. I looked down at my oil-covered fingers.

Goddamn that man.

EIGHTEEN

Lily

BY THE TIME I'D SHOWERED, changed and driven out to the Hollister ranch, it was late afternoon but the temperature had barely dropped. My car had air conditioning but, outside, I knew the hood was probably hot enough to burn skin. The bone-dry weather had left the dirt road billowing with dust. My Toyota was reliable as hell but I still winced at the amount of sandy grit that was getting into the engine. I needed my car to work and not just for going to the store. At the back of my mind, there was always the knowledge that, one day, I might need to run.

I kept telling myself that this was just something friendly. That it was to stop me turning into a hermit, and was nothing to do with the oily finger marks on the front of my panties, or the dream I'd had about him. I'd see the goddamn horses, chat with him and leave. That's it.

When I pulled up outside the stables, a ranch hand was leaning against the wall. A good-looking guy with soft, black hair and snaking tribal tattoos visible under his shirt sleeves. "I'm looking for Bull?" I said as I got out.

The ranch hand nodded with just a trace of a smirk.

"He's a friend," I said quickly. I didn't want him thinking I was one of Bull's casual flings. Would he think that anyway? I didn't look like those girls I'd seen at Lucky Pete's....

But the ranch hand just nodded again. "Inside," he said, nodding towards the gloomy interior. "Have fun." And he started to amble off.

"Thank you," I called after him.

"Don't get too sore," he threw over his shoulder.

"W—*What?*" I felt my face go beet-red.

He stopped. "Don't get too sore," he repeated.

I just stared at him in horror.

He frowned. "You can get sore, you know, if you're not used to it. Some girls come out here and they can barely walk the next day."

Jesus Christ! I was going to kill Bull! Had he boasted to everyone that he was going to—"I'm sure I'll be fine, thank you," I told him.

"Oh. Okay." He grinned. "Just that Bull said he thought it was your first time."

I lost the capacity to speak. I knew guys boasted to each other about sex, but we hadn't even done anything yet. And to just presume that I was a—

I snapped.

"I am *not a virgin!*" I said loudly. "I'm quite experienced and I doubt that Bull's as big as everyone claims so I'm sure I'll be just fine, *thank you.*"

"Your first time *on a horse*," said the ranch hand, straight-faced. "Bull said he was taking you riding."

I flailed around for a response but I knew there was no hope. Inside, all my hot anger was evaporating while my humiliation doubled, *tripled*. Only now, I couldn't blame it on Bull.

Wait...yes I could. This was completely his fault. He'd dragged me out here to this place and seeded my mind with filth—all those wisecracks about the size of his cock and that phone call and...he'd as good as forced me to jump to the wrong conclusion.

I nodded a stiff *thank you* to the ranch hand and marched into the stables...and stopped in my tracks.

Bull was there, stripped to the waist and leaning over a horse trough as he washed himself. It was dim, inside the stables, most of the light coming from tiny cracks in the ceiling and walls that sent a hundred blades of gold through the room, freezing dust motes in midair. Water cascaded down his naked torso, freezing mountain streams winding down his sun-warmed body. They flowed around the smooth, hard hillocks of his shoulders and biceps. They rippled over the angled ridges of his abs and followed the lines down towards the bulge between his legs, the water falling like rain just before it reached his jeans.

I looked at the hay on the floor, at the saddles on the wall...anywhere but at him. "Did you hear that?" I stuttered at last.

He stood upright and then shook the water from himself, droplets flying like rain. "Not all of it," he said.

I relaxed.

"Only the part about you not being a virgin."

I unrelaxed. "Look—" I said tightly.

"You're wrong, you know."

That threw me. "About what?"

"Me." He smiled modestly. "I *am* that big."

Inside, I let out a silent scream. I wanted to run at him and, and—

What? Kill him? Kiss him? Both?

I looked at the line of stalls. Each one held a horse, its head poking out into the main room. 'You didn't say we were going riding," I said weakly.

"You didn't give me much of a chance. Kept trying to hang up the phone. What's the matter—you needed both hands free?"

I stepped closer. "You are the most—"

"What?"

I couldn't speak, I was so angry.

"What?"

We stood there staring at one another, the air growing thicker and thicker between us. The horses watched with interest. I could feel his gaze eating me up and yet his eyes never left mine—it was as if he was absorbing me from the inside out until he owned me utterly. And part of me didn't want him to stop.

"Why are you so infuriating?" I asked at last, dragging my eyes away.

"Why does it say *Department of Homeland Security* on your forehead?"

Dammit! I rubbed at my forehead. "Just show me how to get on a goddamn horse," I muttered, waving at the nearest one.

He grinned. "Well now aren't you presumptuous? You're just going to go ahead and get on one? Just treat it like a *thing?*"

"What, should I buy it dinner first?"

"Don't you think you should at least find out its name before you try to ride it?"

I folded my arms. "Is that what *you* do, with those

girls at the bar? Do you always find out *their* names?"

He grinned wider. "Depends how much I like them, Lily. Depends how desperate they are to be ridden."

I glowered at him, but I could feel the heat washing down from my face and twisting into a dark cyclone between my legs.

"Show me how to get on," I said again.

"Well, you're just *desperate* to climb aboard, aren't you?" He shook his head. "Didn't you say you didn't even like horses?"

I huffed and blew a strand of hair away from my lips. "Obviously you've planned this whole thing," I said tiredly. "Obviously you've told everyone on the ranch that you're taking the"—I almost said *fat girl*—"the latest girl riding and I'd hate to disappoint you."

Now *he* folded his arms. His voice lost its teasing tone. "Why *are* you in such a hurry?"

The silk in his voice flowed like liquid gold over my mind, making it difficult to lie. I glanced at the nearest horse. "No reason," I said.

He stepped a little closer. "You know, there's only two reasons people hurry to do something: because they're really eager, or because they want to get it over with because they're nervous." He paused. "Lily, are you nervous?" And, though I could hardly believe it, he managed to ask the question without making me feel like a complete moron.

I shrugged and looked at the floor. "Not *nervous*. I mean, not *scared* of them like they're going to bite me, but just..." I shrugged again. "You know. I haven't been around animals much. And they're big."

I slowly met his eyes. He was studying me. His eyes betrayed far more concern than I would have thought him capable of. "Go on," he said. His voice was gentle, now. I wasn't ready for that, for how the deep bass throb of his voice would vibrate through me when he spoke quietly.

I looked at the horse. "I don't know what they're going to do," I said helplessly. "They're just big and...unpredictable. I like stuff to be more...controlled."

"Always?" he asked.

I nodded dumbly.

"Must make it difficult to have fun."

He walked towards me. My heart thumped faster with each step he took. I honestly don't know which I viewed as more of an unpredictable animal, in that moment: the horse or Bull.

He reached out and took my arm by the wrist, his thumb warm against my pulse point, and I went weak inside. I had sudden visions of him putting my palm to his cheek but, instead, he led me over to a horse with a rich, reddish-brown coat. It probably wasn't all that big, as horses go. But to me, it was enormous.

He pressed my hand to its neck. I drew in my breath at the feel of it—warm and velvet-smooth, yet with the prickly kiss of short little hairs. I expected it to suddenly jerk or rear up or something. I'd realized I'd tensed up and tried to relax.

"This is Caliope," murmured Bull. "She won't hurt you. Just say hello."

I looked up into the thing's strange, long face. Every time it moved, I jerked my own head back, afraid it was going to side-swipe me. "Hello," I said nervously.

The horse snorted and licked its own nose. I yelped in mixed surprise and fascination.

"It's all about trust," said Bull. "You have to trust it and it has to trust you."

I turned and gave him a look. Did all those girls at Lucky Pete's trust him, too, when they gave him their bodies, only for him to dump them the next morning?

"What?" he asked, reading my expression.

I shook my head. I couldn't put it into words. I began to slowly stroke the animal, the feel of it oddly pleasant. "Now what?" I asked.

"Put your cheek against it."

I looked at him as if he was mad.

"Nothing will happen," he said. "Trust me. Or if you can't trust me, trust the horse."

I took a deep breath, leaned forward, and put my cheek against the horse's neck. It watched me out of one eye, but didn't move away. After a few seconds, it pressed a little closer. I felt my breathing start to slow down. This *was* oddly relaxing. Why had I been so hesitant?

And then something huge and warm and wet dived into my ear. I yelped and stumbled backward. The horse next door, a huge black thing, had leaned over and licked me while I'd been cozying up to its friend.

I stared at the two of them...and then laughed. Bull put a hand on my shoulder and I tried not to admit how good it felt.

"There," he said. "Now—let's go riding."

He strode off down the room and I hurried along behind him. I still wasn't sure about any of this. I'd shown up confused and strangely horny. Then he'd been normal, arrogant Bull with me. Now he was suddenly tender. What did he hope to gain by taking me riding—was this something he did with all the girls, like the ranch hand had implied?

If it was, did that make me one of his girls? I wasn't sure how I felt about that.

When I caught up with him, he was putting on a loose white shirt. I watched his tanned body disappear button by button. Not having to stare at that broad chest and those washboard abs made it a lot easier to concentrate, but I started missing them immediately. *God, what's happening to me?*

I coughed and focused on what he was doing. He'd picked up a saddle and was adjusting the straps. "We're using saddles?" I said, trying to seem knowledgeable and interested.

He looked at me. "Why? Would you prefer bareback?"

I couldn't believe I'd walked into that. I felt the blush crawl up from under my collar, filling my cheeks. *Aaand...back to the old Bull.* As if he'd never been away.

"*I* prefer bareback," he said. "Feels better."

I just stared at him, my whole face turning red.

"You can really feel every sensation," he told me.

I stared back at him as if I was slowly counting to ten, and formed my face into an *I'm very offended* expression. Not because I thought it would stop the teasing; because I didn't want him to suspect what was really going on. Beneath the embarrassment, I was imagining the naked touch of him, advancing inch by forbidden inch inside me. I resisted the urge to press my thighs together.

"You should try it, sometime," he said.

I turned away. The temperature in the stables had shot up ten degrees and I was struggling for breath. *Don't let him know you're imagining it. Don't let him know you're imagining it.*

"Are you imagining it, Lily?"

I studiously ignored him. It was okay, I told myself, because he was still only teasing. I could still kid myself he was talking about horse riding.

"Are you imagining being ridden bareback?" he asked.

I spun around, my mouth open. I was expecting to see him leering at me, maybe with his thumbs in his belt loops. But he was just staring into my eyes with a deep, hot lust that stirred me inside, making me shift my weight from my heels to the balls of my feet. As if I might just fall upward if I didn't hang onto the ground tight. I tried to keep looking him in the eye, but my gaze kept darting off towards his wide shoulders and the swell of his powerful chest under the shirt. He was so...*big*....

He took a single step towards me. The room seemed to spin.

Something was going to happen, right here, right now, if I didn't say something.

NINETEEN

Lily

"How about we get going?" I said weakly.

He held my gaze for a second longer and then nodded. Marching past me, he opened the stall of the brown horse I'd already met and strapped a saddle onto it. Then he did the same with the huge black one next to it.

"I'll take Apollo," he said, nodding at the black horse. "You take Caliope."

The bareback conversation seemed to be over. Thank God. I mean, obviously Thank God. Though I had a feeling I was going to come back to it again when I was safely on my own. My reaction to what he'd been suggesting required further analysis. And possibly a long bath and my waterproof vibrator.

I cleared my throat. "Are they safe?"

He'd stopped with the teasing tone again. "About as safe as it's possible for a horse to be. These two know the area better than I do. Hell, you won't even have to do anything, just sit back and enjoy the ride."

I nodded. And then there was no more delaying it.

I looked for a sensible way up. Was there a ladder, somewhere?

Bull watched me patiently. "Put your foot in the stirrup."

I looked blank.

"The thing that's dangling from the saddle," he said.

I put my foot in.

"Your *other* foot. Unless you want to sit backwards."

"I'm from New York!" I snapped, swapping feet. "Maybe we should do a cultural exchange, and you can try to hail a cab at rush hour in the rain!"

"Why did you leave?" he asked mildly.

That threw me completely. The last thing I'd been expecting was for him to start delving into my past. I didn't have a good answer ready, so I ignored him. "Now what?" I asked.

"Push up using that leg and swing your other leg over."

I tried a couple of experimental hops and then a jump, worried that I was going to wind up on the floor with my leg still up in the stirrup like a hospital patient in traction. I vaguely remembered seeing women do this in movies and they always looked dainty and elegant. I felt like an elephant trying to do ballet.

"Want a hand?" he asked in that low, melodious drawl. He'd moved closer—right up behind me.

Without thinking, I nodded.

Suddenly, the promised hand was right on my ass, gripping my left butt cheek. I just had time for a yelp of shock and outrage and a hot throb of sexual heat to blossom through my lower body. Then I was jumping again and he was powering me up, up, *up*.... I remembered just in time to swing my other leg over and landed with a thump in the saddle. I teetered there for a second, not quite level and worryingly high off the ground. But I was up.

I stayed silent while he grabbed my ankle and fitted it into the other stirrup. I was so pumped full of hormones, at this point, that just the strong grip of his fingers around my ankle and the rattle of the leather and metal as he pushed it in unleashed dark thoughts of bondage.

He swung himself up onto Apollo in one smooth movement. "You okay?" he asked with a grin.

I assessed things. I seemed to be at least a hundred feet off the ground—death was a certainty if I slipped off. I had visions of rotating completely around and dangling underneath the horse, or it could bolt and carry me off into the distance, or hurl me from its back and trample over my body.

"Yep," I croaked.

He made a clicking sound with his tongue and Apollo obediently trotted forward. *Wait—he can speak horse? I can't speak horse!* I looked at him helplessly.

"Pick up the reins."

I'd been completely ignoring the reins. I snatched them up.

"Lily," Bull said chidingly, eying my white knuckles. "You can relax."

I relaxed my grip a millionth of an inch.

"Good. Now press with your legs a little. Gently."

I'd been trying to avoid thinking about the fact I had a huge, warm-blooded animal between my thighs. I looked down at my legs and felt his gaze there, too, which didn't do anything to cool me down. Thank God I was wearing jeans. Why hadn't he warned me he was taking me riding? What if I'd worn a skirt?

Had he been hoping I'd wear a skirt?

I squeezed my legs together, feeling the hot mass of muscle and power between them.

"Not *that* gently. She's not made of marshmallow."

I squeezed a little harder and Caliope started walking. Suddenly, I was bouncing up and down, her warm body pressing hard up against my groin and then falling away. She walked straight past Bull and Apollo and towards the door.

"Um—" I started.

I emerged out into the light, blindingly bright after the dim stable. Caliope turned right and headed down the ranch's driveway, walking faster. I felt about a thousand pairs of eyes on me—ranch hands, visitors, even the horses. All staring at the dumpy girl on the horse.

A horse that was—yes, we were definitely speeding up. *Oh shit.* I made the mistake of glancing down at the ground and the hard-packed dirt was flashing past. This was almost certainly a gallop. I was going to die. *Help!*

I twisted the reins around my fingers, but I had no idea what to do with them. *If Bull comes and saves me now, I'll kiss him. He can have me naked and willing. I'll do every depraved thing he wants—*

Bull rode up alongside me. "How do I stop?" I called.

He blinked. "Stop? You're barely trotting. Relax."

Annoying, arrogant idiot!

We approached a bend in the drive. "How do I turn?" I yelled. "How do I stop? I don't understand the controls!"

"Relax your legs. You're still squeezing."

Ridiculous, I'm not—Oh. I guiltily relaxed my legs and Caliope slowed to a gentle walk.

He showed me how to gently pull on the reins to guide her. "What are you so scared of, exactly?" he asked, sounding genuinely bemused.

"That she'll get out of control!"

Bull made another of those weird noises with his mouth and both horses stopped, very close together. His dangling leg brushed mine.

"I don't think that'll happen," he said, looking at me seriously for a second. "She's pretty sensible. She knows what she's doing."

And he leaned in towards me.

TWENTY

Bull

I GOT WITHIN AN INCH OF HER, my lips close enough to hers that I could feel her trembling breath. Then she sat up straight in her saddle and said, "What are you doing?"

I fixed her with a look. "You know exactly what I'm doing."

She stared at me for a second, those fabulous breasts rising and falling under her blouse as she panted...and then she jerked the reins and Caliope trotted on.

I sighed and fell in behind her. This was getting to be a problem. Any sensible guy would have given up by now. And *me?* I should have given up right back at the arena, the first time she didn't hurl herself into my arms. What the hell was I doing?

Her ass was bouncing in the saddle right in front of me. Perfect and rounded, curved and full. Watching it come up off the saddle and then thump back down into it again, the cheeks separating just a little, the denim stretched tight over them, was poetry in fucking motion. It was impossible to watch it and not think of her on top of me, riding me as she took my cock. However frustrated I was that I hadn't slept with her yet, just the sight of that firm yet pliant ass bouncing up and down was enough. *I'd rather be here, watching Lily, than off in the barn fucking Kirsten,* I realized.

I couldn't remember ever being this into a girl.

And it wasn't just her body, fine as it was. Or even that gorgeous face with those luscious green eyes, all huge and liquid. It was the way she didn't let anyone get the better of her—not even me. Hell, she wouldn't even put up with me, and *everyone* put up with me. No one ever told me "no." So that fascinated me.

I mean, I still sure as hell needed to teach this girl a lesson. Sooner or later, these games were going to get too much for either of us to take, and then she was going to wind up over my knee. Or up against a wall. Or bent over the nearest available object.

There was something else, too. Something was wrong with this girl, and not just her weird city ways. Some folks are loners but Lily was lonely—*isolated*—in some deeper way I couldn't get a handle on. Like she hadn't just foregone friends and family but actively pushed them away. Hell, she'd pushed me away, too. It was only my stubbornness that had kept me coming back.

I pushed Apollo a little faster so I could ride alongside and just slightly behind her. She had her head up, now, gazing at the road ahead, and I thought I could see just the tiniest suggestion of a smile on her lips. She was enjoying herself. She'd never admit it, of course, but she was.

And then my eyes tracked down and I could see

how the neck of her blouse was flapping open and, because I was at just the right angle, I could peek in and see the upper curve of her breast in its bra cup. Her bra had some delicate lace edging right where I'd want my thumb to go as I swept along that smooth skin.

I glanced up. She was looking right at me and, if I could read her eyes right, she was halfway between shocked and turned on that I'd been looking at her. I felt my cock swelling and thickening in my pants.

And then she snapped her gaze forward and trotted on, and I was back to the view of her ass again.

I started imagining what it would look like in a swimsuit, or maybe a short, tight skirt—one that could easily be hauled up to bare her. *Damn.....* I loved the fact that she didn't drape herself in huge, tent-like clothes, like some curvy girls did. Her blouse and jeans fitted well, even if they were a lot more modest than the stuff Kirsten and her friends wore. She seemed shy about her body—maybe some idiot had said something to her, once, and dented her confidence. Maybe the same idiot who'd made her so closed-off and secretive.

I wanted to kill that idiot.

I called out directions when we hit the street. I saw Lily tense up when the first car passed us, but Caliope had done this so many times she plodded on calmly, and that calmness seeped into Lily, too. Soon, we turned off the street and down a trail, heading out into the desert.

"Where are we going, anyway?" Lily asked.

"You got someplace you need to be?"

"I have work to do."

"What *do* you do, for work?"

She shrugged.

"What does *that* mean?" I asked.

"Internet stuff," she said. "You wouldn't understand."

I was riding behind her, so she couldn't see my expression. I made the most of it. "Guess you're right," I said sadly.

I saw her catch herself and look around. I just had time to adopt a tough-but-pained look, staring off at the horizon like I'd been told my dog was going to die.

"Shit," she said. "Sorry. I didn't mean—"

I shook my head. "Nah, you're right. No point me asking what I'm not going to understand anyway. I guess I must seem pretty dumb."

"No! Not at all!" She looked horrified. It was difficult to keep my face straight.

"Truth is," I said, "I don't really get computers. Like, I'm not sure how you people fit all that information about everything in the world in one itty bitty box."

She gave me a pitying look. "Well, it's not *in* the box, it's the internet, it's—" She frowned. "Wait a minute. You're on fucking Facebook!"

I couldn't hold it in anymore. I threw my head back and roared with laughter. Lily's mouth was hanging open, which only made it funnier. "You must think country folk are dumb as hell!"

She gave me a death-ray glare. "Not all of them," she muttered. "Just you."

"It's not in the box...it's the internet," I mimicked, and collapsed into laughter again. And this time, finally, she managed to relax enough to smile at herself.

"Okay," she said at last. "Yes, okay. I'm sorry. I'm

just not used to talking to locals, yet."

"*Yet?* How long have you been in Gold Lake again?"

She shifted uncomfortably. "Two years."

I was desperate to find out why. Why did she live all by herself? Why had she never been to Lucky Pete's until that week? But I didn't want to push her too hard. So I just said, "So what *do* you do?"

She took a deep breath. "I write documentation about web server interfaces."

It was completely unremarkable. Boring, even. Exactly the sort of thing you'd say if you didn't want someone to dig any deeper. And she'd said it as if she'd said it a thousand times before, which didn't make sense given how few people she seemed to know. Almost as if she'd rehearsed it in the mirror.

We rode on into the desert, out where there's nothing but sky, rock and sand. "Are we heading anywhere in particular?" she asked at last.

"Should we be?"

"I thought there'd be a destination. Like, some hill or the world's oldest tree or something."

I studied her. *Interesting.*

"What?" she demanded.

"You always gotta be heading somewhere," I said. "Always doing something. Achieving something. Don't you ever just...relax?"

"Oh, I should be more like you?"

I grinned.

"I do just fine, thank you," she said. "I can *relax.*" She managed to stay quiet for all of five seconds. "So where *are* we heading?"

I couldn't stop myself grinning. God, I liked this girl. I tugged on the reins and Apollo came to a halt.

"We're here," I said.

She looked around blankly.

"Trust me," I said. "Best show in town."

And then I just sat there and watched as the sun started to sink slowly behind the mountains, our shadows drawing out into long tails behind us, the light turning from yellow to gold to red. Distracted by the sunset, Lily finally started to relax in the saddle. She gazed up at the sky, spellbound, as the clouds were lit up from behind in shades of pink and orange and scarlet that no postcard can do justice to. Soon, it looked as if the whole sky was on fire.

There's nothing in the world like a Texas sunset. I'd watched them all my life and I still wasn't tired of them.

But I didn't watch it; I watched her.

I watched as the golden light streamed through her blouse and showed me the faint outline of her body. I watched as a light breeze picked up and molded the fabric to her breasts. I watched the sun paint her hair with bronze and copper and I held my breath as the wind played with strands of her silken hair.

"It's beautiful," she said as the sun sank below the horizon.

It's the second most beautiful thing I've seen tonight. I wanted to say it so much my damn chest ached.

But I couldn't, even though it was true. It'd sound like I was teasing her again or, if she realized I was serious...I'd have no idea what the fuck to say next. I've never been any good with words, except when I'm kidding around. That's what I am—*who* I am.

I'm called Bull, for Chrissakes. What do you want?

So instead, I pulled out my phone. "Let me take a

picture of you," I said.

She twisted around to look at me. "What? Why?"

"So I have something to come up on the screen when you call me."

"Who says I'm going to call you?"

I sighed. "To remember you by, then." I nodded at the sun. The last sliver of it was just disappearing. "C'mon, it'll look great - you on a horse, the sunset behind you—"

She shook her head. "I don't like people taking photos of me."

"Why?"

She didn't answer, just tossed the reins. Caliope started the long walk home.

I shoved my phone back into my pocket, annoyed. Was this because she was a little bigger than other girls? She seemed self-conscious about her size...but this felt like something more. She'd looked almost scared.

She barely spoke as we rode home. The sky darkened to blue and then to black and a thousand pinpricks of light started to appear overhead. But my eyes were firmly fixed on Lily as she rode ahead of me. My frustration started to build. There'd been so many *almosts,* that afternoon, so many moments when something had nearly happened...but she'd backed away at the last moment.

Well, no more. I'd tried taking it slowly.

When we got back to the stables, playtime was over.

TWENTY-ONE

Lily

I WAS GETTING USED TO THE HORSE. Part of me was wondering, *what was I ever scared of?* And part of me was wondering that about Bull, as well. I'd seen another side to him. One that went beyond the teasing and cocky arrogance. One that I liked.

For a moment, when we'd been watching the sunset side by side, I'd had the overwhelming urge to stretch my hand out towards him to see if he'd take it. And then....

And then what? Suddenly, the past rose up out of the blackness to meet me and all of my childish, happy dreams were rammed aside. *And then he'd kiss me and it would be cherry blossoms and fireflies? Is that what you thought?*

I closed my eyes for a moment and cursed myself for being a selfish bitch. I'd been dangerously close to making an awful mistake. Jesus, we hadn't even kissed yet and already he wanted to take my picture! What secrets would he find out in a day or a week or a month? And even if I could keep him oblivious to my past and my work, that didn't put him in any less danger. Just being with me meant that, one day, he could wind up like Annette.

The memories came swimming back. Her eyes. Those beautiful cornflower blue eyes, pleading with me—

I gripped the reins harder, trying to control my breathing. *One one thousand.*

The pills rolling around in her mouth—

My vision swam with tears. *Two one thousand.*

Water spilling down her chin—

Three one thousand.

The counting trick finally worked and I managed to force the memories back down into the depths of my mind. But I knew they could come swimming back up at any time.

The problem with having no life is that there's nothing to fill your head up with—no friends or laughs or pizza or running jokes about cats. Just a void. It acts like a vacuum, sucking at the door to your memories.

I tried to keep that void filled with work and staying organized. Being the best at what I did. But sometimes it was barely enough.

And now there was someone, *right there*, who could be in my life. Someone who seemed to like me, even though he barely knew me and I was being cagey as hell with him.

I felt myself wavering again. A tiny, stubborn part of myself screamed that it wasn't so much to ask: to wake up in the middle of the night because you heard a noise and *just once* not to be all on your own.

And then I clamped down on the feelings, sniffed

and rode on. I figured the night air would dry my eyes by the time we hit the stables.

***

I was so wrapped up in my own thoughts, as we rode the rest of the way home, that I didn't notice the change until it was far too late. Not until we'd dismounted and he was showing me how to brush Caliope down.

His hand closed over mine as I held the brush, taking me through the brush strokes, and suddenly my heart was in my throat. I couldn't think, could barely breathe. He kept his hand on mine for far longer than necessary, staring at it. When he raised his head and our eyes met, I went weak inside because it was obvious he knew exactly what he was doing and what effect it was having.

That's when I became aware of it. There was a feeling in the air like just before a storm. It was thick and charged with emotion—every word was loaded, every glance powerful.

I tried to remember how I'd felt on the ride home. How determined I'd been to politely say goodbye and head home, to end this whole thing right then and there. Suddenly, it didn't feel that simple.

Bull went to brush down Apollo, watching me over the horse's back the whole time, and I just stood there, my hands knitting together nervously. It was the perfect time to walk away. But I stayed there, rooted to the spot.

He finished up and slowly walked towards me. The air was almost crackling, now, every little hair on the back of my neck standing to attention. *What's going on? Why am I suddenly...*

And then I worked out what it was. Before, when I'd found him annoying, that had helped to hold back the other feelings. Now that I liked him, now that we were alone, in this dark, private place....

There was nothing to hold me back.

My brain told me, firmly, *no*.

But I swallowed and stayed right where I was.

Bull marched past me and over to the door that led outside; a big wooden thing with an old-fashioned iron bolt. "I should close up, now," he said.

We stared at each other. I went to say *goodbye* but the word died in my throat. I tried to take a step towards the door, but my feet wouldn't move.

He tilted his head to one side. "Don't play fucking games with me, Lily," he said. "You've run away from me enough times. Don't start what you can't finish."

I swallowed.

And nodded.

And watched as he closed the door and bolted it, locking us inside.

When he walked back towards me, he seemed even bigger—a giant. The crunch of the hay under his boots was shockingly loud. He came right up in front of me, close enough that I could feel the heat radiating from his body. My breathing grew high and tight.

"Lily," he said, the word just a low rumble in his throat. The sound vibrated against my mind and then sank all the way down my body leaving a trail of heat behind it.

I have to do something. I have to do something right now or this is going to happen and that's going to be a mistake.

He leaned forward.

"I can't," I croaked.

"I don't care," he said simply and moved in again.

"I can't get involved with you," I said quickly.

Suddenly, his big hands were on my face, cupping my cheeks. He gazed down into my eyes. "Lily," he said, "if you give me one more goddamn excuse I'm just going to kiss my way right through it. Do you understand me?"

I just looked up at him, open-mouthed.

He moved in again.

"But I—"

His lips crushed against mine and the next word turned into *mmff!* And then I forgot what I was going to say anyway.

It was as if I'd touched a live wire. I wasn't ready for the raw, hot throb of it, shooting down from my lips to right where I lived. It made me arch my back and gasp, sucking his mouth even more firmly against mine. This wasn't like any kiss I'd known back in New York. This was Texas kissing, hot and wild and rough, his lips pressing, *demanding,* taking what he damn well wanted. He twisted and pushed and then his tongue was plunging into my mouth and his possession of me was complete.

I staggered backward—not because I wanted to get away but because my legs started to give way beneath me. It felt so fucking good, all the better for having been missing from my life for so long. He moved with me, his hands grabbing my waist to hold me up. One step, two steps, and then my back hit the hard wood of the wall and he had me pinned against it, my head tilted up to meet his.

He kept one hand on my waist, the heat of his palm throbbing into me through my blouse. The other he slid up my body...over my stomach, up to—*Jesus*—up to my breast. I went up on my tiptoes, groaning through the kiss as he cupped my breast through the thin cotton, squeezing it gently. I could feel the slow, wonderful ache as my nipple hardened under his touch.

When he broke the kiss, my breath came out in a long, drawn out moan. I blinked up at him helplessly. The look he gave me sent a whipcrack straight down to my groin—naked, raw lust, as if he was barely able to keep himself under control. Jesus, was *I* doing that to him?

He captured my mouth again, tilting my head up even more, kissing my upper lip, and then sucking it into his mouth so that I was left open-mouthed and panting. He used his kiss to keep me against the wall while his hands roved over my body. They started at my hips, stroking the curves of them, then over my sides, making me tremble and gasp, before sliding under my breasts. He took both of them in his hands and, this time, his thumbs rubbed roughly over my nipples. I groaned into his mouth.

When he lifted his mouth from mine, his eyes were heavy-lidded with hunger—he looked almost drunk with lust. I'd never had a man look at me that way before and something about it sent a new wave of heat through me, pooling at my groin.

My brain was still fighting a valiant rearguard action, despite every other part of my body having surrendered. "We shouldn't," I said, my voice sounding very far away. "We mustn't—"

He leaned in closer and just *looked* at me.

I swallowed and my protests died away.

His mouth came down on me again, tasting me and

then devouring me utterly. One hand slid like a knife blade between my thighs and I shrieked in surprise and squeezed them shut...then slowly let them open. He pressed upward until the edge of his hand met the softness of my pussy lips through denim and cotton. And then he rubbed.

I grabbed at his arms with both hands. My fingers closed on biceps that felt like rock, and I let out a little moan and went weak again. Every grind of his hand against my groin sent dark heat rippling through me. I could feel myself getting wet, on the other side of the fabric.

He twisted his hand and drew it up over my crotch and I arched my back and pressed helplessly, wantonly against him, desperate to maintain contact for as long as possible. He lifted his mouth from mine as his hands went to my shoulders. He started massaging them, squeezing and releasing with his powerful fingers.

It took me a couple of seconds to realize that he was doing it to help him hold back. He was occupying his hands to prevent him...

"Undo your goddamn blouse," he panted.

...to prevent him from ripping it off!

My fingers felt as if they were made of wax. They kept slipping on the buttons, but I managed to push the first one through its hole, then another and another. I felt his eyes on my breasts, drinking in the sight of them as they appeared.

I was arching my back a little, unconsciously grinding my hips in response to him touching me. So, as I unfastened the buttons, my bra-clad breasts jutted through the opening, my skin pale in the stable's dim light. Bull groaned as he saw the soft upper slopes. A tremor went all the way down my body. *What if he doesn't like me?*

His fingers slid under the shoulders of my blouse, surprisingly gentle given the size of his hands. He pushed the fabric back, exposing as much of me as possible, and drew in his breath. My fingers slowed on the buttons, shyness about my size welling up inside, despite the semi-darkness—

"You're amazing," he rumbled and the fear evaporated, turning into heat. He ran one thick finger down my collarbone and into the valley of my breasts, enjoying the smoothness of me. Every brush of my warm breasts against his rough skin made me gasp. When his finger reached the front of my bra, he teased it for a second, pulling it away from my breasts, stretching the elastic until I thought he was going to rip it clean off me. But he eventually let it relax, though he kept his finger there. "Keep going," he told me between gritted teeth. His whole body was tense with barely-suppressed need.

My fingers started up again, working through the buttons until they reached the hem, and then the two halves of my blouse were falling back around me, my arched back thrusting my chest towards him. Without words, he scooped his hands around behind me and I felt them under my blouse, then under my bra strap and—

I drew in my breath as my bra went loose, then cried out in pleasure as he filled his hands with my breasts, squeezing the soft flesh. "Goddamn," he grunted in my ear. "I've been wanting to do that since I met you in the arena. Feels just as good as I thought."

A dark, hot bolt of energy shot straight down to my

groin even as the blush rose in my cheeks. His hands were lifting and pressing my breasts together, luxuriating in the feel of them. Then he ducked down and pressed his face against them—the hot press of his lips and just a touch of his rough grizzle. He groaned and his heated breath on my nipples made me gasp. "Goddamn!" he said again. "You're perfect."

His thumbs found my nipples, rolling them in slow circles, and I felt his eyes on me as they stiffened rapidly under his touch. The heat inside me was twisting and thrashing, now—something about him looking at me, *seeing* the effect he was having on me. I was utterly helpless—in every sense of the word—under those big hands.

Bull lowered his head and I realized what he was going to do a half-second before he did it. My eyes flicked to the door—I was already essentially topless but to have him lick my breasts, in such a public place... The door was bolted but I wasn't sure if there were other ways in, down at the other end of the building.

I groaned and tried to bend forward as his mouth neared my left nipple, trying instinctively to wrap myself around him and hide myself. But his hands suddenly grabbed my shoulders and slammed me back against the wall, pinning me there. "Stay right there," he ordered me, and that heavy Texan accent did numbers inside my head—strong but never cruel. It just told me how things were going to be.

I stayed where I was, lust overwhelming the fear of getting caught. I felt his mouth close around my nipple, his strong lips as powerful as fingers, his tongue lashing and twirling around my hardened nub, pushing it and stroking at it in a way that made my fingers dig hard into his biceps. I threw back my head and moaned as he sucked my breast into his mouth, enveloping me in heat. He started licking and the slow swirls of his tongue made me grind my hips in response. I might as well have been a marionette with him working my strings.

After a few seconds, he seemed to trust me enough to remain where I was. He dropped one hand to my other breast so he could attend to it, too, and the red fire that was scorching down through me doubled in intensity. My breasts are big—I've always been a little self-conscious of them—but in his big hands they felt exactly right. His fingers kneaded with just a little roughness, making me hump my hips towards him and grind my head against the hard wood of the wall. Then he took my nipple between thumb and forefinger and started to pinch—slow and certain. He knew *exactly* what he was doing. I cried out and he fixed me with his gaze.

"You like that?" he rasped.

The heat was bucking and snarling inside me, now, taking on a new and darker form. I stared back at him...and nodded.

He pinched just a little harder. White-hot starbursts of pleasure and pain joined the rush of heat and I snapped my mouth closed, shutting my eyes, as well.

He lifted his other hand from my shoulder—I was his, now, and he knew I wasn't going to move. He stroked my cheek, then rubbed his thumb across my lips, letting me feel the size of him against my softness. He stroked me there three times and then pushed between my lips. I panted through my nose as he touched my teeth, playing his thumb along them. I still had my eyes closed—I didn't dare open them, because that would mean seeing him and facing up to what I was doing.

I'd been feeling things I hadn't for years...but this was different. What he was doing now was something I'd *never* felt before. I could feel his eyes on me, watching my reaction.

I opened for him. And then his thumb was in my mouth, stroking across the tip of my tongue, trusting me not to bite. I began to tremble and my breath came in shuddering pants. Every hot gasp of air had to pass around that hard thumb, making it impossible to forget the intimate invasion. It turned every breath I took into a new source of heat. I clamped his thumb lightly with my teeth and he groaned in pleasure.

And then, even though some distant part of my brain was screaming at me that I shouldn't, I started to lick at it with the tip of my tongue.

Bull drew in his breath. He licked my breast twice more and then drew back enough to speak. When the words came, each one was a hot little hurricane against my spit-wet nipple. "Oh," he said softly. "You're a bad girl when you get going. Aren't you, Lily?"

My cheeks were flaming red, but the heat was racing up and down my body, increasing by the second.

He moved his hand to the breast he'd been licking and pinched my slickened nipple. "Aren't you?"

The silver starbursts stretched out, elongating into shooting stars. I was grinding my hips against him, now, helpless with need. "*Uh-huh,*" I moaned.

The thumb withdrew from my mouth. I felt the wet touch of it glance off my bare stomach and then my jeans were being stretched away from my body and the button was popping loose. That did it: the easy little slip of the hard metal through that soft denim hole—*we're actually going to—*

"W—Wait!" I blurted.

His hands froze.

I had to swallow a few times before I was capable of speech. My brain, which I'd left many, many miles behind, finally caught up and reminded me of all the reasons I shouldn't let this happen.

I twisted out of his grip and turned away from him. "I can't," I panted. "Sorry."

He was panting, too, his huge chest rising and falling. I could feel the hot waves of frustration rolling off of him. "Why the hell not?"

I shook my head. I was trying to do my bra up, but my fingers were shaking too hard to manage the clasp. "It's complicated."

He put his huge hand on my shoulder and turned me back to face him again. My breasts were covered by my bra but there was still a lot of exposed skin and every inch of it was suddenly aflame again from the feel of his eyes on it. "Make it simple," he grunted.

I couldn't meet his eyes. I gave up on the bra and looked off to the side as I tried to fasten up my blouse. "It's not you. I can't get involved with anyone."

"This is the same horseshit you fed me outside Lucky Pete's. And yet you came back here."

I shook my head. "This was a mistake. I'm sorry."

He stepped closer, looming over me. "Sooner or later, girl, you're gonna have to wake up to what you really need. Your brain's trying to rope in your body but it don't have a hope."

"You won't see me again," I said, determined. I'd

gotten *some* buttons fastened, at least. I stalked off towards the door.

"Lily," he said as I unbolted it. "Just stay. Stay and talk, goddamnit!"

He sounded angry, but not in a way that scared me. However frustrated he was, I never feared that he might push things. I just knew I was hurting him, running out on him. *Again.*

I swung open the door...and ran.

As I drove away, I saw him emerge from the stable and stand watching me, lit up by the red glow of my tail lights. He didn't yell or curse, just stood there staring at me. As if he knew I'd be back.

As if he knew me better than I knew myself.

I glanced down at myself, taking stock. My jeans were still unbuttoned. My bra was unfastened and dangling from my breasts. I'd gotten three buttons of my blouse fastened, but only one of them was in the correct hole. My cheeks were flushed and my whole body was throbbing with tormented, desperate sexual heat.

Goddamn that man, for tempting me into it.

Goddamn *me* for running away.

I slammed the heel of my hand into the steering wheel. Goddamn my uncle, for putting me in this nightmare in the first place.

TWENTY-TWO

Lily

THE NEXT MORNING, I was up early to go running. I have an uneasy relationship with exercise. For weeks and weeks, I'll do none, while a little voice in my head whispers, louder and louder, that I really need to get off my ass. Finally, to shut it up, I go for a run. At which point, I remember how much I hate running. But then afterwards, I get that brief, satisfied glow—for an hour or a day, I *love* running. *I'll do this every day,* I tell myself. And then I don't...and after a few weeks the cycle starts again.

Given the heat, running in Texas means getting up early. This has the added advantage that very few people are around to see me in running gear. My usual route is down the dried-up creek bed, towards the hills, then looping back to the bus along a disused farm track. At first, I used to carry a Taser. After a year of never running into anything more threatening than a lizard, I stopped.

There was another reason to go running that morning, though. I was due to meet with a new client and I wanted a clear head. Specifically, I wanted to clear my head of *Bull*.

It wasn't easy, though. Every impact of my trail shoes on the hard-packed dirt sent a little shockwave up my legs and into my brain, and the rhythm was disconcertingly similar to the night before. The way I'd arched and ground against him. The way he'd taken my nipple into his mouth—

Shut up! I pounded along the creek, trying to go faster, hoping that that would help.

You like that?

His hands on my breasts. That thick thumb pushing between my lips.

My legs went faster still, my muscles burning.

You're a bad girl when you get going—

Shut up!

—aren't you, Lily?

It was impossible. Dangerous. No matter how big and strong he was, if he got involved with me there was a good chance he'd wind up dead.

It wasn't just the danger I lived with, but the danger a relationship would bring. Avoiding *having a life* is exactly how I stayed off the radar. I couldn't even have a Facebook page. How the hell could I have a boyfriend?

I was panting hard, sweat trickling down the back of my sports top. I'd tied my hair back into a tight ponytail in some sort of unconscious effort to take control and be ruthless and efficient. But beneath my jogging shorts, the flex and push of my hips was rhythmically rubbing things, making me painfully aware of just how out of control I was.

Damn him. Damn him, with his muscles and that smile and—

Goddamnit!

I reached the end of the creek and started back along the farm track. Sweat was trickling down my forehead and my upper chest gleamed with it. My boobs—difficult to control even with a sports bra—ached and heaved. That was all normal. The fact that my nipples were hard wasn't. I could feel them pressing into the soft fabric, yearning for the rougher touch of his fingers. God, his hands were so *big*. If they slid underneath me and gripped my ass, squeezing my cheeks, I'd feel like I was just completely *in his hands;* he'd just scoop me up off the bed, opening me up, and—

Shut up!

I staggered to a stop and bent over, huffing for breath. It was impossible. I couldn't get him out of my head—the more I tried, the more he was there, strong and arrogant and larger than life. And it wasn't just the sex. There was something even more disturbing, underneath that. The memory of that horse ride and the way he'd looked at me a few times, especially as the sun had gone down. A different kind of intimacy, one that maybe I needed even more.

That was the real reason I couldn't be with him. Even if I could somehow enjoy a one-time roll in the hay and then walk away—and I wasn't sure I could—it already felt like more than that. Which was nuts, because if there was one thing I'd learned from seeing him in Lucky Pete's and reading his Facebook page, it was that Bull didn't fall for anyone—he was a rutting, pumping sex machine, and that was it. Why on earth would I think he might develop feelings for me? Because I liked him in that way myself? A thousand slimmer, prettier girls probably thought the same thing. *I'll be the one he falls for.*

I snorted in contempt at myself. And then gave a hard little laugh. Looking down at myself, all sweat and curves, the idea was ridiculous.

I forced myself forward, jogging the rest of the way back to the bus. I'd spectacularly failed to get Bull out of my head, but at least I'd decided that I'd done the right thing, the night before. Now I had to focus on the meeting. In my line of work, acting like a lovesick fool is a good way to get killed.

***

The meet was at Momma B's, a diner not far from the arena. It was actually a pretty nice place, all done out in shades of blue and white that made it feel pleasantly cool, and with a lot of polished wood. The morning rush of workers was just dying down and the families on holiday, stopping in for a relaxed breakfast, were just starting to arrive. The menu was good, too. I'd been living in Gold Lake for two years—*why have I never been in here, before?*

Oh yeah. Because I have no one to have breakfast with.

I was nervous, so I arrived even earlier than usual. That left me with a full half hour to kill, so I made the most of it and had juice and coffee and waffles with strawberries and maple syrup.

When the guy and his two heavies strolled in, I was just pushing my sticky plate aside and finishing up my coffee. I sized them up as they approached. Blond hair, expensively styled. Nice suit. His two heavies were typical hired muscle: no neck and carefully blank expressions.

What interested me about the guy was that he wasn't from one of the usual customer bases—not Russian or American or Mexican or even Colombian. He'd flown in from Europe, although he was vague as to exactly where and insisted I call him simply *Carl*.

I'd guessed at Austrian or German. From his accent, as he said my name and sat down, I was spot-on. He smiled and told me how pleased he was to finally meet me. He was charming, in a way—even sort of good looking, but...

Something was off. However much he smiled, I still felt my stomach knotting. It was like a spider asking you to stroke it. Then the two heavies slid into the booth as well—one beside Carl and one beside me. Now I couldn't easily get out, if I needed to run. *Shit*.

"So," Carl said enthusiastically. "To business." He leaned in. "I need European passports. I'm told you can do those."

I nodded. "Which countries?"

"Germany, France, Switzerland, Austria, about thirteen United Kingdom—"

"Thirteen *UK?*" My eyes bulged. "Wait, how many are we talking about in total?!"

"Eighty-seven."

I felt my jaw drop. I'd been expecting five or ten.

"Is that a problem?" he asked, losing his smile.

I swallowed. "Not at all." It would mean a lot of late nights, but it wasn't like I had anything else to do. And it would take my mind off a certain cowboy.

"Good." His smile returned. It was in contrast to the two heavies, neither of whom had smiled at all. He popped the catches on his briefcase and took out a ring binder. "Here are the details," he said, tossing it to me.

Making sure that no one at the other tables could see, I cracked it open and looked at the first page. There was a passport-sized photo, ten neat fingerprints on a card, a name, date of birth, eye and hair color...everything I'd need. The only unusual thing was that the photo was of a woman—a pretty young thing with glossy black hair. Her date of birth was only three days after mine. Normally, in the criminal world, it's all men. Maybe she was someone's girlfriend.

A lot of the people I work with aren't good at organization but this perfect—it would make my job a breeze. "Fine," I said. "Depending on the exact mix of countries, figure three a day, so twenty-nine days. Let's meet one month from now."

Carl raised an eyebrow. "You work weekends? When do you have fun?"

I gave him a polite smile and started to shove the file into my shoulder bag, but the corner caught on the fabric. I had to pull it out and shove it in again, which was when the thing flopped open. I saw another page, about halfway through. Also with a woman's photo. I blinked and, out of some deeply-ingrained paranoia, turned the page.

Another woman.

They were all women. Every single one. All my age...or younger. Eighty-seven women, all needing passports so that they could be sent—*shipped*—all over Europe.

I tossed the file back to Carl. My fingers tingled, as if I'd been tainted just by touching it. "No."

He leaned forward. "Is there a problem?"

"I've always been very clear about what I will and won't do," I said. I glanced around. All around us, families were chowing down on eggs and hash browns, while the moms checked their Facebook feeds and the dads checked out the waitresses. I lowered my voice until he almost had to read my lips. "And I don't do trafficked women."

Carl shook his head. "Mine is a very old, established business. Rich clients. Very discreet. There won't be any problems. Nothing to blow back on you."

I frowned. "I said no."

He opened his briefcase again and took out a thick envelope, put it on top of the ring binder and shoved both across the table towards me. "Half now, as agreed," he said. "Half on delivery." He smiled at me, as if to show how reasonable he was being.

I charge three thousand dollars for a European passport and all the back-end hacking that goes with getting the false name onto the right databases. There was a little over a hundred and thirty thousand dollars in that envelope. All I had to do was reach out and take it.

I pushed the ring binder and envelope back across the table.

Carl stared at me coldly. And pushed it back to me.

I put my hand out to push it back again but, this time, the heavy next to me put his big paw on top of it, weighing it down. He scowled at me.

"Take the money," said Carl sadly.

"Get that thing the fuck away from me," I said in a low, dangerous voice. This had gone south, badly, and it was time to get out. I always keep my purse on my knee during meets. Now I slid my hand inside it, feeling for the glossy touch of mother-of-pearl under my fingers. I wouldn't actually pull the gun out—not yet. I'd just let him know it was pointing at him under the table and—

Where was my gun?

I'd packed it. Of course I'd packed it. I always packed it. I'd have to be really fucking dumb to not pack my gun. I'd gone for my run and showered and dried off, dressed and— And—

I could almost see the gun, sitting neatly in its holster under my bed, miles away.

Carl shook his head, tired of waiting. He scooped up the ring binder and envelope and dropped them into his briefcase. "Let's all go for a drive," he said to his heavies.

Shit. Shit, shit, *shit!*

TWENTY-THREE

Lily

"Pay for your meal," Carl told me, nodding at my plate. "It's not nice to run out without paying."

I pulled out a couple of bills and tossed them on the table, because that gave me time to think. But no matter how fast my brain raced, it wasn't coming up with anything. If I screamed or tried to run, Carl would probably pull a gun—I didn't doubt that he had one, somewhere on him. His heavies certainly would. And if people tried to help, someone was going to get killed.

I couldn't have that on my conscience. Not again.

I stood on shaking legs. The waffles and coffee were churning in my stomach. They were going to take me outside to their car and then...they could take me anywhere they wanted. Out into the desert, most likely. And this was a guy who sold women for a living.

Nobody would miss me. Not one single person. I could be gone for days—hell, I could be gone *forever*. That knowledge was almost worse than the fear.

We trooped through the diner, Carl leading the

way, one heavy in front of me and one behind. If anyone noticed how pale my face was, they didn't think anything of it. Mamma B's was a nice, respectable establishment, which made anything bad that happened in it effectively invisible.

We emerged into blinding sunlight and oven-hot air, the sort of weather the locals all thought was normal. The sort I still hadn't acclimatized to, even after two years. The heat surged down my throat and oozed under my clothes, soaking me in sweat almost instantly.

I saw the car we were heading for—a big four door sedan hire car. I faltered a little, slowing my pace as I thought about what they were going to do to me. The heavy pushed me from behind. *How could I have been so stupid? How could I forget my gun?*

I knew exactly why. My mind had been full of Bull.

My Toyota was down at the end of the parking lot. I glanced towards it, knowing there was no way I could get there before one of the heavies grabbed me.

Something was wrong. I shielded my eyes from the sun to get a better look. There was something...some*one* sitting on the hood. A big enough someone that the front suspension was dipped under his weight—

Oh, shit. My panic took on a whole new dimension. A battle started inside me: fear for him, fear for myself. I didn't want him to get involved but a traitorous part of me soared with the possibility of rescue.

Carl opened the rear door of the car and nodded me inside.

From the other end of the parking lot, I heard my Toyota's suspension creak as the weight was lifted off of it.

"Get in," Carl said tersely. The debate was raging in my head, now: let them take me quickly, before Bull could get involved, or hold out for a few seconds and hope he could help?

No. It was no decision at all and I cursed myself for even hesitating. This was my problem and no one else's.

I could hear footsteps approaching, but I didn't dare look in Bull's direction. I got into the car. One of the heavies climbed in beside me, the other got in the passenger seat, and Carl got behind the wheel. We'd been so quick, in the diner, that the car was still cool. My sweat started to go clammy on my skin. I'd been doing this for two years and I'd never, ever fucked up and got myself into a situation like this. Would they kill me? Or torture me to make me do the job? There were plenty of ways they could hurt me while leaving my hands and eyes intact.

Carl put the car into gear and we moved off.

TWENTY-FOUR

Lily

THERE WAS A VIOLENT JOLT as Carl stamped on the brake, cursing. I'd been staring down at my lap, imagining my fate. Now I looked up, between the front seats and through the windshield.

Bull was standing in front of the car, his hands planted on the hood. His cowboy hat was pulled low against the sun, throwing his eyes into shadow. But I could sense those bright blue orbs staring right at me.

"Who's this?" asked Carl.

I didn't say anything. I was too busy staring back at Bull. Willing him to run. Willing him not to.

"Get out of the way," called Carl through the windshield.

Bull kept his hands planted on the hood. "Right after I speak to my girl there."

I expected the icy wave of dread. This was exactly what I'd been worried about. What I didn't expect was the swell of emotion, right in my chest, at those two little words: *my girl.*

Carl muttered something and put his foot back on the gas. I guess he figured that he'd inch forward and force Bull to get out of the way.

What he actually did was remove any doubt, in Bull's mind, that I was in trouble. The car crept forward maybe half an inch. And then Bull growled and leaned forward, muscles bunching...

...and *pushed*. The car stopped moving.

Carl cursed again and pressed harder on the gas. The engine roared and we edged forward.

Bull frowned. I saw his massive shoulders tense. And then he pushed again and I heard the rear wheels slip and kick up dirt.

Carl cursed and put his foot to the floor. The rear wheels spun in place. Bull grunted as he took the strain. "You know why they call me Bull?" he yelled over the roar of the engine. "'Cause I'm built like one. I can do this all day!"

Carl took his foot off the gas and started to get out of the car, cursing. Before the heavy in the back could stop me, I threw open the door on my side and jumped out.

"You okay?" asked Bull as he straightened up.

I stared at him, still torn. I was debating whether to lie in order to get him out of there safely. But it was too late—the look on my face was enough. Bull's eyes narrowed.

Carl was still getting out. Bull stepped forward and pushed his door closed with one hand, trapping his neck between the door and the car. "Are you *crazy?*" spluttered Carl.

Bull jerked his head, nodding me over to him. I ran around the car to stand beside him. Meanwhile, the two heavies were looking helplessly at Carl. Every time they started towards him to help, Bull squeezed the door against Carl's neck in warning and they stopped again.

"You have any idea who you're dealing with?" Carl croaked, struggling to get free.

"Do you?" rumbled Bull.

Carl glared at him. He wasn't a small man but Bull was a full head taller and much, much bigger. He stopped struggling.

"Now me and Lily," said Bull, "are walking out of here. You got any sort of problem with that...I don't much care."

Carl glared at me and started to say something. But he glanced at Bull's face and bit it back at the last minute.

Bull let go of the door and slid his arm around my waist. He stepped out of the path of the car and, as soon as Carl and his heavies were back inside, it roared off in a cloud of dust and muffled cursing.

When I looked around at Bull, he was staring straight down at me. I stepped back—only an inch or so, just so that I could have enough room to talk to him. But he used the arm around my waist to pull me in tight against him.

"No," he growled. "Not this fucking time. This is the part where you tell me everything."

TWENTY-FIVE

Lily

I BIT MY LIP as I stared up at him. Part of me was already sliding, instinctually, into full-on denial mode. *It's nothing! A misunderstanding. Goodbye, Bull.*

Except...now that the danger was over, I was shaking from how close I'd come to being badly beaten or even killed. *Really* shaking. I shook my head to indicate that I couldn't speak, turning from him, my lip trembling. Shit, I was going to—

And suddenly, he was gathering me into his arms, turning me back to face him and wrapping me against his chest. I gave a sort of hiccupping groan and then the tears started. *Shit!* I didn't want to cry, not about business. *That's so goddamn weak! Don't let him think you're weak!* But I kept thinking of Carl's fake smile and being driven out somewhere lonely by him and no one looking for me—

"Shh," said Bull, almost as if speaking to a timid animal. *"Shh—shh."*

I tried to speak but still couldn't. Eventually, I just

pressed my face to his shirt and clutched at the warm, solid muscle of his sides with both hands. I needed something strong and stable and he was the strongest thing I'd ever felt. I sobbed but, instead of spilling down my cheeks, my tears soaked into his shirt. That made me feel better, as if I wasn't on my own.

When I was all cried out, I gently moved back and looked up into his eyes. The look of concern I saw there almost started me crying all over again.

I knew he'd still want an explanation and that any lie I told wasn't going to convince him. Not after what he'd seen. And the relationship between us had changed again. Just like when he'd saved my life from the bull, I felt that I owed him.

I hesitated for another moment. I'd kept my work a secret for two long years. Telling Bull was like taking a willing step over the edge of a precipice.

I nodded to my car. "Get in."

***

Bull looked ridiculous with his massive body folded into the passenger seat of my little Toyota, but he didn't complain. Nor did he badger me with questions on the short drive out to the bus, which gave me time to compose myself.

When we arrived, he spent a moment just staring at my home. Inside, he eyed the improvements—the kitchen, the stairs down to the bathroom...the bed. Particularly the bed.

To say I hadn't been expecting guests was an understatement. No one had set foot in the place but me for two years. I kept it pretty clean, but maybe my norms were all off, after two years alone.

"You did all this yourself?" he asked at last. He didn't sound surprised that I'd managed it; he sounded impressed.

"Yeah," I said shyly. Then, "I had some time on my hands."

He nodded slowly, still gazing around. "So what do you do, Lily, that involves assholes like those guys?"

I took a deep breath. I was way past lying, now. Opening up, after so long, was intoxicating. I folded back the bed and revealed my desk.

Bull took off his hat and ran a hand through his hair as he stared. He stepped forward and brushed his fingers across the partially-completed passports, fingering the covers, examining the bundles of special plastics and the strips of holograms I used. He gave a long, low whistle. "Holy shit."

"Holy shit," I agreed.

Bull picked up one of the finished passports at random. The gold letters on the dark red cover were in Cyrillic. He opened it. "Grigori Arsenyev," he read.

"His real name's Yuri. Bodyguard of a Russian arms dealer—Luka Malakov. Yuri managed to get himself on a watch list so now he needs a little help getting into the country."

Bull turned and stared at me.

"What?" Then I realized I'd said it sort of nonchalantly. This stuff was just normal, to me.

"Just..." he shook his head. "I thought you were all done surprising me."

I allowed myself a little smile.

He opened another passport. "Mexican. I guess the drug cartels?"

I nodded.

"And Russian arms dealers..." he mused.

"Also the Yakuza, sometimes." I said helpfully. "The Colombians. I don't discriminate." I was smiling. But then the mood changed.

"So you do passports for *anyone?!*"

I crossed my arms. "Of course not *anyone*. I check my clients out. Personal recommendations. No one I think is a terrorist. I've even tipped off the FBI a few times. Anonymously, of course. And that German asshole today was selling women." I shuddered. "That's why I said 'no'."

Bull shook his head again. "Jesus, Lily...."

"What?" I could hear the defensive note creep into my voice.

"I just can't believe you're mixed up in all this."

"*Mixed up* in it? What, you think I fell into it by accident? I didn't get *mixed up* in it. This is what I do." I held my chin up high.

"*Why?* I mean...you're smart"—he gestured at the converted bus—"you work your ass off. Why do *this?*"

I stiffened. "I found I was uniquely qualified. Most criminals aren't too smart." I considered. "Well, Luka's pretty smart. But most of them aren't. I'm good at it, okay? And I can do it quietly. I can stay hidden."

He frowned. "Why do you need to stay hidden?"

Shit. I didn't answer. Instead, I pointed towards my computers. "Most people think it's just about the physical stuff—the passport, the driver's license. But these days, those are the easy parts. As soon as they're scanned, the online records are checked. If they don't match up, you end up in a very small room at the airport, talking to some guys from Homeland Security."

"So you're a hacker, as well."

I shrugged. "By now, it's pretty much routine. I

have ways into anywhere I need to get to." It was the first time I'd ever been able to tell someone and I was surprised at how proud I felt. "If I don't know, I know who to ask and who to pay. Some of it's hacking, some of it's favors for the right clerk at the DMV."

He shook his head again. That stung—I'd been almost glowing with pride as I laid out my whole little empire. "Will you stop shaking your head at me? You wanted the truth."

He stared at me, eyes blazing. Because he disapproved, or because I'd been keeping it from him? Neither alternative was good. At last, he slumped down on my couch. "Why do you need to stay hidden?" he asked again.

Shit. I'd been hoping I'd distracted him from that one. I tried to come up with an answer that was both truthful—because I was sick of lying—and that would close down this line of questioning. "Things got complicated in New York. I had to leave."

He stared at me. "You're gonna have to do better than that," he rumbled.

TWENTY-SIX

Bull

SHE SHOOK HER HEAD. The way all that silky hair tossed around took the edge off my anger—damn it, I was mad as hell at her, but all I wanted to do was run over there and kiss her. Didn't she realize what she was messing with? Mexican drug cartels? And a Russian goddamn arms dealer? I didn't want a guy like that anywhere near my Lily. *Luka Malakov?* I imagined a pale blob of a man with thinning, greasy hair, his stomach straining at his suit. Probably leering at her as he tried to get her price down, and she'd feel she had to flirt with him to keep him happy....

Hell, no!

I just wanted to take her away from it all, rescue her...couldn't she see that? Yet for some reason, she seemed to be getting mad at *me*.

"I've told you more than I should have," she said. "More than anyone else knows. I have some secrets. Get used to it."

I glared stubbornly back at her. I had to know why

she'd left New York if I was going to help her. Why would she have to stay hidden? Some crime she'd committed? She'd told me the other stuff—why not this? "If you never trust anyone, you're going to be mighty lonely."

She glanced around the bus. "I've been doing just fine on my own until now."

I couldn't stop myself. I thought that, if I could make her see what her secrecy had done to her, she'd see sense. I didn't stop to think how it would sound. I nodded at the single bed. "How's that working out for you?"

I saw her face redden, almost as if I'd slapped her. *Shit.* I hadn't meant to upset her. "How about you get off my bus?" she whispered.

Damn it! I hesitated for a moment, trying to think of how to apologize. "Goddamn it, Lily," I said, which probably wasn't the best way to start. "Listen—"

"Just get out!"

I sighed and grabbed my hat, shoving it on my head. I was still mad as hell at her for putting herself in this kind of danger. "You know where I am when you're ready to talk," I told her. And I stalked out. *Goddamn that woman!*

TWENTY-SEVEN

Lily

Goddamn that man!

I stomped around the bus, pacing back and forth for a good half hour. I was pretty sure I'd seen the last of Carl—I always made sure none of my clients knew where I lived. I'd cut all ties and I might even consider an anonymous tip to Interpol. *Jesus!* Selling women? *What happened to nice, normal crime like drugs and guns?*

I thought about that for a second. I was raised by one of New York's most powerful dons. It's possible my moral compass is a little out of whack. But at least I *have* a moral compass.

But the problems with Bull? That couldn't be so easily solved. The argument had angered me but also upset me, leaving me shamefully close to tears. I was proud of what I did: I was one of the best in the world at my gig, I had clients who trusted me, and I kept everything professional. That's why it burned so much that Bull disapproved.

The thing is, however much you hate the person

who raises you, you still learn from them. I'd learned about running a business from my uncle and I'd picked up his respect for hard work and doing the best job you can. On some deep level, I think I'd even wanted to impress him—even though he had no idea what I now did. And the fact that he was so sexist, that he thought women had no place except in the home, made me even more determined to build my own little empire.

I hadn't realized, until I'd told Bull about it, how much I'd been longing to share my achievements with someone. And then he'd thrown it all back in my face.

Why was he so mad? Because he thought I couldn't handle crime—or maybe that *no* woman could handle it? I'd known he was arrogant and kind of a jerk at times, but I'd been getting to really like him. I hadn't figured him for sexist. Or was his problem the morals of what I was doing? That didn't make sense either—Bull didn't strike me as someone who didn't at least bend a few laws. Sure, he might be taken aback at what I was doing, but not *angry*.

Maybe I just didn't understand men.

TWENTY-EIGHT

Bull

Maybe I just didn't understand women.

I was out at the ranch, stripped to the waist and riding a fine, fast stallion, helping the owner chase down a troublesome steer. Exactly the kind of thing I did well. But I couldn't enjoy it as I normally would. I kept thinking of Lily, alone in that bus.

Lily, with her hair like silk and her lips like goddamn satin pillows. Lily, with those full, bountiful breasts and pale, curving thighs that I'd still only seen in my imagination. So smart and so sure of herself, so proud of all she'd accomplished—

Proud?

Aw, hell. The lasso fell from my hand and I pulled my horse up short.

I'd gone and offended her, hadn't I? That's why she'd blown up at me. I'd been worried about her and angry at her for putting herself in danger, and she'd taken it as criticizing her. And then I'd made it worse with that crack about her single bed. All I'd meant was that her damn secrecy had stopped us getting together for the whole time she'd been living in Texas. If I hadn't saved her from the bull, we might never have met.

Maybe I should apologize. But I still couldn't figure out why she wouldn't tell me about her past.

"Hey!" the owner bawled at me. "You gonna rope that steer or what?"

I looked up. Confused by the fact I'd stopped chasing it, the steer had stopped too and was frowning at me as if to say, *"Are we doing this or are we not doing this?"*

"Sorry," I mumbled to the owner. I retrieved the lasso and tossed it over the steer's head with a quick flick of my wrist. The steer snorted as if to say, *"About time!"*

There. Simple. Why did women have to be so damn complicated?

TWENTY-NINE

Lily

"And who is it you're here to see?" asked the receptionist.

"Mr. Hanlow," I told her. "Room 233. I'm his granddaughter."

"I thought I recognized you. What's it been...two months?"

I nodded and signed myself in... as Carol Hanlow. Then I walked all the way through the care facility to room 233...and knocked on 232 instead.

I knew that there were people looking for me and I knew they'd check here at some point. I couldn't have a visitor's book showing I'd been here. But my grandmother was the one link I had to my parents and I couldn't abandon her completely. When I heard she'd had to be moved into the care home, some months after I left New York, it had taken me weeks to pluck up the courage to make the trip to Colorado. It was meant to be a one-time thing but, when I'd seen her here all alone with no visitors, I'd known I'd have to come back.

Hence the ruse. As far as the care home was concerned Mr. Hanlow got a visit from his (actually long-dead) granddaughter every few months while my grandmother saw no one at all. I really would stop in to see Hanlow for a few minutes on my way out—partially because I felt sorry for the poor guy, partially to cover myself if he talked to the nurses. His Alzheimer's helped to muddy the waters enough that no one would figure the time discrepancy.

My grandmother opened the door and her face lit up when she saw it was me. She pulled me inside while simultaneously giving me an enormous hug. "Get yourself in here," she ordered. "I've got two clues I'm stuck on."

She did the Wall Street Journal crossword every Friday. At eighty-three and at least as sharp as I was.

When we were sitting drinking tea and I was trying to figure out ten down, she said, "Who is he?"

"Maybe I just came to visit, like other granddaughters. I could brush your hair for you. Do you want me to brush your hair?"

"Tessa, you touch this 'do and you won't sit down for a week. It's been sixty-two days since you visited and you average eighty-eight. You came here because you want advice and that means it must be a man because it can't be your job or your friends or your house because you won't tell me diddly squat about any of those."

I always suspected I inherited a lot of things from my grandmother. It was one reason we got on so well. "I'm sorry," I said. "It's better that you don't know this stuff." I didn't even dare to tell her which state I was living in. It'd make it easier for her to play dumb if anyone came looking for me. She knew I'd fled New

York, but nothing else about my life.

She shook her head. "As long as you're happy and you're well away from that prick—pardon my French—Erico." She sighed. "Of all the people who could step in and raise you. Your parents would have been horrified. Your father was a goddamn hippy. He *abhorred* violence. Animals, plants...that was always his thing."

I'd never been able to relate to that, before. I'd grown up a city girl, under Uncle Erico's wing. Since the horse riding with Bull, though, the great outdoors seemed just a little less scary.

"So," said my grandmother. "It's a man. Unless it's a woman?"

"Grandma!"

"It's all fine, Tessa." She put her hand on mine. "When I studied in San Francisco, *I* had a few experiences with—"

I put my hands over my ears. "Too much information!"

"So shut me up. Tell me about your man."

I met her gaze...then dropped my eyes. This *was* what I'd come here for. "He's...good," I said. "I mean, I think he's *a good man,* you know? He tries really hard not to be, when everyone's looking at him. He's got this bad boy thing going on. But when he's with me..." I sighed and shook my head. "He's an asshole too, though. He thinks he's God's gift."

"Is he?" she asked sharply.

I bit my lip. And nodded.

"Sounds like a keeper."

"But he's an asshole!"

"The good ones usually are. Your grandpa was kind of an asshole, God rest his soul. So what's the problem?"

"We had a fight. About what I do for a living."

She frowned at me. "Are you stripping?"

"*No!*" I said, horrified.

"Because there's nothing wrong with that. *I* did it. That's how I met your grandpa, actually."

"No! God, look at me! Do I look like a stripper?"

"There's nothing wrong with curves, Tessa. *He* obviously likes them."

"I'm not stripping."

"Hooking?"

"*No!* Just...anyway, he doesn't approve and we had a fight about it. And now I don't know how to apologize."

"Go and visit him. Surprise him. Don't let him tell you what to do with your life, but give him a chance to explain. You don't want to lose this one."

"He's an asshole! How can you be so sure he's right for me?"

"Because you've called him an asshole three times since you've been here. You're never that down on *anyone*...unless you really, really like them."

I stared at her. And then hugged her, which knocked the table and sloshed tea over my jeans. "Goddamnit!" Luckily, I found a napkin in my pocket so I mopped up the worst of it with that.

I spent the whole afternoon with her, then slipped into Mr. Hanwell's room for a quick game of checkers before I left. On the flight back to Texas, I turned it over and over in my mind. By the time the wheels hit the tarmac, I'd made a decision: I was going to go and see Bull. *Not* to carry it on. I couldn't. That would be dangerous for both of us. I'd just apologize and that would be it. I figured that seeing him again, just for a few minutes, would scratch my Bull-itch. It would be, I thought, like giving an addict a carefully measured dose to help them gradually kick the habit.

I hadn't realized just how helplessly addicted I was.

THIRTY

Lily

"Y'all be taking out?" asked the smiling girl behind the counter. Even Starbucks was different, this far south.

"Yep," I said. What would he like? What was safe? "Can I get an iced latte with extra ice?"

"Tall? Grande?"

I thought about Bull for a second. "Venti. Definitely Venti."

"Whipped cream?"

"Probably not."

I told her my name and went to wait at the end of the counter. He'd like an iced latte, right? Everyone liked an iced latte, on a hot day. Even if it showed up unexpectedly.

***

A half hour later, with the latte still relatively cold, I pulled up outside the ranch. It was mid-morning, which was deliberate. I wanted him to be busy and have to run back to work—that way, there'd be no way that things could get out of control.

One of the ranch hands directed me to a barn—a huge, old-fashioned one of red-painted wood, piled high with hay bales. When I peeked through the door, I saw Bull stripped to the waist, heaving hay bales around. *Doesn't he ever wear a shirt?*

I didn't speak, didn't move. I just stood there silently watching him for a moment, taking in the rippling muscles of his back and the solid mass of his biceps. Everything about him was...*physical*. Real. The opposite of my own world of electrons and secrets.

Then I saw him freeze, like an animal catching a scent on the breeze. He turned slowly to face me and I ducked halfway back behind the door. When he saw me, we just stood there staring at each other for a few seconds.

"Hi." My voice quavered. "Um. I came to apologize."

He tossed the hay bale aside as if it weighed nothing and strode towards me.

"I shouldn't have blown up at you," I said, and looked at the ground.

He put a finger under my chin and gently lifted my head so that I was looking up at him. I braced myself for something raw and coarse, some crack about how he wanted to fuck me.

"I'm sorry, too," he muttered.

I just stood there in shock.

"I guess I didn't expect...all that," he said. "But that don't mean it ain't...impressive. Hell of a lot more impressive than roping steers and riding bulls. And better paid, that's for goddamn sure."

Had he just...*apologized? Bull?* The ground

seemed to be slipping away from under my feet.

"I'm still mad at you," he said. "Because I'm worried you'll get yourself killed."

Someone was worried about me? The shock of it was matched by how good it felt. The ground was gone completely, now. I was floating, helpless.

And then I remembered my plan. I had to turn away and leave, now.

I offered up the Starbucks cup. "I brought you an iced latte," I said, holding it out. My hand shook a little.

"Did you?"

"Um...yep."

He moved even closer. He *loomed*. So much power. My insides tightened again and this time the feeling slid lower—between my thighs. Our chests were almost touching. "I don't want a fucking latte," he said.

I stood there in shock, just breathing for a second. It wasn't what he'd said; it was the unspoken message in his eyes. The realization of what he *did* want.

It wasn't much cooler in the barn than outside. The air pressed in on me from every side, roasting me slowly through my jeans and faded red t-shirt. But there was a second kind of heat, throbbing into me from him, pulsing right into my depths. A sort of heat that made me weak inside, all my good intentions melting away.

I closed my eyes and tilted my head up, waiting for his kiss.

"No," he said in a low growl.

I opened my eyes. He was staring right at me.

"No more goddamn games," he told me. "No more letting me kiss you and then running, Lily. You come in this door, it's going to happen. I'm going to take you, my way, so you better be sure you're ready."

The heat filled me completely, washing down to my toes and up to my brain, scorching away any last traces of rational thought. Somewhere, there had been a plan. Somewhere, there had been reasons why this was a bad idea. But suddenly, none of that mattered.

"Yes," I whispered. "I'm ready."

The latte slipped out of my hand.

And he pulled me into the barn.

THIRTY-ONE

Lily

HE SPUN ME AROUND and I went staggering backwards across the floor in my sneakers. I would have fallen if he hadn't kept hold of my hands. Then I whumped into a soft, prickly wall.

His lips were on me instantly, his tongue slipping into my mouth, and I was panting and opening for him. His urgency, his hunger made me weak. I could actually feel my legs giving a little and I sagged, held up by his hands on mine and the press of his body against me. *I'm being kissed up against the hay bales by a cowboy,* went through my mind. Along with: *this doesn't happen in New York.*

He put one hand on my hip, squeezing me there, while his other hand roamed over my body, sweeping over my shoulder and side, teasing me, making me moan with need before it finally settled on my breast. When I felt his hot palm through my t-shirt, I trembled and gave a little mewl of lust. He didn't even squeeze at first, just pressed gently, making my breast pillow and bulge under the cotton. I could feel my nipple stiffening in response and knew that he'd be able to feel the hard outline even through my bra.

"You particularly attached to this t-shirt?" he growled between kisses.

It seemed like a strange question. I swear I honestly had no idea what he had in mind. "No."

His mouth pressed to mine again, taking my upper lip and sucking on it until I moaned and thrashed, then sealing me into a kiss. I was vaguely aware of his hands in the neckline of my t-shirt, stretching it away from my body—

There was a violent renting sound and my t-shirt was suddenly hanging off my arms in two halves, torn clean down the middle. My *MMF!* of shock was muffled by his kiss. I could feel the oven-hot air wafting over my stomach and the upper slopes of my breasts. For a second, all my insecurities about my body flooded back. Then his hands started to work over me, starting at my shoulders and sliding all the way down my front, following the shape of me. It was as if he was luxuriating in me, worshipping my shape. My brief protest died away and my shyness about my body melted like ice in a furnace.

A hand slid behind me. Some men have trouble getting bra clasps open; Bull was not that sort of man. I felt my bra loosen and then he was pushing it impatiently up and out of the way, both hands capturing my breasts and rolling and squeezing them, thumbs stroking across my nipples.

It hit me, for the first time, that we were doing all this in the middle of a goddamn barn. We hadn't even shut the door, never mind locked it. And this was the middle of the day—wasn't Bull meant to be at work?

I broke the kiss for a second. "Won't someone

come looking for you?" I panted.

"Maybe," he growled. "Why, you want to stop?"

I stared at him for a second and then grabbed his biceps with both hands and pulled him into a kiss.

I moaned as he kissed right the way down to my jeans and then slowly back up in a lazy "S" across my stomach. No man had ever paid that area much attention, but he was almost reverent. Then he reached my left breast and sucked it into his mouth, bathing my nipple with his tongue, and I very nearly exploded right there. I let go of his arms and dug my fingers into the straw behind me, growling into his mouth. He slowed down, teasing me or maybe savoring the feel of me in his mouth. I could feel every slick millimeter as his tongue played back and forth across my breast with agonizing slowness. Every raised dot and tiny crinkle around my nipple became the epicenter of new tremor of pleasure.

His hands were on my jeans, just like last time. Except this time, I didn't stop him. This time, my own hands were exploring his back, tracing over the hardness of the muscles, sliding down his torso as it narrowed towards his ass. At the same time he popped the button free and pushed my jeans down, I clasped his ass in both hands. God, he was so firm through the denim. All muscle. Power to ram and thrust and pound....

He shoved my jeans down my legs and I helped by kicking until they were a tangle of fabric around my ankles and I could prise my feet free. The feel of loose straw and warm stone under my feet was a shock—it reminded me where we were and how risky this was. It nearly made me stop.

Nearly.

His hand came up between my legs, cupping me through my panties. The heat of his palm surged through the thin fabric, melting any last traces of my resistance, adding to the twisting storm of heat that was building inside me. The one that had started as soon as I'd seen him...or maybe even earlier, maybe since the night before, when I'd lain in bed horny and frustrated.

And then his thumbs were hooking into the edges of my panties and he was tugging them down, kneeling as he did it, escaping my clutching fingers. I gave a low, shuddering moan as the kiss was finally broken, then another as his face drew level with my sex. I could feel his eyes on me, his panting breath sending little currents of air through the soft hair to blaze against my damp flesh. He leaned forward and licked me, just once, and I went crazy, folding at the waist as the pleasure exploded outward from my groin. But he reached up with one hand and pushed me hard against the hay bales, trapping me there. He hooked my panties off one foot, leaving them dangling from the other ankle. Then he was nudging my legs apart—

I hadn't had much chance to make a noise before, most of my moans and groans swallowed up by his kisses. Now, though, my mouth was free and I couldn't stop myself crying out, a long, keening sob of pleasure as his tongue speared into me. *Jesus!* I tried instinctively to shut my legs—the sensations were almost too much. But his hands were on my thighs immediately, his thumbs hooking around the inside of them so that he could haul me open and—

Ah! His lips found my clit, sucking and teasing it, sending the heat inside me spiraling upward. His tongue plunged between my lips again and again, tasting me. My eyes were tight closed, so I had to feel for his head: then I buried my fingers in those soft brown curls. I started to pant, tasting sun-heated air, and the scent of the straw. I cursed and begged, squeezing and rubbing at his head in time with his ministrations. "Ah! Oh God, Jesus Bull please—*OH God* like that don't—AH God DON'T STOP—"

My legs couldn't hold me. My knees bent and only the strength of his arms kept me standing, my back pressed against the hay bales and my thighs in his palms. I was grinding my ass back against the hay, its scratchy touch the perfect antidote to the soft, wet pleasure. But I still wasn't going to be able to hold back the storm for long. It was rolling towards me, huge and mighty and I was a matchwood house in its path.

Bull suddenly drew his tongue from me and lashed over my clit, at the same time as he plunged two thick fingers deep inside me. I let out a scream of release as the pleasure blasted me apart, shattering me and sending me sailing away in fragments.

I still hadn't touched down when I heard him get to his feet. There was the distant leather creak of his belt opening and then the jangle as his jeans fell around his ankles. Another rustle of cloth—*that'll be his boxers,* I thought vaguely. I was still gasping, rolling my head from side to side against the hay bales, eyes tight closed.

My hands had fallen away from his head as he stood up. Now one of my hands was gripped in his and drawn towards him. I let it happen, still drunk on pleasure.

I only really came awake when I felt my fingers

being closed around his cock.

The first sensation was heat—throbbing, almost scalding. Then the size. As my fingers wrapped around it, they stopped far too soon. He couldn't be that thick—

My eyes flew open and I looked down. He *could* be that thick. And that...long.

You know why they call me Bull?

It was beautiful and just as big and strong as its owner, hard as rock and with a silky, arrow-shaped head. I felt myself getting wetter, just looking at it. It would fill me...*stretch* me. *Jesus.*

I began to stroke it with my hand, showing him how much I wanted him. He gave a low growl, pressing so close to me that his pecs mashed against my breasts. He laid kisses up and down my jaw line as I pumped him, but he only endured it for a handful of seconds before he knocked my hand away and pushed my legs apart. I almost slid down towards the floor, but he used his body to pin me firmly against the bales.

I wanted it so much and I was so far gone on pleasure that I almost didn't realize, at first. Not when the hot length of him slapped against my thigh. Not when that silken head stroked my moist lips. He'd actually started to enter me, splitting me apart with that arrow-shaped head and sliding inside, before I clutched at his forearms. "Wait!" I squeaked. "Condom!"

He licked at my earlobe. "I already told you how I want to fuck you," he said. "Bareback."

The word went off like a bomb in my head, scattering all sense. It fell all the way down to my groin and seemed to detonate there a second time, making me twist and buck. That sent the naked tip of him a little further inside and the sensation of it, of bare flesh on flesh, made me heady. "We can't," I said.

"The hell we can't." He moved his own hips just a fraction, angling into me, and I felt another millimeter of him slide inside. I clutched at him and let out a silent scream of pleasure.

"Do you want it, Lily?" he growled, his breath hot in my ear.

The storm had returned, bearing down on me, ready to lift me and carry me again.

I nodded.

THIRTY-TWO

Lily

HE PLANTED HIS HANDS on the hay bales either side of my head. He started the slow push into me and I gasped as the girth of the head spread me wide, silky-smooth and *God* so hot, so raw and real inside me. I grabbed for his shoulders, digging my fingers into the muscles there, as I began to stretch—

Ah! He surged into me, my body clamping down around him. My eyes went wide at the sensation of him naked inside me. It was so completely different without a condom. I could feel every hot millimeter of him.

His hands closed on my hips, pinning me to the hay bales, his thumbs stroking at the creases at the tops of my thighs and drawing whirlpools of pleasure from them. And then he began to thrust.

I drew in a breath, squeezing my eyes shut, as I felt the orgasm begin to spiral around me, building speed and pressure. On every stroke, I could feel him deep inside me...and he wasn't even in me all the way, yet.

My ass was tight against the hay, held there as securely as if we were lying down. All I could do was to tilt myself up to meet him and he groaned as I did just that, wantonly offering myself up to him.

He gave a sudden grunt and pressed and *ground* and I cried out as I felt the hard base of him rock against my pubis, and knew he was in me all the way. *God! What are we doing?!* I was suddenly aware of the throbbing tip of him, naked and deep inside me. It was wrong and risky and insanely hot, all at the same time. And then the climax was pressing in on me, stealing my breath and my thoughts. Nothing mattered except—

He started to fuck me. *Really* fuck me. Hands locked tight on my hips, chest rubbing against my breasts. His cock was so hot, so thickly long inside me: solid, heated rock wrapped in satin. I thrashed my head against the hay, mouth open and slack.

But that wasn't enough for him. He scooped his hands under my hips and lifted me, pulling me away from the wall of hay bales for a second and then slamming me back against it. My feet came off the floor and I lifted them, wrapping my legs around his waist and my arms around his shoulders.

I was more open to him like this, and he moved even faster, pounding into me with long, hard strokes that made me heady. His mouth laid a trail of kisses up my neck and along my jaw to my mouth. We kissed, gasping and panting, as he fucked me, both of us now coated in a thin sheen of sweat. *"God!"* I managed, the first proper word I'd managed in a while.

He sped up even more. Every part of him felt hard, from the press of his pecs against my nipples to the muscles of his ass against my ankles. He was made of rock, and I was softness and warmth around him. "I love fucking you," he gasped. "Goddamn, Lily, you're mine."

The storm finally rose up and overwhelmed me, obliterating me from the inside out. His words echoed in my head and I clung to him with all my strength as the pleasure rocketed through me, making me arch my back and dig my fingers hard into his muscles. I felt myself spasm and clench around him and heard him groan. And then—

He said my name and humped his hips against me one final time, grinding his groin against me—

I felt his cock twitch and—

My eyes opened as awareness hit. I stared up at the barn's rafters, at the cracks of sunlight streaming into the darkness—

Ah! A sudden, hot jet inside me, thick and heavy and potent. *OH JESUS!* My orgasm had been winding down, but now it spun back up to full strength. Another jet. Another. *Another.* I clung to him, rocking and gasping, as he filled me, my eyes wide, all but the most basic thoughts torn away by pleasure.

When he finally went still against me, I just hung there panting. The barn was suddenly very quiet, our breathing the loudest sound in the place. He raised his head from my shoulder and kissed me, but I was too weak and drunk on sensation to do more than open my mouth and let him plunder me.

He carefully turned, his boots scraping on the floor, and walked us over to a stack of bales that was about level with his hips. He set me down on it, lying me down full-length on my back like a slumbering princess.

I didn't *feel* like a princess. I was naked, save for the scraps of t-shirt hanging off my shoulders and my pushed-up bra. My hair was festooned with bits of straw. My whole body was shining with sweat and I knew that, all down my back and ass, I had pink imprints from where I'd been pressed hard against the bales. But most of my attention was focused lower down.

I...*ached*. Not in a painful way but in a been-to-the-gym way. As if I'd been worked hard. I'd just never felt it *there,* before. I could feel it every time I moved my legs and I could feel something else, too. Deep inside me, hotly thick and sticky—

I put my hand over my groin. "Jesus," I whispered.

THIRTY-THREE

Bull

I HAULED UP MY BOXERS AND JEANS and buckled my belt, doing it all by feel because I couldn't take my eyes off of her. God, she was beautiful. Her near-naked body shone in the shafts of sunlight, her magnificent chest rising and falling as she recovered. She put her hand down between her thighs, feeling what I'd done to her, and that made my cock swell all over again.

Even near-naked and just-fucked, she managed to look classy. She looked like one of those society girls, the kind you see in movies riding around in Mercedes with blacked-out windows, about to inherit the family fortune. But there was something about her looks that was slightly different. Exotic. I hadn't picked up on it before because her skin was so pale, but was there a trace of Spanish or...

Italian. That was it. Italian. An Italian-American princess.

She'd gone very quiet, so I strolled over there. "You okay?" I asked, unable to keep the dumb grin off of my face.

She lay there for a second, staring up at the ceiling. "What did we just *do?*" she asked, horrified.

I smirked. "What I do best."

She sat up, shutting her thighs tightly. "I'm not like that," she said firmly. She was staring off into the distance, as if she was speaking to herself.

"Hate to break it to you, Lily, but *yeah you are.* You came in here damn near dripping for it."

Her head jerked around to glare at me. At the same time, her hand whipped across my cheek. Not a very hard slap—she definitely wasn't used to doing it. I let it bounce off my cheek and laughed.

"Shit!" she gasped. "Sorry. I just—" Then she frowned. "Stop laughing! It's not funny!" She ran a hand through her hair. Little bits of straw fell out. "I can't believe we just did that. Did we really just do that?"

"Oh, for the love of God," I muttered, and kissed her, which felt damn fine *and* quieted her down. When I pulled back, her breathing had slowed a little. "Stop thinking like a damn city girl," I told her sternly.

"I *am* a city girl."

"Not anymore."

She looked down at herself, as if she'd never seen her own body before. Then, for some reason, she touched that gorgeous, softly-smooth stomach.

I leaned close. "I'd love to fuck you again," I told her. "Or just lay down in the hay with you and hold you. But sooner or later, someone's going to come looking for me, and they're going to see you all laid out there...."

She yelped and tried to pull her t-shirt back together, then realized it was useless. She dived for her jeans and I enjoyed watching that ripe ass wiggle its way into them. Then I threw her my t-shirt. "Here," I said. "I barely wear it anyway."

She caught it and stared at me for a moment, as if I'd just given her a Gucci dress. Then fastened up her bra and pulled it on. The t-shirt was ridiculously big on her, but at least she wouldn't have to suffer the other guys gawping at her.

I walked over to her and took her hands. "Now, I don't know how you do it in the big city," I told her, "but out here, this means we gotta get married."

She looked up at me, eyes huge.

"Joke," I told her.

Her face relaxed and she sort of shook herself, like, *of course it was.* But for just an instant there, I'd thought I'd seen a flash of...*disappointment?* Shit. I'd misjudged her again. She always seemed so distant, pushing me away—I'd just been kidding around, letting her know I wasn't some hick who'd get all clingy, and it had backfired.

"But you're not going to do your disappearing act again, are you?" I asked.

She shook her head, but in a very doubtful way.

"*Lily,*" I grated. "Don't run out on me again. I got a lasso and I know just how to use it."

"I have to go," she muttered, and pulled away.

I grabbed her by the hand and pulled her up short, then dragged her across the floor towards me, her sneakers sliding on a bed of hay.

I pulled her into my arms, lifted her up off the floor and kissed her. After a second of resistance, she opened her lips and allowed it, and then I felt her melt. I relaxed. Everything was going to be okay. I hoped.

"I'm serious," I whispered in her ear. "You run off again and I'm going to have to teach you a lesson."

She squirmed against me and nodded. Then she was sliding down out of my arms and hurrying out of the barn.

I stood staring at the door for a long time after she'd gone. In theory, I should be celebrating. The sex had been the best ever, just how I'd imagined it. And if she wanted to keep it casual and just show up for sex and then disappear...wasn't that what I wanted? Wasn't that what every guy wanted?

But something wasn't right—about the way she'd reacted, after the sex, and on a deeper level, too. Something in her past. Something that kept scaring her away.

I was worried about her.

I couldn't remember when I'd ever worried about a girl, before.

THIRTY-FOUR

Lily

I STUMBLED DOWNSTAIRS to the bathroom, only just making it to the toilet before I threw up. *Isn't morning sickness meant to only last a month?*

I ran my hands over my huge, swollen belly. The last eight months had shot by. I still hadn't told Bull. *Why hadn't I told Bull?*

My whole life was in ruins.

The sound of a car engine outside sent me waddling over to the door. Three black BMWs were pulling up. My blood turned to ice water. I recognized the type of car. The first man out was Antonio and the second was my uncle, followed by a small army of goons. They started towards me.

They'd found me. I'd been invisible for two years, but the baby had made me noticeable.

I jumped down out of the bus and tried to run away down the creek bed, but I could only manage a stumbling walk, hands holding my stomach, terrified that I'd trip. I was so worried about the baby. How was I going to protect it, if I couldn't even protect myself?

They'd catch me and now they'd want Bull and the baby, too. I'd brought them into my life and I was going to get them all killed. How could I have been so irresponsible?

Footsteps behind me. Expensive leather shoes pounding through the dust. Hands caught my arms—

THIRTY-FIVE

Lily

I HEAVED IN A MASSIVE LUNGFUL OF AIR and sat up in bed. Everything was still and quiet. I sat there in the darkness for a few seconds, terrified the nightmare was going to come back. My hands searched my belly. No swelling.

I slumped back on the sheets, my heart rate gradually slowing. I was soaked in sweat. *Fuck!*

It was the night after I'd met Bull in the barn. *Met* being a euphemism for *gone there in the middle of the morning and allowed him to fuck me.*

Hard.

Bareback.

And now my slumbering brain had gone to town with the potential consequences.

Too shaken to get back to sleep, I went to get a glass of water. The dream had been so real that I actually relished each easy, unladen step to the sink.

What had I been thinking? The few times I'd had sex, back in college, I'd never, ever not used a condom. Had my brain just shut down the moment I'd stepped inside the barn?

Yeah. Pretty much. The sight of him, the words he'd said...it had sent all the rational parts of me on vacation.

I'd started to come back to myself straight after the sex—that's why I'd left so abruptly. And almost immediately, I'd started running through dates in my head. By the time I was back in my car, I'd already reassured myself that I was just about due to get my period, so I couldn't possibly get pregnant. The instant I got back to the bus, I dug through my store receipts and checked the dates to see when I'd last run out for tampons. By the time I'd gone to bed, I was 99% certain that everything was just fine.

And yet I'd still had the nightmare.

I knew that it wasn't just about getting pregnant. I'd broken all of my own rules. I'd gotten involved with someone when I said I never would. Sex had moved our relationship to a whole new level. Even without the bareback thing, this morning still would have been watershed moment—that realization that you're connected to a person in a whole new way, that they've known you, *felt* you in a way few men have. It's a big deal for any woman, but for me the shock of it came wrapped in dark, dark fear.

I was putting myself and Bull at risk: myself, because if I started getting all dewy-eyed I'd get sloppy and make a mistake; Bull, because if my uncle's men found me, he'd try to save me. And they'd have no hesitation in shooting him.

I'd taken two big chances, in sleeping with Bull. Risking getting pregnant was the smaller of the two.

I hopped up onto the counter, sitting on the edge as I sipped my water and stewed on the problem. The loudest sound in the bus was the dripping of the faucet. Outside, I could hear the cicadas.

Was it really too much to ask, for me to have just a *little* happiness? To have one thing in my life that wasn't related to crime? *I could be really careful.*

But what about Bull? Would he be careful? Hell, I wouldn't even be able to tell him to be careful, or he'd start asking *why*. I couldn't get into my past with him. He'd demand I take steps I wasn't ready to take—steps I'd *never* be ready to take, like testify against my uncle. I didn't need to change. I was fine just as I was.

I gazed around the darkened bus. *Yeah, right.*

I went back and forth on it for so long that I actually dozed off, perched on the edge of the kitchen counter, and only woke up when I leaned so far forward that I nearly fell. At that point, I headed back to bed, still undecided.

The next morning, I woke to that familiar cramping. Sure enough, by mid-morning my period had started. I slumped against the bathroom wall. I hadn't even realized how tight my chest had been. The fact that I'd been 99% sure was irrelevant. That last 1% is everything.

One problem down. Now for the much bigger one.

***

For two days, I managed to avoid the Bull issue completely by burying myself in my work. Most of it was coming from the arms dealer, Luka. I made a whole slew of fake IDs for a small army of surly-looking Russian guys with crew cuts, and shipped them all over the country: New York, Boston, Chicago. Luka seemed to be building an empire.

One of the passports, though, wasn't for a man. It was for a very pretty girl about my age, with long, glossy brown hair. For a second, I was worried that he'd started trafficking women, but there was only one woman and I really didn't get that vibe from Luka—he'd always seemed honorable. And the note that arrived with the woman's details said to take extra care with this one.

A lover?

I wasn't sure how I felt about that. I mean, not that Luka would be interested in me. Obviously not. And we'd only met five or six times. And I wouldn't want to get mixed up with a guy like that. He's an arms dealer, for Chrissakes. Even with those cheekbones and that super-sexy Russian accent. I absolutely wasn't jealous. At all. *I'm sure she's lovely and I wish them all the luck in the world.*

I put Arianna *bitch* Scott's photo down and started making her a fake French passport. *Veronique Sardou,* Luka had requested for the name. Going through all the French databases to set her up with a fake life was a welcome break, after all the Russian. French was such a romantic language. I wondered what Luka and this Arianna woman might be doing in France. Paris, maybe. A romantic vacation, walking hand-in-hand on the banks of the river Seine. Or filthy sex in some cheap hotel in Pigalle—

I caught myself. *Wait. Really? This is my life, getting jealous of a client's lover and thinking that a French social security database is romantic? Fantasizing about what they might be doing in Paris because I'll never go there myself?*

There had been a time in my life when I'd thought about going to Europe—had actually planned it out, in fact. Before I'd woken up to what my life in New York was, I'd been just another college student, ready to take on the world, instead of isolating myself completely from it. Now...I was never going to go there. *Ever.* Not with a guy, at least. I couldn't put someone else at risk, not after what happened to Annette.

She wasn't the only one who'd suffered, either.

There was a guy in high school, Russell. You would have thought it would be some hormone-pumped football captain who'd dare to show an interest in the don's daughter, but no—they were all too scared. Russell was a slender little guy, barely taller than me but good looking. He wore his hair long and had a guitar and wrote god-awful love songs that we both laughed about and...I'm not sure I even liked him in *that* way and I wasn't sure he liked me in that way either. I was just so glad to have some male contact at last. We never actually did anything, but we hung out and I used to pretend he was my boyfriend.

Then I made the mistake of hugging him within sight of Antonio, as he picked me up from school. And Antonio immediately wanted to know *who's the faggot?*

I was the only kid at our school who hadn't caught on to the fact Russell was gay, even if he wasn't out yet. That's how starved of social contact I was.

Faggots, as my uncle called them, weren't people he wanted me hanging out with. I was forbidden to see him again, but that wasn't enough. He quietly applied pressure to the school board and, suddenly, Russell's parents were told that maybe their son would be happier elsewhere. His parents had to move him and, because word got around, none of the upmarket private schools would take him. He eventually landed at a nearby public school, where his posh background meant he was targeted and beaten daily. After that, no one dared to be my friend at all except Annette.

Or there was the time, in my freshman year at college, when I came home stinking of air freshener, because I'd doused myself in it to try to get rid of the smell of weed. Just one shared joint with the cool kids in the old boiler room. I barely even got a buzz off it. I just wanted to fit in.

But my uncle guessed. He questioned me for a solid hour about who'd given me drugs and then, when he got tired, Antonio had taken over. I'd eventually broken down and told them the name of the kid who'd passed around the joint. He wasn't at college the next day. He showed up days later with one leg in plaster and from then on he walked the other way every time he saw me. That was the worst part—he was so scared of me, I never even got to apologize.

More memories rose up inside me, rushing towards the surface. Suddenly, the cool, clean, air-conditioned bus felt a lot like our house, back in New York.

I needed hot desert air, a reminder I wasn't there anymore. I jumped up from my desk but found my legs would barely hold me, I'd started shaking so hard. I staggered down the bus, tears turning everything blurry. I had to feel for the door button—

And then I was outside, and for once the Texas sun felt good. It was reassurance that I wasn't trapped in New York anymore.

My breathing slowed and I managed to push the

memories down below the surface again. I slumped against the bus, even though its metal sides were almost hot enough to burn me.

When I felt strong enough, I went back inside and focused on Arianna's French passport. I did my very best work, despite my lingering jealousy. I'm nothing if not professional.

I did give her twenty-seven French parking tickets, though. I'm not *that* professional.

Three days later, I was making coffee, still stewing over what to do about Bull, when my phone rang. I was so focused on what I was going to do about the problem, it didn't occur to me that the problem might pick up the phone all on its own.

"You ran away again," Bull admonished in that deep Texas drawl.

THIRTY-SIX

Lily

SUDDENLY, Bull didn't feel like a problem anymore. Each sweet syllable melted into my brain like molasses and I pressed my thighs together. All I wanted to do was to run over there and let him do whatever he wanted to me.

And he was calling me. Men like Bull *never* called girls. Certainly not when the girl runs out on them and goes silent. So what did that mean?

My heart did a somersault. Immediately, I clamped down on the feelings.

"I've been thinking about you," he told me. "Can't seem to think of much else."

I pressed my lips together, *hard*. But then it slipped out anyway. "I've been thinking about you, too." It felt weird, telling the truth for a change. *But this is wrong! I can't put him at risk!*

He started to speak again, but it sounded for a second like he was struggling to find the words. And then I realized what it was—he'd never made this kind of call before. Calling the girl after he'd slept with her was precisely what he *didn't* do. "I guess I wanted you to know that, um—"*Wait...is he really getting tongue-tied?* "I want to see you again. Today."

He was reassuring me that it hadn't been just a one-night stand. I wasn't ready for the way my heart soared. He was changing. For me.

I looked around the bus. I'd escaped one prison in New York, but had I wound up just making another one for myself?

Maybe *I* needed to change a little, too.

"Okay," I said slowly. "Today." Then I remembered my nightmare. "No, wait. Tomorrow. There's something I have to do this afternoon."

"Tomorrow," he echoed. "Can you stop by the stables, about six? Everyone else will have headed out. We'll have the place to ourselves."

"How romantic!"

His voice dropped from a rumble to a low, seductive growl. "You want romantic, now? ' Cause last time I saw you, what you wanted was a good, hard—"

"Tomorrow!" I yelped and hung up. A wave of heat was sweeping through me, flushing my cheeks.

As soon as I stopped talking to Bull, the fear came back. *What the hell am I doing?*

But it was too late. For the first time, the feelings inside me were strong enough to overshadow the fear. I started to rationalize it away. *It's been two years and my uncle hasn't found me yet. Maybe he's stopped looking.*

I started to wonder if, if I was very careful, I could actually make this work.

Well, if there was even a chance...I was going to give it a damn good try.

***

That afternoon, I headed to my doctor's office. She had no problem writing me a prescription for the pill and I popped the first one in the parking lot. I'd only just finished my period so I was—I squirmed inside—*good to go.*

I hadn't had that sensation in years: the feeling of *planning sex.* I'd forgotten how good it felt. My next stop was the nail salon. If I was going to do this, I was going to do it properly.

"Toes, too?" asked the nail technician. "A pedicure?"

Money was the one thing in my life that wasn't a problem. The work was well paid and my living expenses were virtually zero. Cash just built up in my bank account because I didn't have anything to spend it on...until now. "Sure," I told her.

She was like a shark sensing blood. "A leg wax? Bikini wax?"

I went to say *no*... and then nodded my head, instead. "Go nuts," I told her. She ran to get help. I stumbled out of the salon over three hours later, my purse much lighter and various parts of me tender.

Finally, I hit the mall and bought a little denim skirt that would show off my—laughably pale—legs and a shirt I could tie beneath my boobs. I had to look at it for a long time in the changing room mirror before I decided and, even then, I wasn't sure about showing off so much of me. But I'd been wearing blouses and jeans for two years. I needed something appropriate for dating.

I figured that, with enough attention to detail, I

could control the relationship and manage its risks just like I did with my business. The pill? That was just a different kind of Taser.

I hadn't realized that relationships are a hell of a lot more complicated.

THIRTY-SEVEN

Antonio

I'D SPENT A FRUITLESS WEEK searching New York. Tessa's old college classmates, the few boyfriends she'd had...all the same people I'd questioned two years ago. And it had gone just the same as before.

I hated the little bitch. I'd wasted the best years of my life driving her to fucking band practice when I should have been doing real work for the family. Now, finally, she was gone. But just when I was making a name for myself I'd been pulled back to running around after her again.

When I found her, she was going to fucking pay.

There were precious few possibilities left, though. Her parents were dead and she'd been an only child. There was only one surviving relative and she was in a goddamn nursing home. I was almost certain that she would be a dead end, too.

"I'm here to see Abigail Oates," I told the receptionist. "I'm her nephew." I wasn't even related to Tessa, Erico or the rest of the family, but I looked as if I could be.

She handed me the visitor's book and, just as I'd expected, there were no entries on the preceding pages for Tessa's grandmother. Just to be sure, I said, "I'm the only one who's stopped in? My cousin hasn't been by?"

The receptionist shook her head. "Nope. Mrs. Oates never gets any visitors."

I sighed. A four hour fucking flight for nothing. I headed for the door.

"Wait—aren't you visiting?" asked the receptionist.

"I changed my mind."

I kicked open the door to the parking lot, which drew an angry shout from the receptionist. I was halfway to my rental car when I stopped.

Tessa pissed me off. Always had. Partially because of how I had to follow her around as if she was a fucking princess, partially because of how close she was to Erico—closer than I knew I'd ever get. She was family and I wasn't. Hell, she'd tried to leave and he'd *still* taken her back in. If it had been my call, I would have killed her along with her prissy friend.

But however much I hated her, I had to admit she was smart. It takes brains to disappear completely, like she'd done.

I turned around and marched back into the care home.

"What now?" asked the receptionist glaring. "And I'd appreciate it if you didn't kick our—"

I held up a photo of Tessa. "Has this woman been here?" I demanded.

She balked, then lifted her chin and folded her arms defiantly. "We don't give out information on visitors," she sniffed.

I looked left and right. No one else was around. I vaulted the counter and muscled in on her, backing her up against the far wall. She dropped the tough girl act instantly, her eyes going wide with fear. "I—I'll call the cops!" she bleated.

I grabbed the phone and pulled it out of the wall. Then I showed her the photo again. This time, I caught the recognition in her eyes. "Talk!" I snapped. "When did she come?"

"You've got it wrong! That's Mr. Hanlow's granddaughter. She comes every few months."

I frowned. "Hanlow?" Who the fuck was Hanlow?

"He's a resident," the receptionist said. "Room 233."

Then I got it. "And which room is Abigail Oates in?"

She checked. "232."

Oh, clever, Tessa. Very clever.

I grabbed the visitor's book. Mr. Hanlow had had a visitor just two days ago.

I jumped back over the counter and marched straight to 232. The receptionist would call security, or maybe the cops, but I had a few minutes before they arrived. And I only needed a few minutes.

The doors to the residents' rooms were cheap, crappy things. I broke the thing open with one good kick. Tessa's grandmother was sitting there doing a crossword puzzle.

"Oh my," she said with a start. "Who are you?"

I frowned. Had there been a second of recognition, when she'd first seen me? Had she guessed who I was and why I was there...or was I just imagining it?

"Tessa," I snapped. "Where is she?"

"Tessa!" she said happily. "Is she coming? I haven't

seen her in so long."

"I know she was here! Where is she living?"

She frowned at me. "In New York, of course. Why, she must be starting school, by now."

I groaned. *Senile.* Of course she was. She was in her eighties. She probably didn't even know what day it was.

Unless...

I narrowed my eyes. Unless she was acting.

She smiled happily back at me, quite unafraid. "Would you like some tea?" she asked.

No. Not possible. Not at her age. I sighed and looked around. Tessa had been here, but I wasn't going to be able to get anything useful out of her grandmother. And I only had a few minutes before the cops showed up.

I checked the wastepaper basket. Empty.

Then I saw something behind it. Someone had tossed a napkin and missed. I unfolded it without much hope.

Printed in the center was a cartoon gold prospector. Coffee or tea or something had blurred the name of some bar or restaurant below it, but I could read the last word of the address: *Texas.*

THIRTY-EIGHT

Lily

THE NEXT EVENING, I drove out to the ranch. No one had to ask who I was there to see—my little Toyota was known, now. I flushed. Did everyone suspect what we'd been doing in the stables and the barn?

Then I remembered that this was Bull, and flushed deeper. They didn't suspect. They damn well *knew*.

I pulled up, the engine coughing on dust. I made a mental note to take the car in for a service sometime soon

I'd stopped on the way to pick up a box of pastries from the bakery. I figured munching our way through those would give me time to talk with him—there was some stuff we had to cover, before we got to the sex.

I pushed open the door of the stables, glad to step out of the sweltering air and into the shade. My eyes took a while to adjust to the gloom, but I could see Bull coiling ropes. He was wearing a t-shirt, for once, but the thin fabric didn't do much to hide his muscles. He was bending slightly and his hard ass was outlined through his jeans. "Hi," I said nervously.

He turned and his gaze raked over me. I'd forgotten the raw, primitive effect his eyes had on me. I swore I could feel them sweeping down over the scarlet shirt, tied to show off a little cleavage and leaving my stomach bare. It felt weird, walking around with my navel on display, but I had to admit it was a hell of a lot cooler.

So was the skirt. His gaze skimmed down my thighs, sliding around to the sides and I stiffened as I felt invisible hands stroke down the denim and hit bare skin. It wasn't indecently short, by any means, but compared to the jeans I normally wore, I might as well have been in a bikini.

"Well, *hello,*" he told me, already starting to walk towards me. The words blazed through my mind. It wasn't what he said, it was the hunger in his voice. He might as well have said, "Just stand there—I'm going to fuck you."

"I brought pastries," I told him, holding the box up defensively in front of me. I was desperate to maintain control of the situation.

"First a latte. Now pastries." He was close enough now to touch. "You really don't get me at all, do you?"

He finally stopped, so close that the front of his shirt brushed one side of the bakery box and my naked stomach brushed the other.

"Now wait," I said quickly.

He put a single huge finger under the bakery box and lifted. The box tilted, turning vertical, and he stepped closer.

"Wait," I said again. But I didn't move. His size, his hard bulk...they did something to me. Suddenly, I was gazing up into those fierce blue eyes and I couldn't move at all. "Wait," I croaked again.

The box went vertical, the pastries sliding down to the bottom. And then he was leaning forward, bringing his lips down to mine.

I didn't move my feet, but I dodged my head to one side. "Wait," I said weakly.

He followed me. I dodged to the other side. "Just a minute," I said.

He gave me a *look*. One that said I better damn well keep still. And I did. As he moved in again, I clutched the box to my chest and said, "Bull, I—"

His mouth met mine and it felt so good I actually groaned. His tongue explored my lips, tasting me, and he drew back just a little, testing to see if I'd follow.

I lifted up onto my tiptoes to avoid breaking contact. My mind was suddenly adrift, all moorings severed. I closed my eyes as my tongue found his, darting and twisting. My hands crushed the edges of the cardboard bakery box, and then he was pressing up against me, his hands in my hair, and the box was crushed between us.

I gasped in a little moan of air. The kiss moved and changed, tracking across my lips and down my jaw. His hands were stroking through the hair behind my temples, strong and firm and so damn big. His leg pushed against mine, the denim of his jeans rough against my bare legs, and I pressed hard against him, opening my legs instinctively, hooking one leg around his. I felt the hot throb of his cock against my thigh and a tremor ran through me.

The box slipped from between us and fell to the floor, sending pastries cartwheeling across the hay. Bull's body slammed against mine, mashing my breasts against his chest. One big hand slapped down on my ass, his fingers spread onto both cheeks, and held me against him. "There," he growled, lifting his lips for a second. "Now I can finally get you to hold still for a second."

He squeezed my ass and I moaned. A finger pressed the fabric of my skirt between my cheeks, probing, and I gasped, only to have my gasp swallowed up by his kiss. His kisses were such a perfect blend of hard and soft, power and heat.

I used both arms to push myself back from him. "*Wait!*" I panted. "I need to talk to you."

He gave me a look but then crossed his arms. "You got thirty seconds," he told me.

THIRTY-NINE

Bull

SHE STARED AT ME IN HORROR, as if thirty *hours* wouldn't have been enough to explain everything she wanted to explain. But I knew I wasn't going to last any longer than a half-minute before I grabbed her again. *Damn,* she looked good. Something was different, aside from the clothes. She'd done her make-up, or her hair, or her nails or any of those other hundred things women do that are too subtle for guys to notice straight off, but that just make them ooze femininity. Standing there in that barn, she looked like the perfect Texas cowgirl, all tied shirt and denim skirt, but her pale skin and black hair made her exquisitely exotic—voluptuous and sexy, yet vulnerable at the same time.

My eyes were locked onto her...but the weird thing was, I wasn't staring at her boobs, the way I usually would with a girl. It was her eyes I couldn't stop looking at, those gorgeous, liquid green eyes. And her lips. I could still feel them against mine and, every time I glanced down at their softness, my hands bunched with the need to grab the knot of her shirt and tug her against me.

"*Look,*" she said, still panting. "I need to set some limits."

I grinned. "Like a safeword?"

Her eyes bulged and her cheeks flared red. "*What?! No!* Not like a safeword!" But I saw her give a little twist of her hips, as if the idea touched a nerve, deep inside. *Well, now. Ain't that a thing?* I filed that little nugget away.

"I mean," she said, "I have some secrets. I don't like to talk about my past. If this is going to work, you'll have to respect that."

I went to take a step towards her, but held myself back at the last second. "Okay," I said.

"And my business...I know you don't like it, but I'm going to keep doing it."

I raised an eyebrow. "Girl, I don't want you getting hurt. I care about you too damn much."

She bit her lip when she heard that, but stared back at me determinedly.

I sighed. "At least let me know what's going on, so I can look out for you?"

She considered. "Okay," she said at last.

Thirty seconds was long since up. I moved in to kiss her.

"One more thing. How's your health?" she said, dodging.

I grabbed her upper arms to hold her still. "I got an old muscle tear in my shoulder from wrestling a steer."

"I mean..." Her eyes looked in every damn direction except at me. "Is it safe for us to...without a...."

I suddenly got it. "Oh!"

She blushed, which looked so damn cute I had to will myself to hold back. "I just mean—You obviously...you *know* a lot of the local girls. *Very well.* And regularly. And you prefer to...you know. *Go bareback.* And—"

"My health is just fine. But what makes you think I do that with the other girls?"

That seemed to throw her completely. "Don't you?"

I shook my head and just told her the truth. "Lily, when I saw you, I had to have you. Completely. That's something that's for you. You're not like the other girls. That was just fucking."

She closed the gap between us.

"Are we done talking?" I asked.

"Shut up," she muttered, grabbed the front of my t-shirt and pulled me down to her. My lips met hers. I closed my eyes and just went for it, me all sweat and stubble, her all sweet, perfumed softness. I devoured her, eating her up like a goddamn candy bar, my hands stroking her cheeks and winding into her long, silky hair. I was so hungry for her, I couldn't stay still. I started twisting her around as we kissed, moving in slow circles across the barn as if we were slow-dancing.

When we finally came up for air, I muttered without thinking, "Damn you, Lily, I think I'm falling for you."

Which, it turned out, was the wrong thing to say. Because suddenly, she pushed me away and staggered back, her mouth open in shock.

FORTY

Lily

Falling for me? Oh God. That was too much...*way* too much. My carefully constructed plan to control the relationship had just veered off of a cliff.

"Lily?" he asked. "What the hell?!"

I stumbled backwards towards the door. "*Falling for me?*" I croaked. "You can't fall for me!" It was exactly what I'd wanted to hear...and it was terrifying. I didn't *deserve* someone like Bull falling for me.

"I can't—" I shook my head. "This was a bad idea."

I turned back towards the door and put my hand out to grab the handle—

There was the sensation of something falling around me, then a high-pitched whine and a snap. My legs shot out from under me and I landed, face-down, in the hay.

I lay there stunned for a second and then rolled over onto my back. I went to get up and discovered I couldn't...because my ankles were roped together.

He'd just lassoed me!

He began to wind the rope around his hands.

I opened my mouth to speak, but his voice came like a bullwhip. "Don't you say a fucking word," he commanded.

I shut my mouth.

He took up the slack and kept winding the rope. I began to slide on my ass across the hay.

"You goddamn, over-thinking, Gucci-wearing, latte-drinking city folk," he muttered.

My feet met his. I stared up at him and he glared down at me.

"Bull—" I started.

"Shut up."

"Bull—"

"Quiet!"

"B—"

"You say one more thing and I swear I'll take you over my knee."

I went quiet. A dark heat rippled outward from my groin.

He crouched down by my feet, the muscles of his legs bulging. He looked even bigger, looking up at him like this. "Now for once in your life, Lily, shut up and listen."

"But I—"

"It ain't all about you!"

We stared at each other. *I completely underestimated him,* I realized. This man was an unstoppable force...and I'd tried to control him, to put him in a convenient little box. For the first time, I saw how frustrated he was. Not just about the sex but on a much deeper level.

"What happened to that guy I met in Lucky Pete's?" I asked. "The one who just wanted to fuck me?"

"He stepped out," Bull growled.

We stared into each other's eyes and something about the way he was looking at me made my heart lift and pull like a balloon that wants to be released. I felt my eyes grow moist.

"You're *Bull*," I protested. "You're not meant to— You shouldn't be falling for anyone!"

"Yeah, well, I never met anyone like you," he muttered.

The barn was incredibly still. I could feel the words bunched up inside me, jostling for space, eager to come out...but releasing them was the hardest thing imaginable. "I think...I'm falling for you, too," I said at last. And that admission changed everything. It reverberated through me, leaving me humming like a tuning fork. My resistance began to crumble.

Bull's hands slackened on the rope. "There," he said. "That wasn't so fucking difficult, was it?"

I put my hands to my face and shook my head. "I don't deserve this. I don't deserve...you."

"Well now you're just being dumb." He hunkered down further and stared right into my eyes. "I'll tell you what you deserve, Lily, and it's a goddamn prince in a fairytale castle." His voice softened. "But will you settle for me?"

I nodded, choking up a little. I was just starting to realize what an idiot I'd been. And how much I'd been denying myself any chance at happiness, ever since Annette died. "Sorry," I said quietly. I don't think I've ever communicated as much in two syllables as with that word.

He leaned down and brushed my hair from my cheek with a finger. "I'm sure we can figure out a way to punish you." His smirk had come back and I felt my heart lift and tug, rising a little higher as I relaxed. It felt incredible. I shifted a little and the rope rasped at my bare ankles. I really was tightly bound.

Helpless.

He reached down to the rope, his big hands warm on my bare skin. I drew in my breath.

He looked up at me. "Relax. I'm just going to take the rope off," he explained.

Our eyes met and held. We stared at each other for a few seconds. He tilted his head questioningly to one side.

I wriggled, a whole new sort of delicious, dark heat winding upwards through my body. "Rhinoceros," I whispered. "That's what I want my safeword to be."

"Lily!" He sounded stunned, but there was a note of dark lust in his voice, too. "I didn't know you..."

I swallowed. "I didn't know either," I blurted, blushing.

"Rhinoceros?" he asked, considering.

"Rhinoceros," I confirmed. My heart was hammering. I felt as if I was standing at the very top of a long, sweeping hillside, about to roll all the way down. I'd never done anything like this before. *You're supposed to only do this with someone you really trust.....*

I really trusted him.

I nodded again, confirming that it was really okay.

He knelt down atop me, straddling me, his knees like tree trunks either side of my hips. Then he planted his arms either side of my head and I was completely caged in by him, trapped. I let out a soft little moan as he leaned down to kiss me again, my head sinking back into the soft straw as we pressed and moved and his tongue slipped into my mouth.

It felt different, now. You wouldn't think you *use* your feet, to kiss, but I couldn't seem to stop moving them. I kept twisting them and trying to jerk them apart, just so I could feel the rope tight around my ankles.

The heat started to build inside me, throbbing outward from my core, and it was different, too. Darker, somehow. Before, it had been clean and bright, like the Texas sunshine. Now it was roiling, oily smoke rising up from ruby-red, smoldering coals. And I could feel the same darkness in Bull, too, a side of him he'd only hinted at before. With every passing second, we were burning hotter, growing darker. It was even more powerful because relinquishing control was such a completely new experience for me.

I realized I'd never trusted anyone enough, until now. That's why I'd never even thought of doing this with the few boyfriends I'd had.

I felt his hands on my tied shirt, undoing the knot with expert fingers. He went to pull the two sides apart and I reached up and caught his wrists. I'm not even sure why I did it, because I wanted to feel myself naked against him more than anything.

He stared down at me...and then grabbed one of my wrists. I went unexpectedly squishy inside at the feeling of his muscled fingers gripping me. So big. So strong.

He pulled my wrist up above my head and pinned it to the hay-covered floor. That feeling inside doubled in strength. I made little pushing movements against his hand but I might as well have been pushing against an iron band. Then he grabbed my other wrist and pinned it down alongside the first, and took them both in one big hand so that he had a hand free.

He opened one side of my shirt, laying the fabric out to the side of me. Then the other side, and I was panting and exposed, my breasts throbbing in their bra. I looked up at him, pleading with my eyes.

Pleading, but not to be let go.

He took a penknife from his pocket, an old scarred thing with cracked casing. A thing that cut barbed wire and tightened the bolts on gates. A working tool. Somehow, that made it even better. Everything—the rough scratch of the hay against my legs, the burn of the rope around my ankles—it was all real and raw.

He moved the knife towards my bra. Slid it between my breasts and underneath the strap that connected the cups. The blade lifted and the strap lifted with it and then there was a snapping sound and the cups fell away to either side of my body. My breasts were revealed, milky-white, moving with each breath, their nipples already hardening from the sudden kiss of the air.

Bull's eyes were locked on them as he put the penknife away. He leaned down over me, his face coming closer and closer. I panted up at him, faster and faster, until—

Ah! His mouth engulfed my hardening nipple and my back came up off the floor. I tried to buck and move in response to the pleasure, but with my wrists pinned and my ankles bound all I could do was twist and writhe. That made my other breast slide against his hand, the nipple rasping against his palm, and I felt it grow harder with each contact. Then he captured it with his hand and squeezed, just roughly enough. I gasped.

He was working my nipple with firm strokes of his tongue, spiraling around and around. The other breast he fondled, his thumb rubbing across the nipple. Then he trapped the little pink bud between finger and thumb, just as he lifted his mouth and looked up at me to see my reaction.

He pinched. All the air in my body seemed to leave me in one hot gasp as pain and pleasure twisted together into a rope and lashed down to my groin.

He released his fingers. Pinched again. Released. Pinched again. I was sucking in air through my nostrils, now, my out breaths shuddering pants. He stared into my eyes the whole time. Then he ducked his head and took the nipple into his mouth, bathing it, and his fingers went to work on the other one. I groaned and thrashed, rapidly losing the ability to think.

He bent and kissed me again. His tongue met mine and it was as if the dark heat inside us was combining and mixing, becoming stronger than either of us could control. I felt his free hand snake down the length of my body, passing over both breasts and then over my stomach. His fingers brushed the waistband of my denim skirt.

I was aching for him to touch me. I could feel how wet I was. But my hips jerked to the side, trying to evade him, prolonging the chase. His fingers followed me, sliding under the denim and then under the elastic of my panties. Every touch felt magnified and the newly-smooth skin down there was extra-sensitive.

"You feel different," he growled. His fingertips rubbed over the new, smaller boundaries of my hair. Then he pushed his hand further under my skirt, the size of him stretching the waistband until I thought the button would pop. His fingers slid through the soft curls, then brushed my aching clit. I cried out, a high little *oh!*

He grinned.

His fingers slid deeper, two of them tracing the line of my lips and then hooking to spear up into me, finding me wet and ready. I groaned as they slid inside. He started to pump them and, with my ankles trapped together, I was tight around him. I could feel every knuckle as he thrust and twisted, the pleasure rippling out in frantic waves. "*God!*" I hissed.

He released my wrists because he needed another hand to undo my skirt. But as soon as I was free, I found myself sitting up, pushing him away with both hands. It wasn't unconscious, exactly. I knew I was doing it but I didn't know *why*. I didn't want to escape but I had to try.

So he could stop me.

Capture me.

Possess me.

You can't be chased if you don't run.

He growled and put a massive hand on my chest, pressing me back down to the hay. "Oh," he grinned. "It's like that? I gotta tie you up to stop you moving?"

I stared up at him, my eyes huge and my heart thumping. I'd never felt like this before. It was like being on a rollercoaster, fear but with the certainty of safety. I trusted him completely. I knew he'd release me, the second I said "rhinoceros."

He grinned...and grabbed something from a hook. Not a rope, I saw, but a long brown strap—part of a set of reins, maybe. It passed close enough to my face that I could smell the tang of the leather. Then he crossed one of my wrists over the other and started to bind them together, wrapping it around and around them.

I craned my head up to look, staring at my pale skin and the hard, dark leather.

In seconds, he was finished. Now I was bound wrist and ankle, unable to move. He stood for a second, staring down at me, enjoying the sight of me. And I stared up at him.

Standing above me like that, one foot planted either side of me, he looked like a colossus. He slowly stripped off his t-shirt and I was hypnotized by the way his chest rose and fell, solid slabs of tanned, hard muscle. I twisted, grinding my ass against the straw. The heat inside me was raging, the dark smoke completely impenetrable now. I was out of control. *God, he's so big and I'm lying here so...powerless.*

I had to get away. I mean, I had this overwhelming urge to *try* to get away. I started to heave myself along the floor like an earthworm, making an inch of progress at a time.

He shoved his foot between my calves, so that my tied ankles caught on it and stopped me. And he grinned.

My eyes locked on the bulge in his jeans and I just went weak inside.

He bent and unfastened my skirt, tugging it down my hips inch by inch, taking my panties with it. With each tug of the fabric, I felt myself getting hotter and hotter, the heat turning to moisture as it soaked down to my bared groin.

He left my skirt and panties bundled around my bound ankles. Then he ran both hands down my body, from my shoulders to my calves, taking in all the treasures along the way. I gasped and panted under his touch. Then we stared at one another and I could see the raw lust in his eyes. *God,* I'm *doing that to him. Me!*

I waited to see what he'd do next. Obviously he couldn't fuck me like this, with my ankles tied together, so he'd have to cut the rope or—

He turned me over onto my face, straw prickling against my naked breasts. Then he hauled my hips up so that I was on my knees, and I understood.

I got my bound hands under me a little and lifted my head enough that I could crane around and look at him. He was getting to his knees behind me and lazily undoing his belt.

My eyes locked again on that bulge in his jeans. He grinned when he saw me looking.

I watched him take out his cock, already hard and ready. I watched him guide it towards me, felt the soft breeze of the room on my moistened lips...and then jerked as the head of his cock brushed me there. The blood was roaring in my ears. I could feel how soaking wet I was.

His hands gripped my hips, hauling me back towards him. I gasped and panted, my breasts pillowed against the floor, my nipples throbbing as they stroked against the hard fibers of the straw. I felt the shape of that naked, satin-smooth head opening me up—

I squeezed my eyes shut. I wanted it so much.

He plunged into me, filling me with one long stroke. I felt every inch of his size, my bound ankles making me tighter than normal. The dark heat had taken me over completely now, thought giving way to raw sensation. He groaned as he slid inside me, a slow groan that spoke of hours, *days* of frustration finally released. I could feel each vein, each bulge—God, he was shockingly big, stretching me deliciously. "*Jesus,*"

I whispered.

His fingers squeezed my hips hard and he drew himself from me like a sword from its scabbard. I hissed in air through my gritted teeth, it was so good. So tight, so wet. It felt as if my whole being was wrapped around him, a gleaming, gossamer membrane shot through with silver. For a second, I existed only where I touched his cock.

Then he slammed back into me again and the force of it jolted me forward a little on my arms, reminding me of the leather strap that bound me. My feet twisted and pulled but the rope held them fast. He was straddling my lower legs, I realized, his shins either side of my ankles. This time, he went even deeper and my eyes opened wide as I felt myself stretch and open to accommodate him. "G—God!" I moaned.

He plunged into me again, holding me completely still as his hardness slid past my sopping walls, curving up inside me, making me jerk and gasp at how deep it went. Pleasure fluttered up from each millimeter of his stroke, overwhelming me. I pressed my cheek to the floor. *"Ah!"*

He pulled back again, wrapping his hands around the sensitive creases at the front of my hips and holding me rock steady against him. Then he thrust into me again and I couldn't move away even an inch. I thrashed with my bound hands, kicked with my ankles. It did nothing to free me, but I didn't want to get free. I just wanted to release some of the insane pressure in my head, to gain some space from the pleasure. And then I felt the wiry hair at his groin press against my lips and the soft slap of his balls against my clit, and he was in me as deep as he could be.

He stopped moving, then. The sensation of him there, so hot and hard inside me, kept the pleasure radiating out in waves, even with him still. My eyes were wide and staring—I was off in my own little world, for a second. Then I felt his hand slide across to my groin, fingers toying with the soft curls of hair and then moving down. Seeking out my clit....

I closed my eyes and groaned as he touched it, brushing my soaking lips to gather moisture and then using it on the sensitive nub. He didn't touch it directly. He rubbed two fingers in a Y either side of it, trapping it, using my own skin to touch where his calloused skin would be too rough. I shuddered as the first tremors of an orgasm started to roll in, like the smaller waves that precede a huge one.

I started to pant through my nostrils. My bound body began to twist and arch. He was doing very little, just a tiny back-and-forth movement of his fingers, simple and exquisite. I needed friction, needed him to fuck me, and I started to hump back against him, feeling my body move around his length.

Only after a few seconds did I realize what he was doing to me. He was making *me* fuck *him*. Making me show him how much I wanted it. The dark shame of it lashed through me like rain in a gathering storm, and it only seemed to spur me on. I started to buck against him harder, faster. It was okay, because I was tied up and helpless and I couldn't control my own body and—

I started to twist my hips, circling them, and he rewarded me by rubbing me faster. "That's it," he breathed in my ear. "You can be a good girl when you want to, can't you?" The words soaked into me, adding to the heat. "Next time, you can show me what else you can do with that smart mouth of yours. And another time...."

His other hand left my hip and stroked across my ass. Following the curve of it inward, between my cheeks—

My eyes opened wide as he touched me there. A jolt went through my body, as if he'd touched me with a live wire.

He chuckled.

And then he started to fuck me. *Really* fuck me. One hand gripping my hip to hold me firm against him, the other rubbing faster and faster at my clit. I could feel the orgasm approaching, could feel it roaring towards my shores, engulfing everything in its path.

With every thrust, his groin slammed against my ass, making a slapping sound that reverberated around the barn. Each time, I arched my back in response and my breasts dragged along the straw, making me tremble.

I didn't think it could get any better but, as he sped up more, it did. It became a hard, pounding rhythm, one that melted away everything else in my brain except for him and me and that delicious friction. As the trembles became shudders, I croaked, "*Yes!*"

His cock was as merciless as a machine, pumping into me, drawing me towards orgasm whether I wanted it or not...and I did. Oh, God, I did. "Louder," he grunted.

"*Yes!*" I was almost vibrating with the force of the approaching orgasm, now, fully in its shadow.

"Scream it for me, Lily." His voice had gone tight with the effort of holding back. "Scream my name."

"*Bullllllll!*"

With a final grunt, he rammed into me—and it was only when I felt the first thick spurt of him inside me that I remembered how he was taking me. *Naked. Bareback.* That threw me headlong into the orgasm, all sense lost as it consumed me. My whole body went rigid and I felt myself tightening and squeezing around him. He groaned in response, shooting again and again, and that made me twist and grip even more...*God!*

The climax washed over me for long seconds, completely immersing me. I couldn't breathe or speak or even think. And then finally, it drained away and my legs quivered, unable to support me anymore. Bull carefully let my hips down and laid me down on my stomach, drawing himself from me.

I lay there almost naked in the straw, face turned to the side, throbbing from head to toe. He lay down next to me, propping himself up on his elbows, and for a few seconds we just lay there panting. "Goddamn, I love fucking you," he said at last. "I don't care how much work you are."

I opened my eyes and turned to look at him. "I'm a lot of work?"

He gave me a look.

Okay, he had a point.

"I didn't know you were into that," he told me.

"*I* didn't know I was into that," I said, flushing. "I'm not...I mean, I don't think I want to do that every time."

He chuckled. "Calm down, girl. Plenty of other ways I can ride you."

I squirmed. Then we just sort of stared at each other. I got the sense he was thinking the same thing I was: *what now?*

"Come with me to the fair," he said.

I blinked. It was so completely out of the blue. "What?"

"The town fair. Come with me."

"The town fair?" I was dimly aware of something about a fair, round about this time each year. I'd always stayed hunkered down in the bus when it came around. I'd presumed it was very Texas and very country—beer and cattle and cotton candy and not my thing at all. That was probably completely unfair. If I was going to be with Bull, I should try to come to this stuff with an open mind. "What's it like?"

"Oh, you know. Beer. Cattle. Cotton candy. You'll hate it. It'll be great." He reached back and ran a hand over my naked ass cheek.

I drew in my breath. "You don't want to go with one of your local girls? Someone more...*Texas?*"

"I'm with you now." He looked at me questioningly. "Right?"

I nodded. "Right." And the thought of it, of being with someone after so long, made my heart swell and rise and finally break free of everything that had been holding it down. It soared high into the air. I grabbed him and kissed him, partially because it felt so good and partially to prove to myself that it was real.

He kissed me back, long and hard enough to convince me it was.

I looked at him and, for the first time in years, I truly smiled. I was happy—shell-shocked at what I'd just done, but happy. And at least some of it was because I was *allowing* myself to be happy.

I hadn't realized, until he'd made me admit it, just how much guilt I'd been carrying. I'd thought I'd been hiding myself away out of fear of getting someone else hurt, but at least some of it had been to punish myself.

Maybe, just maybe, this could work. I had to try, or I was going to die in that bus all on my own. And this town fair was the perfect place to start. A nice, normal thing for a newly-country girl and her boyfriend to do together. I was already looking forward to it.

FORTY-ONE

Bull

"What time is the greased pig-catching?" Lily asked.

"Two-thirty," I said with authority.

"I still think you're kidding."

I pulled her closer. "I ain't kidding. There's greased pig catching every year."

I'd been going to the fair since I was a kid and it was one of my favorite places on earth. Everything was big: hulking bulls and fine, glossy-coated horses competing to be the best animal in their classes. Giant pumpkins and squashes, nursed and nourished for months as carefully as any baby. And everywhere there was food. My stomach rumbled. Cotton candy, turkey legs and corn dogs, popcorn and ice cream. And most of it was fried. And on a stick.

But none of it could distract me from Lily. I walked arm-in-arm with her, proud as a kid with his prom date. She looked amazing. When I'd gone over to the bus to pick her up, she'd stuck her head out of the door and tentatively shown me her dress—white, with black polka dots, cut tight on the waist and with a long skirt the wind kept catching, licking it upwards to show glimpses of her bare legs. I'd whipped off my hat and told her that she was the prettiest darned thing I'd ever seen.

She'd thought I was kidding.

The local girls had gotten dressed up, too, whether in little strappy tops and shorts or full-on dresses like Lily's. Girls I'd lusted after and sometimes fucked—sometimes more than once. Any other year, I would have been swaggering around and showing off for them. Now, though...I was having trouble remembering what I'd ever seen in them. They just seemed so plastic, next to Lily.

Sometimes, they'd start to flounce towards me, either not noticing Lily or studiously ignoring her presence. Then I'd grip Lily a touch more firmly around the waist, and she'd pull me closer, and sometimes we'd kiss, and I'd feel the girl skid to a halt, staring at us, and then turn and march off the other way, her nose in the air.

"I guess it all seems kinda silly to you," I said. We were strolling past a tiny stage, where a country band was belting out a song, the audience lounging on hay bales. "Ain't exactly New York. Not a whole lot of bling, or Krystal, or dot-com billionaires."

"I'm pretty sure that's *West* coast," said Lily.

"Okay—not a whole lot of cocktails and canapés, then."

She patted my arm. "You have a very weird view of New York."

"Maybe we should go visit, sometime. You could show me around."

She nodded and smiled, but I saw the momentary panic in her eyes. It popped up whenever I mentioned

New York, or her past. "Mmm-hmm," she said, noncommittally. "Hey, that looks like fun."

I followed her pointing finger and groaned inwardly. She was pointing to the Ferris wheel.

I have a thing about heights. You want me in an arena with a pissed-off bull? I'll tip my hat and go to work. Got five or six liquored-up cowboys trying to cop a feel of the barmaid? I'll wade in there and knock seven shades of hell out of them. But heights?

The thing with Texas is, it's mighty flat. If I grew up in mountain country, I'm sure I'd be climbing like a damn lizard.

"Sure," I said, giving her my best smile. 'Why not?"

FORTY-TWO

Lily

Oh Christ, Lily, why did you say that?

I hate heights. I have a thing about it. Even indoors, in a tall building, if there are floor-to-ceiling windows I have to stand like ten feet back from the glass. I'd just been trying to get us off the subject of New York. I'd pretty much just stuck my arm out at random and said, *"Hey, that looks like fun."* I was lucky I hadn't pointed at the burrito eating contest.

But anything was better than talking about my past. So I grabbed Bull's hand and damn near *skipped* towards the line for the Ferris wheel. "I don't, you know," I told him as we approached.

"Don't what?"

"Don't think it's silly. I love it." And I squeezed his hand. It was true—I *did* love it. The sun felt amazing on my bare arms, like I was sucking up all my vitamin D for the entire year. I was only just starting to realize how starved of fresh air I'd been, cooped up in the bus. Fresh air and *life*. Sure, the fair was incredibly country and kind of cheesy, but it was *real*. Real people with real lives, not the shadows and ghosts I hung around with, with their dual identities and fake passports. I didn't know anyone, but Bull knew everybody and introduced me to them all. *Proudly.* And that made me feel amazing. I remembered how good it felt to smile.

I want to bottle this, I thought. *So I can drink it when I'm back on the bus on my own.*

I suddenly realized what I was thinking and the shock of it made me stumble, pulling on Bull's hand. If it had been any other guy, we both would have gone down in a heap. But this was Bull and I might as well have pulled on a bulldozer. His warm, strong grip held me up until I got my feet under me, and he just gave me a puzzled smile. I gave him a sheepish grin and we joined the line.

I'd been assuming it was going to end.

I'd been assuming that this was just temporary, that sooner or later I'd go back to my old life—on my own, with no one to protect me, no one to love me...no one even knowing I existed.

I squeezed Bull's hand. *The hell with that.* I'd found something good and I was going to cling the hell onto it.

A nagging voice in my head told me that, if this was really going to work, I'd have to share everything with him. *Everything.* Including my past.

No. No way. Not that. My stomach twisted into a cold knot. *It could still work, right?* I could just keep that one secret, that one part of me—maybe the most important part—hidden away from him, but be honest about everything else.

"I'm allergic to radishes," I blurted.

He blinked at me several times. "Okay," he said

slowly. "Duly noted."

"When I was six, I lied and said the dog knocked a can of paint all over the rug, but really it was me."

Now he turned to me, concerned. "Lily, what's—" He stopped when he saw my face, eyes wide and desperate.

It wasn't going to work. There was no amount of trivial shit I could tell him that would make up for lying to him about the big one. If I really wanted this to work, I had to level with him about my uncle. But I couldn't. Once he knew I was running, he'd want me to stop. And there was only one way to stop—to go back to New York and testify. To revisit everything I'd locked away in a dark corner of my mind and confront the monster I'd escaped. And even if I could face doing that, I'd have to go into witness protection. I'd never see Bull again.

No. Fucking. Way.

"Nothing," I told him. I took a deep breath and pushed the nagging voice in my head deep, deep down inside. "I was just being silly."

He nodded doubtfully and I squeezed his hand.

The guy running the ride showed us into a car and put the safety bar down across our laps. I'd been so distracted by what was happening in my head that I'd forgotten to be scared. As the car lurched into the air, rocking forward and back, I made up for lost time.

"Wow," said Bull happily. "This is really...yeah."

He was obviously loving every minute of it. I gave him my best grin. "Yeah. Awesome!"

We rose higher into the air. The ground fell away, the people becoming toys and then blobs. The wheel suddenly seemed much, much bigger than it had from down below and we weren't even a quarter of the way around, yet.

"Look," said Bull. "You can see the greased pig pens."

I followed his finger and saw dark blobs in cowboy hats chasing after a smaller pink blob. Then I was looking down *on top* of tents and my stomach lurched. I clung onto the safety rail, knuckles white.

"You okay?" asked Bull. His voice was oddly tight. I guess he was worried about me.

"Fine," I said. "Just excited."

We reached the top of the circuit...and stopped. My eyes bulged. Bull and I looked at each other.

"That's normal," he told me.

"Right. Yeah. You're probably right."

"To give us time to enjoy the view," he explained.

"Yup." I made a show of looking around, a delighted, fake smile pasted on my lips. I pointed at a stall. "Look—deep fried iced tea on a stick."

He'd almost looked as if he'd gone pale, but it must have just been the light. This was *Bull,* after all. "Yeah," he said. "Have to try that."

I could feel the panic starting to build. My feet wouldn't stay still on the floor of the car and, every time the wind rocked us, my grip on the safety rail tightened until I thought I was going to tear right through it. Bull, meanwhile, had one hand lazily resting on his hat to make sure the wind didn't take it, while the other arm was wound around my waist.

Quite *tightly* around my waist, actually. I guess he wanted me to feel safe.

I turned to him suddenly. "Kiss me," I said.

He licked his lips. "'Scuse me?"

"Kiss me! I mean, I want to kiss you, right now." Any excuse to shut my eyes.

He leaned across, pulled me along the seat to him and—

Suddenly the world became still and warm and glorious. His lips were like givers of life, sending energy and comfort flooding through me. I gave a contented little sigh. The wind must have died because the car seemed to stop rocking altogether and hung dead still.

His tongue played with the join between my lips, meeting my own tongue there and dancing with it. I groaned softly against him and opened and then we were twisting and moving, luxuriating in it. It was very different to how we'd kissed before, a kiss that was all about security and warmth.

Someone coughed, right in front of me. I opened my eyes to see the guy who ran the ride, and the people waiting to get on. How was that possible? Weren't we still at the top?

The guy swung the safety bar out of the way and we guiltily broke the kiss and stood up.

"Unless you want to go round again," offered Bull.

"No, no. Someone else should have a turn."

FORTY-THREE

Bull

I FELT BAD that we only rode the wheel once, because she'd so obviously enjoyed it. She probably would have happily ridden it all day if it hadn't been for me, but one more look at those tiny little cows down on the ground and—well, I got my limits. *For her birthday, I'm going to have to get her a parachute jump.*

Not far from the Ferris wheel there was one of those vintage photo booths where you get dressed up in old-fashioned clothes and get a photo taken of you. I still didn't have a photo of Lily and I figured it'd be a good opportunity. Besides, the place probably had corsets and the idea of Lily's curves, spilling out of a corset...oh, sweet Lord. I towed Lily over there.

"A photo?" she said immediately. "I don't really like photos."

I frowned at her. "Why not?"

She shrugged as if embarrassed. "I don't like people looking at me."

I wasn't totally sure I bought it. She sometimes

seemed a little shy about her body, but.... "No one's going to see it except us."

She looked so nervous about it, I nearly abandoned the whole idea. But then one of the dresses they had on display caught her eye—a scarlet thing, all silk and ribbons. I could feel my cock rise just at the thought of her in it. "No one?" she asked tentatively, fingering the fabric.

"No one. Look, it's authentic, old-fashioned - you get a printed photo. It can go on the wall at my place." To be fair, there was an option to get a copy emailed to you as well, but we didn't have to do that.

She stared at the dress for a moment, then at me. "Okay," she said at last.

Twenty bucks and thirty seconds later, we were "backstage" in the booth, looking at costumes. I took off my hat and set about choosing a new one.

Lily stood in front of a full-length mirror and held up the dress she'd seen outside. "You think this is too much?" she asked, fingering the bodice.

"*NO!*" I said, more firmly than I'd intended. She looked up at me, startled, and I almost blushed. I was just so damn eager to see her in it.

"I don't know," she said. "It's kind of...I always thought of myself as more of a schoolmarm, you know? This is more saloon girl."

I sidled up behind her and wrapped my arms around her. "Lily, I mean this in the nicest possible way, but you're *definitely* a saloon girl." She slapped me playfully. "Oh, come on! Who wants to be a schoolmarm?"

"Schoolmarms are the ones who wind up married," she said distantly, holding a long black skirt up in front of her. "Saloon girls are the ones who wind up murdered in some outlaw's hotel room."

"You looking to get married?" It was out before I realized I'd said it.

Her cheeks flared red. "No! No, of course not. God, are you kidding? People like us don't get married."

I kissed her neck, then drew back enough that I could see her face in the mirror. "*People like us* meaning you and me, or people like us meaning *you and me,* together?"

We just stared at each other in the mirror for a few seconds, the air growing heavier and heavier around us.

Then she took the scarlet dress and raced off into the tiny changing area before I could stop her.

"You realize I've already seen everything you've got?" I called.

From behind the curtain, rustling fabric. "Even saloon girls have to preserve some mystery."

I looked for something for myself. I settled on fancy pants and a dark shirt, with a silver belt buckle and a badge. A sheriff's outfit. After much debate, I picked out a suitable hat.

Lily emerged from behind the curtain and I forgot how to breathe.

The scarlet dress clung to her like a second skin, outlining the full curves of her breasts and the swell of her hips and ass. The bodice, still partially unlaced, displayed her pale breasts nearly down to the pink of the areolae.

"What?" she asked. "What's wrong?"

"Nothing," I said honestly. "I'm just wondering if I can sneak you out of here and off to my place in that dress."

She gave me a look and then turned around. The

sight of her partially-naked back, from her lower spine up to her shoulders, was more erotic than seeing Kirsten and her friends stark naked. *How is that possible? Goddamnit, this woman works some magic on me.*

"I need you to fasten me up," she said.

I stepped forward. My hands were shaking like a teenager at the high school dance, about to fumble for his first bra strap. It didn't matter that we'd already done the deed twice. This girl had me harder than a tree branch every damn time I looked at her.

I hauled on the laces of the bodice, which cinched her in at the waist and did fascinating things to her breasts. Her already hourglass figure became the stuff of wild fantasy.

I stopped cinching while she could still breathe and tied the bow, then gently turned her around. Her pale breasts had been pushed up and together and the effect was...

"Seriously," I growled, licking my lips. "What are the chances of us sneaking you out of here in that thing?"

She tossed her hair. "Sir," she drawled. "Unless you got five dollars or a good bottle o' suppin' whiskey, I'm afraid you'll be lonesome tonight." She looked at my outfit and blinked. "That's *it?*" she asked in her normal voice. "I get my ribcage crushed and you just have to put on a shirt and pants? I was expecting chaps, at least."

"It needs the hat," I said, and made a show of putting on my chosen hat.

She just stared at me, unimpressed.

"It's *white,*" I explained. "Because I'm the sheriff." She still looked blank. "My normal one's *black.* This makes me a good guy." I knitted my fingers with hers. "Come to save the fallen woman from her life of ill repute."

She stared at me strangely for a long time. "It suits you," she said at last.

We strolled outside and had to wait our turn while another couple had their photo taken.

"So you're the sheriff," she mused. "And you've married me."

"Arrested you," I corrected. I ran a finger under her chin. "You've been a *bad* girl."

"Arrested me *then* married me," she countered.

I thought about it and nodded. Meanwhile, Lily seemed to be slipping off into her own little world. "And now we live in a little house just outside town, by a river..."

I narrowed my eyes. "You've really thought about this."

She reddened and coughed. "No. Hey, we should think up names."

"Names?"

"You know. For..." she indicated her outfits. "Us."

"Lily's a pretty good name for a saloon girl, you ask me."

Her eyes got that faraway look again. "Mary. I like Mary."

I nodded. "Okay. Good, solid, country name. Mary." I looked down at myself. "I could be Cletus."

Lily let out a snort. "*Cletus?* Oh, come on. Who's called Cletus?"

I blinked at her, then lowered my eyes.

She put a hand to her mouth. "Oh my God. Your real name is Cletus, isn't it?"

"No," I said, looking off into the distance.

"Oh God, it is, isn't it? I'm so stupid. *Cletus*. There's nothing wrong with Cletus. I *like* Cletus."

I just stood there stoically.

"Bull—Cletus. I'm really sorry."

I couldn't hold it in any longer. I erupted into laughter, doubling over.

"Oh, you *bastard!*" She looked around for something to hit me with. "You...*Argh!*"

I pulled her close and hugged her, still quaking with laughter. "Your *face*," I told her. "I wish I could have kept it going. You were so damn guilt-ridden. You would have agreed to *anything*, in bed tonight."

Lily drew back and stared at me, shocked. Then she gave me a tiny smirk and muttered, "Not *anything*."

God, I loved this girl.

We took our turn in front of the camera and for a while we couldn't keep a straight face. But at last, we found a pose that worked: me standing behind her with my hands around her waist. I looked solemnly into the camera, the sheriff who's caught his quarry, and Lily gazed into the lens with a sort of pride. As if being caught was exactly what she'd wanted.

We waited while the guy printed out the photo. He seemed surprised when we turned down the offer of an emailed copy—he said we were *a real sweet couple*. But Lily insisted. I pocketed the printed copy and told her I'd get it framed.

"So what *is* your real name?" she asked, when we were back in our street clothes.

"Bull *is* my real name."

"No, but really."

I just looked at her. Eventually, she shook her head. "I'll get it out of you eventually," she said.

FORTY-FOUR

Lily

WHEN WE'D EATEN our fill of food-on-a-stick, Bull drove us home. I felt like even more of a country girl, being driven around in a pickup.

When we reached a junction, he stopped. I looked at him quizzically.

"Your place?" he asked. "Or..."

I could see the concern in his eyes. After all the times I'd run out on him, he was worried that I was going to get cold feet again.

"Your place," I said firmly. "I only have a single bed." And I smiled at him, he smiled back at me and then we just sat there grinning at each other like idiots until someone pulled up behind us and honked their horn.

Bull's place turned out to be an old, aluminum caravan a half-size Airstream, parked on an overgrown patch out near the ranch. It seemed impossible that someone his size could fit into it, let alone live there, but I soon discovered his trick—

everything important happened outside. There was a table for eating, a mirror nailed to a tree for shaving and—

"That is *not* for real," I told him.

"It is."

"It is *not.*"

It was an old copper bath, the kind with a raised back that lets you sit up in it.

"Let me get a fire going," he said, "and I'll show you."

And, when he'd boiled a few huge pans of water, he did.

Stripping off in front of him made me a little antsy, because of my size. It had been easier when it was sex, because the heat of the moment had stopped me thinking too much. Now, all I could think about was how much of me there was. But it was getting dark, which helped, and I did it quickly and then slid into the security of the water. Bull sat behind me, with me between his thighs and his arms around me, and I cuddled in as we watched the stars come out. Between the hot water and the hard press of his muscles against my back, it was just about the most relaxed I'd ever been.

And then I felt his cock hardening against my ass. And I became very aware of his strong arms, wrapped around me not so very far from my breasts. And suddenly, the heat of the water paled next to the heat throbbing through me. I resisted for a good few minutes, drinking in the feel of his hard body against me, but eventually I couldn't take it any longer.

I twisted around in the tub and pushed myself up against him, my glistening breasts pillowing against his chest. My head tilted up, seeking his mouth.

"Well, hell," he said in delight. "Now ain't you eager tonight?" And he leaned down to kiss me, tipping his hat back out of the way.

Yeah, he kept his hat on in the bath. This was *Bull*.

I let out a long groan as his lips met mine. I needed him so much. It was the first time I'd been the one to initiate things and it felt fantastic.

We gasped and groaned as we kissed, kneeling up in the water and running our hands up and down each other's gleaming wet bodies, the steam wrapping around us. When we couldn't take it anymore, he lifted me out of the bath and laid me down on the grass next to the tub and entered me with such slow, tender care I wanted to weep with joy. It became fast and then frantic, his muscled ass rising and falling between my thighs, the stars above us and the cool grass below as our bodies cooled and then warmed again.

I came, arching my back and thrusting my breasts up as he bent to kiss them. And in the afterglow, I hugged him tight. I finally felt that things were all going to be okay.

I was wrong.

Down in the town, the photographer from the fair was getting a call from the state newspaper. *We're running a piece about the town fair, but our editor just nixed the picture we were going to use. Says he doesn't want another goddamn greased pig this year. Do you have anything we can use?*

Why, yes, I surely do. Got a lovely photo of a sweet young couple, her in a scarlet dress, and him in a sheriff's uniform. And the guy's a minor celebrity around these parts, too, a rodeo rider.

Well, that sounds just perfect. Please email it right over. We go to press in an hour.

FORTY-FIVE

Lily

FOR THREE DAYS, I lived an idyllic life with Bull. I'd wake up each morning in his tiny trailer and we'd have slow, sensual morning sex. He'd go off to the ranch to work and I'd drive my Toyota to the bus so that I could work. It was weird—the work wasn't any different to before but now I practically whistled to myself as I did it. It was the knowledge that this wasn't all there was in my life.

And when I did step out of the air-conditioned cool of the bus, the sun felt good. The heat felt good. I let it soak into my bones instead of fighting it. I'd finally acclimatized to Texas.

In the evening, we'd venture into town...or, more often, just cozy up in Bull's trailer. Long summer evenings filled with good food: steaks cooked outdoors, sticky ribs you ate with your fingers, corn that was perfectly barbequed and dripping with butter.

And the sex. Oh, God, the sex. Up against the wall of the trailer. Bent over Bull's bed. Twice, in the stables again (I don't know what it is, there's just something about stables). I'd fall into bed pleasantly exhausted with Bull spooning me from behind.

We were *disgustingly* happy. And the nagging voices in my head, the ones that said it was wrong to keep my past from him, seemed very small and far away. How could it be wrong, when it felt this good?

Besides, I found out lots of other things about him. I found out that he liked his coffee not strong and black but milky as all hell. I found out that his dad was in oil and that he was considered the family misfit because he'd wound up riding horses. His brother, who *had* followed in his dad's footsteps, was seriously rich.

So we *were* getting to know each other…even if it was a little one-way. He didn't need to know about my uncle.

Right?

FORTY-SIX

Lily

THE NEXT MORNING, Bull had to pick up rope for the ranch from the hardware store, so we figured we might as well grab a coffee in town. We took both cars so that I'd be able to head back to the bus when we'd finished, and I bought the coffees while he bought the rope.

I was dumping huge amounts of cold milk into Bull's Americano when it happened.

"Miss?" A voice that didn't belong in Texas. A voice as out of place as my own. I spun around to look.

Big. As tall as Bull, although not quite as massively built. He was clean-cut where Bull had stubble, his hair neat where Bull's was tousled. Even his face was refined, with high cheekbones to offset the strong jaw. He could have been sculpted by some Renaissance artist, cast in marble for ladies to drool over. The sort of smart, good-looking guy who could have been a banker or a stockbroker.

But his suit and his shoes didn't say *banker* or *stockbroker*. They said three letters that I'd been half expecting to hear for the last two years. Letters he was going to say any second, right after his name.

"Samuel Calahan," he said with a smile. Then he opened his mouth again.

Time seemed to slow down. I felt my body locking up. It didn't matter that I'd been preparing myself for years for exactly this situation. I knew I had to run, but I couldn't fucking move.

"F—" said Calahan.

I looked behind him, towards the coffee shop door. He'd catch me before I got anywhere near it.

"...B..." said Calahan.

I picked up Bull's coffee..

"...I," finished Calahan.

I swung my arm, squeezing the cup as I did so to pop the plastic top off. Twenty ounces of hot coffee hit Calahan square in the chest and he staggered back, cursing and flailing at himself. I bolted past him and crashed through the door. I was panicking too much to think clearly. *He's going to take me back to New York! He's going to make me testify and—*

Outside, the blinding sunlight restarted my brain. All my planning kicked in and I knew exactly what I had to do. I ran across the parking lot.

In my car was my Go Bag. A simple little backpack stuffed with clothes, money and enough fake IDs to get me into almost any country I wanted, plus a Taser, water, energy bars and an encrypted USB flash drive with a backup of all my work. That was Plan B - get in my car and drive.

There might still be time for Plan A, though. Plan A was to drive back to the bus and pick it up. Most people make the mistake of thinking that because the bus has been parked in the same spot for two years, it can't move. But I keep it fully fueled and even give it a little test run every few months. Everything I cared about could come with me.

And that was when I realized my plans were out of date. I froze, standing beside my car, for fatal seconds.

None of my plans had ever accounted for a hulking cowboy I was crazy about. *Shit!* What was I going to do? I couldn't ask Bull to come with me to Mexico (my first choice) or Canada (my second). He had a whole life here. He had family and—

A hand landed on my shoulder and whipped me around, keeping a tight hold of me.

Calahan's shirt was still steaming and the soaked, brown fabric was sticking wetly to his skin, showing off a muscled chest.

"That," he said tightly, "was *not polite.*"

I tried to wriggle out of his hand, but he had a grip like a vice.

"I just want to talk, Tessa," he said. "Just talk."

Just hearing that name again brought it all crashing back. I hated him for that. I glared at him and tried to yank my shoulder out of his hand again.

"Do you want me to put cuffs on you?" he asked. "I've got some." He patted a pocket. "They may be a little damp, but they'll work."

I glanced around. A few passers-by had noticed us, but so far they were studiously pretending they hadn't. Just a woman arguing with her boyfriend. That would all change as soon as the cuffs went on. Everyone in town would know my secret in about thirty seconds.

If I talked to him, it gave me options. I stopped trying to wrestle out of his grip. "Talk," I snapped.

He cautiously took his hand off my shoulder, ready

to clap it back on again if I tried to run. When I stayed where I was, he reached into his pants pocket and pulled out a piece of paper. It was limp and soggy with coffee, but I recognized the image as soon as I saw it: Bull and I in period dress, at the fair. A screenshot from a newspaper's website. "What the ever-loving *fuck?"* I whispered.

"I'm kind of surprised," said Calahan mildly. "You've stayed off our radar so completely. Not a Facebook photo, not an Instagram...and then *this* pops up. What were you thinking?"

I slumped against my car in defeat. I'd been so careful. All my paranoia *hadn't* been paranoia. It had been working...until I'd fallen for Bull and gotten soft.

"Two years!" Calahan said. "When the facial recognition software flagged the photo, they had to blow the dust off the file to figure out who to call. And that would be me. I've been working your uncle's case for five years, now—long before you ran away. I watched you growing up."

I raised an eyebrow. "Well, *that's* not creepy at all," I muttered.

He gave me a look. "We were worried about you. For a while, we thought your uncle had murdered you. But he was pissed off as hell when you disappeared, so that didn't make any sense." His voice softened a little. "I'm glad to see you're okay."

I looked at my feet. I'd been lectured by my uncle about the evil, manipulative FBI for years. Then I'd lived in fear of them showing up and dragging me back to New York. I hadn't figured on one of them being...*human.* It occurred to me that it was lucky Bull took so much milk in his coffee, or I would have really scalded the guy. I shrugged, embarrassed. Then I nodded at his shirt and mumbled, "Sorry."

He shook his head. "I'm fine," he said breezily. "Didn't even feel it." *Jesus,* he was as much of a determined hard-ass as Bull.

Calahan took a deep breath. "There's going to be a trial."

Immediately, I turned to run.

"*Wait!* Relax. I can't *make* you testify."

I turned back to him suspiciously.

"I'm not even here officially. Technically, I'm on vacation. My boss thought the chances of tracking you down were so slim, he wouldn't authorize it. But I wanted to give it a shot."

I folded my arms crossly. Why did he have to be so *nice?* "Why?" I asked.

"I want to take down your uncle. I know what he did to a lot of people. Including Annette."

Now I did meet his eyes. I looked up and glared at him, enraged that he'd use such a low blow. But almost immediately, my eyes were filling with tears. It was the first time I'd heard anyone say her name in two years. Her memory had only been kept alive in my own head.

And the most annoying part was, when I checked his expression, he wasn't just using her murder to persuade me. He actually gave a shit.

But that didn't change anything. I couldn't face my uncle in a courtroom, not on my own. And I would be on my own—going into witness protection with the FBI would mean I'd never see Bull again. "No," I said. "I can't testify."

"If I found you, they can too. They'll be looking for you, Tessa. You're a crucial witness. Your testimony could swing the whole case."

He was right. I'd watched him murder someone, right in front of me, not to mention all the other beatings and bribes and contract killings I'd heard him order over the years. I sniffed, blinking back tears. "Without me, will he go to prison?"

"Maybe. Maybe not. Maybe not for as long. What I *do* know is, if *they* get you and force you to testify in his defense, he'll walk."

I knew he was right. My uncle had men like Antonio, men who were good at making people do things. If I was back in that house in New York, I didn't kid myself that I'd be able to resist them. "They don't have facial recognition software," I said, pointing at the newspaper picture. "They're not going to see it."

"Something else, then."

"I'm careful." I turned to my car.

Calahan put his hand on the door to stop me. "We're not done."

"Yeah," said Bull's voice from behind him. "You are."

FORTY-SEVEN

Bull

I FIGURED he must be one of Lily's clients. Another criminal getting pushy with her. From the few words I'd caught as I approached, he sounded American—a city boy. Drug dealer, maybe. I didn't much care what he was; what mattered was that he was hassling my girl.

"Now hold on," the guy said, straightening up. "I was just—"

"Leaving," I told him. "Leaving is what you were doing."

I stepped an inch closer to the guy. "The girl in the coffee shop said Lily threw coffee over some guy." I looked at his shirt. "That'd be you."

"Luckily," said the guy, straightening his tie, "I'm fine."

"What makes you think I gave a rat's ass about you?" I growled. "That was *my* coffee she threw at you. You owe me three bucks."

The guy squared up to me. "You want to try and take it?"

"You sure you want to get that fancy suit dirty?" I looked again at the coffee stain. "*Dirtier?*"

"You think you're a hardass because you play cowboy?" asked the guy. "Yeah, I know who you are, '*Bull.*' Let's go for it, I'll show you how we do things downtown."

I lifted my chin a half inch. "You know why they call me Bull?" I asked. "'Cause when I get mad, there ain't no stopping me."

"*Enough!*" Lily's voice made us both turn around. "Bull, let's go." She looked at the guy in the suit. "And you—you have my answer." Then she grabbed my hand and pulled.

I resisted for a second, just long enough to glare at city boy, and then let myself be led away. I slipped my arm around Lily's waist and pulled her hard against me, crushing her softness against me as we walked.

"I'll be in town a couple of days," the guy called after us. "I'm staying at the Stallion Inn. In case you change your mind."

Neither of us turned around, but I saw Lily bite her lip at his words. I could feel the hair on the back of my neck standing up, my whole body going tense with rage. *No one* upsets my Lily.

But if she wanted me to leave it, I'd leave it. For now.

We climbed into my pick up and I pulled out of the parking lot, heading towards the ranch. But as soon as we were out of town, I pulled off the road and turned to Lily.

"It's time for some goddamn answers," I said. "Start talking."

FORTY-EIGHT

Lily

"About what?" I knew it wouldn't work to throw him off; I was just trying to buy time to come up with a convincing story.

I didn't expect *how badly* it would work, though. With a sort of snarl, he rose as far out of his seat as the cab roof would allow, swung around to face me and put his open hand against my breastbone, pinning me back in my seat. "Goddamn it, Lily!" he roared. "Quit it!"

I gulped. It *should* have been scary—*was* scary, in a way. A huge guy like Bull, angry as hell, pinning me to my seat in the middle of nowhere. And yet….

And yet I knew he'd never, ever hurt me. I knew it in the way I knew the sun would rise in the morning. We stared at one another, both of us panting. The hot throb of his hand through my t-shirt, the way my breasts pressed softly against the heel of his hand. I could see the need in his eyes, only just restrained by his anger. The thought that I was doing that, that I could defuse even a raging Bull's anger, made me swell with pride. But at the same time, I could feel myself melting and weakening inside—when I was this turned on, lying was impossible. I was ready to tell him anything if he'd just move that hand down and left a little.

"His name's Calahan," I said. "He's FBI."

Bull gripped my upper arm with his other hand. His anger was gone, replaced with concern. "He's after you for the passports?"

I stared at him. Of course he'd assume that. Why else would an FBI agent be hounding me? Calahan didn't have any idea what I did for a living, but Bull didn't know that. My heart lifted. Here was exactly the explanation I needed!

Unless...unless I told him the truth. I bit my lip, hesitating for a second...

No. If I told him about my uncle, he'd want me to do the right thing and testify. He'd do the noble thing and send me off to witness protection and never see me again, just so that I could finally stop running.

Well, the hell with that.

"Yeah," I lied. "The passports."

His gaze hardened. "Ain't no man on earth gonna put my girl behind bars."

My heart gave a frantic little *boom-boom*. His sheer, hard-headed stubbornness was endearing—he was ready to take on the world for me. "Thank you," I told him. I tried to make it light, but it came out a little choked. *What happened to badass, independent Lily?* This guy just turned me to mush every single time. "But it's okay. I made a deal with him."

He nodded, relieved.

My brain was working overtime. *If I can just keep the two of them apart*...Calahan would go home and

Bull would be none the wiser.

And somewhere, far away, maybe my uncle would go free. *That's not my fault! I can't go back there—I just can't!* I pushed the guilt down inside and thought hard. Calahan didn't know where I lived, but he'd have no problem finding Bull's trailer. And if he came round that evening to try to convince me again, he might say something to Bull before I could stop him. "Could we maybe get out of town for a night?" I asked. "I don't want to run into him again."

Bull nodded and then smiled. "I know just the place. It's perfect." His mood was picking up and I realized it was because he thought I'd finally told him the truth. The guilt welled up inside me again. *It's for his own good,* I told myself. It didn't make it feel any better.

But then Bull brushed his hand through my hair, so gentle despite his size. *I can't give this up,* I thought, the emotion swelling up inside me. *Not to put my uncle away. Not for anything.* And then I couldn't fight it any longer—I *had* to kiss him.

I grabbed Bull's cheeks in my hands and dragged his face to mine. He jerked in surprise for an instant, not used to a woman taking the lead. Then I felt him grin against my lips and he was pushing and probing hungrily, his lips forcing mine apart, the hardness and power of him against my softness. I panted faster, letting my head go back against the headrest. His arm folded against me, his wrist and muscled forearm between my breasts, and I groaned as they throbbed and ached, desperate to be touched.

Bull had killed the engine when he pulled over and, without the air-con, we were sitting in a glass and steel box on a scorching hot morning. I could feel the temperature rising second by second, but I didn't care. My hands went around Bull's shoulders—God, I couldn't even get my hands to meet around him! I clutched him to me, tracing the shape of his muscles.

I put my hand on his cheek. The size of him, the *solidness* of him always calmed me. I felt my heart slowing. I hugged him, pulling him close. I had a plan, now, and I always felt better when I had a plan. *Everything is going to be okay.*

For a few seconds, it was just tender. But with the air conditioning off, the temperature was rising and we seemed to throb heat into one another. We started to kiss and then move, almost unconsciously, a slow, sinuous grind. Slow, but getting faster. I became aware of my breasts, squashed against his chest, my nipples hardening. And of how the bulge at his crotch was swelling and pressing against my hip....

Bull suddenly growled, grabbed my hips, and lifted me up out of my seat, handling me as if I weighed nothing at all. He twisted around and sat down in the driver's seat with me astride him. He reached under his seat, pulled a lever, and slid his seat back to give us room.

Then I realized what he wanted room *for*.

"We can't," I said. "Not *here!*" I twisted and looked out of the window at the road beside us. Anyone passing by could glance straight in.

"Fuck 'em," growled Bull, and hauled my t-shirt up around my neck. I yelped as I was suddenly bared. It was getting seriously hot in the pickup, now, the sun blasting in through the windows and baking the air. I could feel the sweat slippery on my back as he deftly unhooked my bra and pushed it up and then his hot hands were squeezing my breasts, thumbs rubbing across my nipples. My fear of being seen rapidly slipped away. I threw my head back in pleasure, my face almost up against the ceiling. *God!*

I was wearing a short denim skirt so my bare legs were against his jeans. I'd had to open my knees wide to sit astride him, especially since his own legs were open a little. That meant that my pussy was suspended above his crotch with just air beneath it. I found myself grinding my hips instinctively, trying to find friction where there was none.

He noticed. Taking his hands from my breasts, he shoved one of them roughly down between our bodies. I cried out as his fingers found the stretched-tight cotton of my panties, massaging lips that were already slickly wet. His other hand pressed on my sweat-wet back, tipping me forward, and his mouth engulfed the tip of my breast, his tongue lashing my nipple. I closed my eyes in ecstasy. The sucking wetness was a new source of heat, throbbing through my breast and down into my core, making me grind against his hand.

He rubbed more firmly. He couldn't speak, with my breast in his mouth, but he rubbed so deliberately, working the damp fabric against my lips, that I knew exactly what he meant. *You're wet for me,* he was saying. I flushed and ground harder against him.

He moved his mouth to my other breast and slid his hand up my back to the nape of my neck, gathering my hair into a rope and using it to tug my head back and expose my throat. His mouth worked hungrily up my body, from my breast to my neck and up along my jaw line, leaving me gasping. He used my hair as a handle, gently but firmly guiding me to where he wanted me, while his lips left little explosions of pleasure all the way to my ear.

I shuddered, back arched and tight as a bow, as he nipped my earlobe with his teeth. Sweat was trickling down my front, running in rivulets between my breasts. But no way was I going to stop, even for a second, to fire up the air conditioning.

Under my skirt, his fingers nudged aside the edge of my panties. My lips were already held open for him by my position, presenting me to him like a sacrificial offering. He speared up into me with two thick fingers and I groaned in delight, rolling my hips. I could feel my tightness stretching around every knobbly inch in just the right way. *God!*

He started to pump me like that, returning his mouth to my breast at the same time. I could feel how hot he was getting, too, his whole body throbbing with it, as if I was atop a huge, sun-warmed granite statue. His thumb found my clit and I gasped, trying to climb up his body, clawing at his back. He chuckled, making his tongue do amazing things to my nipple.

My hips traced circles in the air as his fingers thrust slowly back and forth. The sweat was pouring off both of us, our clothes just an inconvenience, now. I panted into his ear, my hands cupping and massaging his shoulders through his shirt. His skilled fingers took me higher and higher, spiraling towards a climax. His mouth on my breast was like a furnace, pouring more heat into me, while his other hand on my cheek completed the circuit. I felt as if my whole body was melting away until only the feelings remained.

His thumb circled my clit, getting faster. His fingers *pushed* and *pulled*...so *deep* and then suddenly they *hooked*—

I bit my lip, sinking my fingers deep into the

muscles of Bull's shoulders. My whole body went rigid and my sneakers clattered against the steering wheel. My whole body rippled as wave after wave of pleasure went through me. Then I slumped, sweat-soaked and exhausted, atop him.

I was barely aware of him lifting me, or of him unbuckling his belt and shoving his jeans and boxers down his legs. But I woke up fast when he lowered me again and I felt the thick, rubbery head press against my lips. He'd stretched my panties to one side with his hand. I opened my eyes, having to blink several times before I could focus on him. He was looking up at me with raw, undisguised lust. And, I realized, I was looking back at him with exactly the same expression.

He lowered me onto him and I groaned as he split me apart, driving up into me. I was so wet that he entered me easily, despite his size. His hands slid down my back and grasped the cheeks of my ass through my skirt, then flipped it up so that he could hold me skin-on-skin.

He adjusted our angle and then pushed up with his hips as he guided me down and—*Ohhh*...he slid right up into me, stretching me exquisitely. It really did feel different without a condom—hotter and more real, and I could feel the satiny texture of him that a condom concealed...I rocked forward atop him and had to bite at his shoulder to keep from screaming, it felt so good.

I knew that this position was meant to be all about the woman taking control, setting the pace and fucking their man with powerful thrusts of her perfectly gym-toned thighs—*Yeah! Girl Power!* But my legs were so shaky and weak from my orgasm that I didn't have a hope of powering myself anywhere, even if they *had* been gym-toned.

It didn't matter, though, because this was Bull. His hands tightened on my ass cheeks, then started to rhythmically squeeze me there as he lifted and lowered me. I groaned as I felt him slide from me, moving easily on my wetness, then plunge back into me, filling me in a way that made molten silver erupt in the dark heat inside me.

I was like a doll in his hands, his to do with as he pleased, and all I could do was tangle my hands into his hair and use my thumbs to wipe the sweat from his brow as he built up the pace. Each sudden lift made my breasts bounce and shake, sending ripples through my rising pleasure and making me ache inside with the need to be filled again. We were still touching but we were *too—far—apart* and I'd grind my teeth and moan. Each powerful push downward flattened my ass against his thighs, his cock plunging into me to the very root, our groins grinding together until we were as close as it's possible for two people to be.

I leaned forward and gasped as my clit started to rub against him with each thrust. My building climax started to rocket upward. And now my breasts were dragging along the front of his shirt each time he lifted me, making me squirm and raggedly pant. I traced my hands down his arms, loving the way his muscles bulged as he lifted me.

I was thumping up and down atop him, now, vaguely aware of the pickup rocking on its suspension and of just how exposed we were, out here by the side of the road. But my eyes were tight closed, my orgasm close. I didn't care if anyone could hear or see. I just cared about what he was doing to me, my huge, rock-hard cowboy *stud*, his cock naked and throbbing inside me—

God, naked! It was dirtier, somehow, filthier and more exciting. Everything was hidden by my skirt, but I could visualize his balls beneath me, heavy with seed and ready to—*God!*

There was something primal about it. Something I couldn't quite explain, but it was a turn on like nothing else. I felt myself spinning out of control, as if someone had flipped a switch and multiplied my arousal by a factor of ten.

I clung to him even harder. My ass was bouncing hard on his thighs, my nipples like pebbles against his wet, clinging shirt. I could barely breathe, my hair sticking to my damp forehead and my whole body shining with sweat. But all I cared about was that beautiful friction inside me, the feel of *him* driving up into me, making me his.

My orgasm was on top of me, taking control. It made me put my lips to his ear and gasp, "*Do it.*"

Hearing myself say those two words sent me over the edge and it nudged Bull past the point of no return, too. He grunted, pounded me up and down even faster for a few strokes, and then rammed me hard down onto him, until his cock was throbbing at my very limits. I was already shuddering and bucking atop him from my own climax when I felt the first thick jet of his seed erupt inside me. I wrapped my arms around him and pressed myself to his chest as I felt the hot spurts continue, each one making me tremble. I felt as if my whole body was welcoming him in, draining every drop from him.

We gasped and panted our way down from our peaks and then I lifted myself off of him. I slumped back onto my own seat, eyes closed and chest heaving.

I heard Bull thumb the ignition. There was a few second's pause as the fans spun up and—

Heavenly, icy air washed across our sweat-soaked bodies. We both groaned in blessed relief. I opened my mouth and drank the cold air in, gulping it down like water. I offered up a little prayer to the inventor of air conditioning.

I didn't want to open my eyes. I was so exhausted, so shell-shocked by what we'd just done, that I just flopped there. God, had I really just done that by the side of the road...and had I really gone so out of control at the thought of his naked cock inside me? It had been so powerful—instinctual, almost.

I was still trying to figure it out when I felt his huge hand grasp mine. We held hands like that for a full minute, just panting and cooling down.

"God, Lily," he whispered. "You're incredible."

It went off like a warm bomb in my chest. I leaned against him. "So where's this perfect place you're taking me?" I asked. "A hotel? A seedy motel? Some mom and pop guest house?"

He smiled. "Ever been camping?"

FORTY-NINE

Antonio

I WAS READY TO GIVE UP. It's not easy, searching for a place when all you have to go on is its mascot. I didn't even know if I was looking for a bar or a restaurant or a goddamn bowling alley. I just knew it was in Texas...and Texas is a big place.

I didn't even know if this was a genuine lead or a wild goose chase. For all I knew, that napkin had been dropped by a nurse. Or Tessa may have passed through Texas but barely stopped there and she was in fucking Brazil by now. But it was all I had to go on. Every other avenue I'd tried had gone nowhere.

But I'd spent days Googling and hadn't found a damn thing. Now I was slumped in front of my laptop, glowering at the screen, half-drunk on Scotch. The bearded prospector grinned at me from the napkin I'd pinned to the wall. I'd nearly torn the thing to shreds more than once. He was just so fucking annoying—

On a whim, I typed *bar annoying prospector* into Google.

Immediately, a photo taken in a bar appeared.

Grinning, drunken faces...and, beside them, a puppet version of the prospector. The text below griped about how annoying the thing was.

It was so unexpected, after days of failure, that I just stared at it in shock. Then I saw that they'd tagged the bar's Facebook page. I grabbed the mouse and clicked.

Lucky Pete's. Gold Lake, Texas.

FIFTY

Lily

I GRINNED AS I unloaded my last bag from the trunk of my Toyota and added it to the pile. Bull walked out of the stables...and stopped dead.

My grin faltered. "What?" I asked blankly.

He stared at my bags. "What's *that?!*"

I looked down at my backpack. And suitcase. And laptop bag. And the bag for my spare batteries and cables. And the garbage sack holding pillows and blankets. "My stuff?"

He pushed back his hat and scratched his head. "I said only bring the essentials."

"These *are* the essentials." I looked at his pick up. "There's plenty of room."

He burst out laughing—that big, booming laugh that was as large as he was. "This is a camping trip. We're not taking a car." And he led Caliope and Apollo out of the stable.

I looked at the horses and then at my stuff. "How much *can* I take?" I asked.

"I already got food and bedding rolls. You can take

one little bag. Some clothes. That's all you need."

One small bag?! I looked at my laptop bag. *If I don't change my clothes for the whole trip, or take any toiletries....*

No. I had to face up to it: I was going to have to go a day without a computer. Glowering, I packed everything except a few changes of clothes and my wash bag back into the car.

This time, I managed to get up onto Caliope after only a few attempts and I wasn't half as nervous. Maybe I was starting to get used to being around big, powerful animals.

I glanced across at Bull and my smile came back.

FIFTY-ONE

Bull

THERE ARE SOME MIGHTY FINE SIGHTS in Texas. Sunsets. Cattle drives. A pitcher of ice cold beer. But the sight of Lily's perfect, round ass bouncing up and down in her saddle...that beat every last one of them. It was even better than when we'd been horse riding. Back then, I'd had to imagine what it'd feel like to have her bouncing on top of me. Now I knew and the memory of it made my cock rise every time I saw that tight denim hit the leather.

And now, we'd gotten rid of all the tension because she'd finally spilled her big secret. I should have figured it out on my own. What *would* make a forger so twitchy and nervous? Of course the FBI had been on her tail. I could fill in the blanks myself. They must have nearly caught her in New York and that's why she'd had to skip town. It explained everything.

I even knew why she hadn't told me. She'd figured—correctly—that I'd beat the hell out of anyone who tried to take her away from me. If I ever saw that Calahan guy again....

"Your boss is definitely okay with this?" Lily asked over her shoulder. "I don't want you getting in trouble."

I shook my head. "He was eager to get me outta there. Truth is, I barely ever use my vacation time. I enjoy what I do, you know? Why would I want to sit around at home when I can be on the ranch?"

I was taking us in a different direction, this time, into some low hills where there was some greenery and a lake. Only a short ride—two, two and a half hours.

After only an hour, though, Lily was getting antsy. She was looking around at the desert scrub, clearly seeing something I wasn't. "What?" I asked.

"There's just...nothing," she said. "No buildings. No roads. Not even a telegraph pole. I bet I don't even have a cell phone signal." She dug her phone out of her pocket. "I don't."

"That's the general idea."

"What if we run into a snake?"

"I'll stamp on it," I told her.

"What if the horses run off and we run out of water and die of thirst?"

"I'll find us a creek."

"What if—"

"You really don't like the country, do you?" I asked, amused.

"I do like it. I mean, it's beautiful. I like looking at it." She gazed around, shrinking down in her saddle. "I'm just not sure about being *in* it."

I rode closer and leaned sideways in my saddle so that our shoulders touched. We rode on like that for a few minutes and I gradually felt her relax.

We began to climb into the hills. We weren't

following any trail, but the route was clear in my mind. I'd ridden out here to clear my head plenty of times when some local girl had flipped out and raged at me, just because I'd slept with her best friend. It was weird, but I couldn't imagine doing that to Lily.

It was starting to hit me just how little I'd cared about all of those girls I'd fucked, and how much I cared about the woman beside me now.

I thought of all the girls back in town. All those tight, toned bodies and those flicks of long, golden hair. Their giggling and bitchiness as they backstabbed each other, the way they thrust out their tits and slipped arms around my waist, cozying up to me before I even knew their name. And I didn't miss them. Not for a second. I'd take Lily over any of them...*all* of them.

"Lily?" I just kinda blurted it out.

She turned and looked at me expectantly, green eyes huge, black hair glossy and shimmering in the sunlight. We were just passing under some trees and, in the green dappled light, she looked like a goddamn fairy queen, soft and pale and perfect.

My words died in my throat. I only now realized what I'd been about to say: something along the lines of *I love you. What? What the fuck?* I'd already told her I was falling for her and that'd freaked her out for a while. If I unleashed the L-word she'd likely split and gallop right back to town.

At least, I told myself that's why I was scared. Deep down, I was horribly aware of the real reason: I like to think of myself as an honest guy, at least in the sack. All of those local girls I'd bedded, and not once had I told them I loved them because it had never been true. The thought that it might be, with Lily...it was terrifying. Even for me, and I'm not scared of a goddamn thing. Except heights.

"What?" asked Lily, frowning.

I swallowed. "You want some water?" I asked. "It doesn't do to get dehydrated."

She nodded, took the bottle I offered and glugged some, and I tried to remember to breathe as I watched her chest move under her blouse.

"It's just up here," I told her. And rode on ahead before I said something dumb and messed things up. What I wanted to show her was just around the next bend and, as we got there, I looked back to see her reaction.

It wasn't a disappointment.

FIFTY-TWO

Bull

LILY SAT THERE looking around in amazement as Caliope slowed to a halt. "It's beautiful," she said at last.

The spot I'd picked out was next to a lake, nestled between three low grassy hills. The lake was crystal clear, fed by a river that wound down out of the distant mountains. And the finishing touch was that the river dropped into the lake over a waterfall. The place was goddamn perfect. It would have been easy to bring some of the local girls out here and let it work its magic on them—a guaranteed panty-dropper. Yet I'd never wanted to share it—I'd wanted to keep it as my own private getaway. Until now.

"This is Gold Lake," I told her. "This is where the town got its name."

"*Gold* Lake?"

"You'll see." I tied the horses to a tree and set up camp—which consisted of unrolling the bedrolls.

Lily tilted her head to one side. "I don't get it," she said, squeezing the bags I'd packed. "Where's the tent? Does it fold up really small?"

I just grinned at her.

"We're sleeping *outside?*" she asked, sounding appalled.

"Remember the stars when we went horse riding? That was still pretty close to town. Light pollution. Here, with the hills around us and no lights...trust me."

She nodded, still looking uncertain. But, bless her, she was willing to give it a go. I loved that about her. She was doing a hell of a lot better out here than I'd probably do in New York, trying to figure out which fork to eat my sushi with.

"So what now?" she asked, looking around.

I grinned and started to strip off my shirt.

"Oh!" She flushed. "Just like that? You expect me to just...I mean, no warm up or anything?"

I laughed. "Hold your horses, city girl." I tossed down my shirt and tipped my hat back on my head. "I was heading in for a dip." And I nodded my head at the lake.

"Oh!" Then her eyes widened. "Shit! I didn't bring a bathing suit. I didn't know we were going swimming!"

"Who needs a bathing suit?" I asked. And pulled off my boots. And jeans. And boxers. And finally my hat.

She stood there staring at my naked body. "Out *here?!*" she squeaked.

"Well, I've already seen all of you. And the horses were with us in the stable that time, so they've seen it too, and there ain't no one else for miles."

She glanced around her, arms wrapped around her for protection. "Umm..."

"What?"

"I'm just not...you know."

I put my hands on my hips. "What?"

"I'm not comfortable...naked, okay?"

I frowned. "You've been buck naked in front of me plenty of times. In the stables. And in the barn. And in the tub at my place."

"But not outdoors!" She looked around. "Not in broad daylight!" She looked at me standing there. "How are you so relaxed about it?"

I looked down at myself. "I guess I never thought much about it," I said. And I realized I hadn't. "It's just a body, you know."

"Easy for you to say," she muttered.

I frowned again. "What? What's that supposed to mean?"

She flushed more. "You know."

"Lily, I swear I don't."

She waved her hand at me. "You're all big and muscled and...*rippling*. How a man should be. You're goddamn perfect, okay?"

I looked down at myself again. Okay, true. But so what?

When she saw my bemused expression, she got even more frustrated. "I'm...*not*. Okay?"

I finally got it. I walked slowly towards her, my cock bouncing against my leg. "Lily..." I started. As I got closer, she turned her face away from me, red-cheeked and ashamed, and I saw that her eyes were moist. She'd held back the tears, but only just. "Lily," I said again, my voice softer. "I'm sorry. I didn't..." I shook my head. "I didn't know. I guess it plain didn't occur to me that you'd be...shy."

She gave me a frustrated glare. "You can't see

what's in front of you?" She waved her hands at her body.

I frowned. "I *can* see what's in front of me," I told her. "That's why it makes no sense to me, because you're goddamn perfect."

She blinked back tears, twisting her head around to look out at the lake, still avoiding my eyes. "You really mean that?" she whispered after a second.

My stomach was knotting. It killed me to see her in this much pain. "Of *course,*" I said. "Look at you!" I gently put my hands on her shoulders, then ran them slowly down her front. "You got the best ti—*breasts* I've ever seen. You've got this gorgeous curve that drives me wild"—I traced it with my hands—"right here, allll the way down here and then out again." Her hips moved against my palms as she wriggled. I slowly crouched down and continued. "Your legs—sexy and gorgeous with so many great lines I don't know how to even describe them, so I'll just show you." I swept my hands down her thighs and spiraled around her calves, then worked my way up again. "And your ass. I've been staring at your ass all afternoon and I could keep right on staring at it all night. Full and ripe and so perfectly round."

"It's enormous—" she whispered.

"It's exactly the right goddamn size, is what it is," I said firmly. "Hell, why would anyone want one of those skinny-ass asses that ain't even there? How the hell are you supposed to squeeze one of those?" And I gave her ass a hard squeeze to show her. She wriggled and, at last, a tiny smile appeared.

I stood and looked her in the eye. "I'm sorry." I nodded at the lake. "I shouldn't have just sprung this on you. It's just...you never...I mean, you never seemed self-conscious when we were...you know."

She reddened and looked at her feet. "I was distracted, those times. Or it was dark." She looked around. "This is different. I'm all...exposed."

"Your perfect body, out of the shadows, so I can see every inch? I can't think of anything better. Hell, that's why I got you up here." I'd been thinking about skinny dipping with her ever since she suggested getting out of town.

"Really?"

"How about I show you what your body does to me?"

FIFTY-THREE

Lily

I HAD TIME to draw in one shuddering gasp before he lowered his head and touched his lips to mine. Not his normal kiss, all hungry and urgent. This was slower and more gentle—gentler than I'd thought him capable of.

When his kisses moved away from my mouth and down my neck, it was as if he was following the lines of me so that he could draw them indelibly in his mind.

All my lines. He started to unbutton my blouse and I caught my breath, my hands automatically rising to catch his. But he leaned closer and made a *shh*-ing sound in my ear and I slowly lowered them. He was right—it was crazy that I was self-conscious when we'd already had sex. But what I'd said to him was true, too—the sex had been hot enough that it had burned straight through all my insecurities. This was different—more intimate, in a way. It's surprising how close you have to feel to someone, to be happy for them to see all your imperfections.

As he folded the fabric of my blouse back away from my chest, opening up a deeper and deeper sliver of skin down my front, he trailed the edge of it with his mouth. Every shocking gust of warm, outdoor air against my breasts was followed by a reassuring touch of his lips. It kept me just on the edge, hovering between allowing this and stopping it.

He kept going. By the time my blouse was down to its lowest button, he had it pushed back to reveal my shoulders, still creamy-white despite the summer sun. I always stayed covered up, outside. Until now.

The tension inside me made me stand as stiff as a mannequin. He pushed the blouse down my arms and it fell to the ground behind me. My whole upper half was exposed to the sun and the wind and a million billion pairs of imagined eyes.

He kissed me just above the navel—did he know that that was the part of me I disliked most?

"I love you here," he said. He'd been so quiet that the shock of his voice almost made me jump. "I love how smooth your skin is. Soft and warm and sexy."

My insides did a somersault. No one had ever described my stomach like that before.

He unfastened my jeans and then knelt to push them down my legs, kissing his way down the length of one and then up the other. It sent warm waves up through my thighs and they became a slowly-twisting heat in my groin...it was sexual, but not in the same way normal sex is, if that makes any sense. It felt more giving. It felt as if we were connecting soul to soul instead of body to body.

It felt like being worshipped.

He nudged me backward until I stepped out of my jeans, sneakers and socks. The grass was crisp under my feet, the blades warm from the sun but the earth beneath still cool.

He stood, using just his fingertips to trace up my legs and over my hips. "I love you here," he said. I cringed inside, thinking of the width of my hips. "They're perfect," he said. "Full and curvy and they make the perfect frame for *this.*" And he moved one hand inward, cupping my pussy through my panties. I gasped and stepped my feet a little farther apart, the heat changing and spreading. His hand pushed upward just a little, so that I opened under the cloth. "But I can't figure out if *that's* my favorite part of you," he said.

He stripped my panties down my hips and let them fall around my ankles, then drew them off and tossed them aside. He came around behind me and I began to pant. I'd never felt so *studied* before. I'd always pushed thoughts of my own body down into the depths of my mind, and the sex with Bull had helped because it had always been so urgent—there hadn't been any time for doubts. Now, all I could think about was how huge I must look, how unlike the slender, tanned girls he knew. *What if he realizes his mistake?!*

He kissed my shoulder and I felt my fears calming. Then both big hands slid down my back and cupped my ass. "I especially love you here," he told me. "I think this is my favorite part of you. I love to watch it when you're riding a horse—or when you're riding *me.* It's so ripe and juicy and it feels just right in my hands." He gave a squeeze to demonstrate and I gasped.

Then I felt my bra loosen. A second later, he stripped it from my body, tossing it away. But he didn't come around in front of me—he stayed behind, close enough that I could feel the warm press of his chest against my back, and he looked down at my front over my shoulder.

"Your breasts—they were the first thing I noticed about you. Yeah, I know, I'm supposed to say your face. But it wasn't. It was these." He scooped them up in his hands and, immediately, I felt waves of heat radiating out from where his palms touched me. "Gorgeous and *big* and just the right weight. Pert, but they hang just enough. Goddamn perfect." He squeezed gently, then harder and I gasped. "All of you is goddamn perfect. Every damn inch."

I felt his cock, rising between my thighs and bumping against my ass cheeks. "I told you I'd show you what your body did to me," he said. "Can you feel it?"

I nodded dumbly. I felt it growing rock hard, throbbing hotly as it rose to stand vertical, nestled between my cheeks. He moved closer and I could feel the soft kiss of his balls, heavy and...*full*. "Can you feel how much I need you?" he growled.

I nodded again.

His muscled arm wrapped around my waist and his hand slid down between my legs. I gasped. My knees softened as his fingers stroked down my lips. Then he thrust them inside me.

I could feel him moving on my own slick heat. I'd been listening so hard to his words, focusing so much on the differences between how he saw me and how I saw myself, that my own arousal had crept up on me. The heat had built slowly, throbbing outward from every place he touched, and it had silently filled me up. Now I was aching and trembling, needing him as much as he needed me. Suddenly, every breath of wind against me made me gasp.

He pulled me back hard against him so that he touched me from shoulder to ankle, the warm press of his body the perfect counterpoint to the cool breeze against my front. The fingers inside me began to move and even *that* was different to normal sex. Instead of pumping me, driving me towards orgasm, they were gently sliding deeper, making me appreciate every millimeter of my sensitive flesh. I was rediscovering myself.

It might not have been what I was used to, but the slowly-moving fingers, coupled with that deep, gravelly voice telling me how much he wanted me, made the heat swirl and build inside me. I was heading for a climax, but not like any I'd known before. This was a slow-burning fire instead of an explosion, but all the hotter for it.

When he wrapped his other arm around me and cupped my breast, gently pinching my nipple, I moaned. The heat was spiraling and twisting inside me, drawing me inexorably towards ecstasy. I'd started to unconsciously grind my hips, swirling myself around those questing fingers, really feeling—maybe for the first time—how my body moved, instead of glossing over it in my mind. My breast in his hand felt heavy. My ass, pressed against him, felt rounded and ripe...but suddenly, neither of those things felt bad.

The heat inside me rose higher, becoming molten silver and then white-hot lava. I'd had my eyes tightly closed for what felt like hours now, imagining laughing, jeering people staring at me. Suddenly, I opened them and it wasn't just that the hills around us were empty and peaceful—it was that I wasn't scared anymore. I was proud of my body.

Bull rubbed his thumb across my clit. It took me a notch higher, my whole body growing tense, but it wasn't quite enough to take me to orgasm—

"I'm going to fuck you right here on the grass," he growled in my ear. "Harder than you've ever been fucked before."

I cried out and came, the orgasm doubly intense because of how gradually it had been built. I rammed my ass back against him, folding at the waist, and trembled and shook as my body spasmed around his fingers.

When I finally straightened, I felt different. I was red-faced and a little embarrassed, but only on the surface. That deep-seated worry and guilt I'd been carrying around, without even realizing it, was gone.

I turned and looked at Bull in wonder. Then I swallowed and glanced at the grass beside us, remembering what he'd said.

"First," he said, "let's take a dip."

FIFTY-FOUR

Bull

THERE'S ONLY ONE THING better than Lily's perfect, naked body. And that's seeing it shining wet. I'd seen it in the tub at my place, but that was just an appetizer. I wanted to see those perfect tits bobbing in the water, those long legs flashing and kicking as she swam.

I grabbed her by the hand and ran down to the water's edge because I knew that, if she had time to think about it too much, she might hesitate. I jumped off the bank but, just as my feet left the ground, she pulled her hand from mine.

I hit the water—sun warmed, but still cool enough that it was like a wake-up slap across my whole body. I surfaced and whooped, shaking my head and throwing shining droplets out across the surface.

Lily was standing at the edge, eying the lake suspiciously. "Wait," she said. "How cold is it?"

"Beautiful," I told her. "Fantastic."

She narrowed her eyes. "Give me a temperature," she insisted. Then she stuck a toe in. "*Jesus!* It's freezing! Are you trying to kill me?"

"It's great once you're in." I clapped my hands together and held my hands out to her. "Come on."

She dipped her foot in and then snatched it back, gasping.

"Just jump in! Do it quick!"

She gave me a look.

"Do you trust me?" I asked.

She tilted her head to one side. Then she took a deep breath, backed up a step, and launched herself into the air.

She hit the water and went under, then shot to the surface and almost into the air again, kicking frantically. "You *prick!*" she yelped. "It's *freezing!*"

I frowned. Now that I thought about it, it *was* kind of chilly, but then skinny dipping always is. I swam over to her, "You'll get used to it," I said.

She thumped me on the arm. I grabbed her and pulled her close. Her wet breasts pushed up against my chest, her nipples hard as pebbles. She glowered up at me as I brushed strands of soaked hair from her face. With an arm around her waist, I leaned down and tried to kiss her, but she twisted sulkily away. I chased her mouth and claimed it, wet lips against wet lips, droplets of water coursing down our chins. As my tongue invaded her mouth she wriggled...and then gave a sigh and relaxed into my arms. The kiss changed, our bodies writhing together as we tasted each other. When we broke apart, she was heavy-lidded and panting.

"I wasn't kidding," I growled. "I'm going to fuck you. Right there on the bank."

She stared at me for three quick breaths. "Remember my safeword?"

"Rhinoceros," I said without hesitation. "Why?"

"Because you've got to catch me first." She used my surprise to get a head start, twisting away and launching into a powerful stroke.

A split-second later, I flung myself after her. By then, she was already ten feet away. I really was going to have to catch her before I could—

I could see her ass through the crystal-clear water, the creamy moons of her cheeks gleaming wetly. When she rippled sinuously with her stroke, I caught a glimpse of pink lips beneath them and dark curls of submerged hair.

I splashed to a standstill, transfixed. She pulled away another ten feet and only then did I wake up and swim after her. She was fast, too. She must have been a serious swimmer, at some point in her life. Her gleaming body sliced through the water, her shoulders and ass just breaking the surface. Meanwhile, I blundered along behind her, making up in power what I lacked in finesse. I was like a sailor chasing a mermaid, eager to claim his prize but hopelessly outmatched.

Then she twisted to look back at me, her whole body lifting up onto one shoulder, and one naked breast came into view, shining as if varnished, milky-white skin and hard pink nipple—

I growled and went for it, full power. No matter that I was about as good at cutting through the water as a barn. I just pushed the damn water aside.

Her eyes grew big as she saw me pick up the pace. She kicked for the shore, but I'd already closed the gap to half what it was. By the time she made it out, I was already splashing through the shallows.

And then we were on land. My territory.

She checked over her shoulder again, panting and giggling...and something else. That wild-eyed, heady arousal I'd seen when I'd tied her up. The thrill of being chased. Of being *taken.*

She ran. I ran faster.

I thundered across the field like my namesake, eating up the ground in long strides. Every time she glanced back to see where I was, she lost a little more of her lead. And panted a little harder.

I caught her just at the base of one of the hills, where the ground started to rise. Grabbing her wrist, I jerked her back and threw her to the ground, keeping hold of her as she fell so that she didn't hurt herself. She landed with a *whump* on the soft grass, surrounded by wildflowers. She looked like some goddess of nature, naked and pure.

Her legs were a little way apart. I dropped to my knees, opening them farther. She'd given up on the game of resistance, now. She was too turned on, staring up at me with half-closed eyes, her chest heaving.

My cock had softened—an icy dip will do that to you. Now, it rose and stiffened and I enjoyed the sight of her eyes locking onto it hungrily.

"Now," I said. "I'm going to fuck you."

FIFTY-FIVE

Lily

I SWALLOWED AND LOOKED UP AT HIM. More specifically, I looked up at his cock, angry and erect, throbbing above me in a way that sent dark tremors through me.

If what had happened before the swim had been spiritual and beautiful, what had happened afterward had been base and kinky...in the best possible way. What better feeling than to be chased, naked, by a powerful man who wants to throw you down and— *God!* It was the knowledge that he'd never hurt me, that he'd stop as soon as I said the word, that made it fun. He was so big, as he climbed down on top of me, so hugely powerful. Those broad shoulders, the heavy swell of his pecs. Intimidating, but in a good way. In a *makes-you-feel-weak-and-helpless* way.

His knees pushed mine apart. I bent them, so that the soles of my feet were flat on the ground, and opened myself to him. Bull planted his hands on my thighs and the feel of his touch there made me groan. Then he was moving forward, positioning himself. I felt the kiss of his naked cock against my lips, damp from the lake on the outside and slickly wet inside.

Both of us were still dripping. The sun was warm on our skin, but it was the heat inside that kept me from shivering. I felt charged up and ready in a way I'd never been before. Each time, with Bull, it had been about losing control, about my feelings for him taking over. For the first time, there were no arguments in my head. Even my fears about our future had retreated. Maybe it was because we were away from town or maybe it was something to do with my new-found body confidence but everything was *right. This* felt right, me and Bull together, with green grass and water. It reminded me of something....

And then all conscious thought ceased because he was driving slowly up into me, the blunt head of him spreading me, sliding on my wetness, slipping inside—

I groaned as he entered me, his size making me stretch in that delicious, bite-your-lip-it-feels-so-good way. He surged up inside me, groaning himself as he felt my tightness. I saw his toes dig into the soft ground as he pushed on, determined to fill me completely in one, long thrust. And at last he did, my back arching and my eyes going wide as his balls kissed up against my ass, his muscled thighs pressing my own legs wide.

He stayed there for a moment, not moving, and I reached up and gripped his shoulders, staring at him wordlessly. Something was happening, something I didn't fully understand. The feel of him there, so big and naked. *This,* the two of us outdoors under a massive sky with just a couple of horses tethered and not a modern trapping in sight. It could have been a hundred years ago, two hundred—

And then I realized what it reminded me of: my dream. A simple life in the old west.

With my husband.

Bull moved his hands up to my breasts and deftly stroked them, my skin wet under his fingers, my nipples achingly hard. Then he began to move, sliding from me and then thrusting into me again, filling me so fast and hard that my pleasure escaped as a high little cry.

He pushed his hands under my ass and lifted me a little, presenting me to him more fully. We both groaned as the angle changed. His hips rose and fell, his muscled ass powering him again and again into my wetness and heat.

My hands searched across his back, tracing every muscle, my fingertips digging in. I clutched him to me, wanting him harder, deeper, *more.* I started to toss my head against the grass, wet strands of hair sticking to my forehead. "*God,*" I moaned, relishing the hardness of his body, the sheer size of him. "*God!*"

His lips drew back from his teeth—almost a snarl. I remembered what he'd said, then—that he'd fuck me harder than I'd ever been fucked before, and the thought made the heat whirlpool down to my groin. His pace picked up again, his body brutally strong between my legs, his groin pounding mine. Every thrust sent bolts of silver pleasure rippling through my entire body.

I ran my hands down his body, just managing to reach his ass. So smooth, so hard, flexing and plunging. He growled as I fondled it. I could tell from the tension in his arms and shoulders that he was getting close, holding himself back until he was sure

I'd come first.

I suddenly gripped his arm. The orgasm was blasting up towards my brain now, seconds away. We were in the old west and I wasn't some lonely girl eking out a life making fake passports, I was a normal, happy woman and I'd found my man.

I wrapped my legs around Bull, my heels kicking at his ass—

His cock was so, so deep inside me, throbbing and hot and—

I lifted my head off the ground, eyes still squeezed shut. My whole upper body came up, my breasts pillowing against his chest. "H—Husband!" I blurted.

The orgasm arrived a micro-second before the horrifying realization of what I'd just said. My arms and legs clenched tight around him as the explosion went off in my mind. I tightened around his plunging cock, triggering a whole new wave of sensations. My head and shoulders fell back against the grass but my chest thrust up, back arching and breasts mashing against his pecs.

—*WHAT DID I JUST SAY?!*

My eyes flew open and I just had time to see Bull's expression. He was startled, for once, genuinely thrown. And then the feel of my body spasming around him took him over the edge and he groaned. He stared down at me and his eyes took on a look of such burning, all-out lust that my climax collapsed in on itself and exploded again like a dying star, blowing away all coherent thought.

He shoved his hips forward, burying himself, and I felt the long, hot streams of him.

And then I was collapsing back onto the grass, panting and sticky with sweat. And I wondered what the hell would come next.

FIFTY-SIX

Lily

HE ROLLED OFF OF ME, but caught me around the waist as he did it so that we were lying on our sides, facing each other. "*That* was unexpected," he said, when he got his breath back.

"What do you mean?" I said hopefully. *Maybe he didn't hear it.*

He looked me in the eye. *Yes he did.*

I jumped to my feet, my face scarlet, and started walking around the lake towards our clothes. I heard the rustle of grass as he got up and, after only a few steps, he grabbed my arm. "Hey!"

I turned to him.

"Talk to me, Lily!"

"What? It was just some stupid—" I sighed. He was doing his stern expression. "I had this dream, okay?"

He wrinkled his forehead. "Mary? *That's* where that came from?"

My jaw dropped. He remembered the fair! I dropped my eyes to the ground, cheeks flaring even hotter. Now he'd *really* mock me.

Strong hands cupped my cheeks, lifting my head so that I was looking at him.

"I'd marry you," he said.

I forgot how to breathe. I just stood there staring into his eyes for a second. But however hard I tried, however much I wanted to see it, I couldn't see even a trace of his usual teasing.

"People like us don't get married," I said hollowly. "Remember?"

My hand was swallowed up in his warm grip, the heat radiating up my arm. "But if we did," he said, "I'd marry you. And kids, someday. The whole damn shooting match."

I opened my mouth to speak once, twice—but couldn't find any words. Eventually, I just nodded quickly and pulled my hand away, then hurried off towards our clothes.

Before we were even halfway there, the Texas sun had blasted the remaining water from our bodies. But my cheeks still hadn't cooled to their usual color. I stumbled along, trying to process it all.

All that time out there on my own in the bus…I'd never needed anyone. Never *been able* to have anyone. Of course some vision of idyllic family life would gradually become a fantasy, bubbling away under the surface. That's what I told myself. That's all it was.

But I knew it was more than that. This hadn't started until I'd met Bull.

It wasn't about some need to get married. It wasn't that literal.

It was about sharing my life with someone. Finding someone I could finally open up to about everything:

what I did for a living, my deepest insecurities...even, one day, the horrors of my past.

I looked over my shoulder at Bull and he smiled at me. I whipped my head back to the front, wide-eyed and almost panting with fear and excitement.

For the first time in a very long time, I dared to hope.

***

When we'd dressed, Bull showed me how to build a campfire. Which involved an axe.

"Aren't I meant to just sit here?" I asked. "While you go off and be a lumberjack?"

He rested the hand axe on his shoulder. "I could," he said. "I can if you want. But then you'd never learn how to do it yourself."

It took me by surprise. I'd got it into my head that cowboys were, in some quaint and sort of understandable way, sexist. *Especially* ones like Bull, with his rodeo riding and arrogant attitude.

He must have caught my expression because he said, "I don't know what it's like in the big city. But Texas girls learn to shoot and ride and make fires just the same as the men. 'Least, they do if they've got a dad like mine."

"You've got a sister?"

He nodded. "Just the one." He grinned. "I guess that has something to do with it—my dad raised her just like the boys. What about you? Your family still in New York?"

Shit. Now it was more difficult to dodge the questions because he thought I didn't have any more secrets. I nodded quickly. "Yeah. I've, uh...sort of lost touch." Then, because that sounded suspicious, I added, "I miss them, actually. I wish I saw more of them but...you know how it is." *There.* That was good. I held out my hand. "Can I have a turn with the axe?"

We worked together, stopping only to watch the sun go down and turn the lake to gold, just as the name promised. Chopping the wood and building the fire was strangely therapeutic—very different to the painstaking work I normally did. And the payoff was huge. As night fell, we cuddled up in front of our very own crackling fire, the smell of wood smoke in our noses. I tried to remember the last time I'd seen actual flames and not the sterile glow of light bulbs and computer screens.

We ate chili and drank our way through the one luxury Bull had brought with us—a very good bottle of red wine. When the meal was over and we lay back on our bedrolls under the stars, my head slightly buzzing from the alcohol.

"I can see the stars, reflected in your eyes," said Bull.

He snuggled up beside me and I nestled my head into his shoulder. Underneath that huge Texas sky, I felt tiny. Insignificant. But not lonely.

Not anymore.

I pressed the whole side of my body against his, from head to toe. I was convinced I'd made the right decision, back in his pick up. Bull never needed to know about my past. Tomorrow, Calahan would go home. And then we'd be safe.

FIFTY-SEVEN

Antonio

I STALKED OUT OF LUCKY PETE'S, shoving the photo of Tessa back into my pocket. The guys there remembered her—she'd ridden the mechanical bull a little while ago, they said. And now she was fucking some cowboy *named* Bull. No one knew where she lived, but they knew all about him. He was some sort of rodeo rider, a local hero.

I fingered the gun I had stashed under my jacket. Part of me really hoped he'd get in the way. I'd enjoy seeing Tessa's face when I offed her boyfriend.

Christ, but it was hot. I ran a finger around my collar. I'd already taken my tie off and still it was unbearable. Who the fuck would want to live in a desert?

I tried the ranch first, but it was all closed up for the night. Then I tried Bull's trailer but there was no one home.

Well, fine. I knew they were here. I could wait it out.

I found a motel to stay in—the Stallion Inn,

cowboy-themed like every other thing in the fucking state. I grimaced. I was sick of cowboys already.

It was when I was getting a soda from the machine that I saw him going into his room. *Calahan.* One of the FBI pricks who'd been hounding Erico for years. *Shit!* No way was that a coincidence. Tessa must be talking to him.

I ducked back into the shadows so that he didn't see me. Then I hurried to my room, called Erico, and told him to send me some men.

FIFTY-EIGHT

Bull

LILY WAS STILL ASLEEP, but I'd gotten up early to make her breakfast. I had bacon sizzling on a skillet over the fire and coffee brewing in a metal jug.

The real reason I'd risen early, though, was because I couldn't sleep.

I couldn't lose her. I'd never felt this way about anyone. What if, when we got back to town, she ran again?

I was scared of saying the wrong thing and driving her away. I was scared of *not* saying anything and losing her because she didn't know how I felt.

I rubbed my hand over my face and went over to Caliope. I needed to practice this. And if I was going to practice on a horse, I figured it should be the female.

"Hey," I said softly. I glanced over at Lily, but she was still fast asleep. "You and I need to talk."

Caliope blinked at me expectantly.

"Look. I know I'm not much good at stuff like this." I scratched the back of my neck. My stomach felt like a nest of rattlesnakes. "But I gotta tell you how I feel."

Caliope gave a little snort. But I plowed on.

"Ever since I saw you, I wanted to bang the—I wanted to fuck you like—I *wanted you.* But I never said—" I swallowed. "I never said that I—"

FIFTY-NINE

Lily

Mmm, bacon.

I could smell coffee, too. I sleepily opened my eyes to see that Bull had gotten a campfire going. My heart swelled. He was cooking me breakfast! God, he was too much!

Then I heard him talking in a low voice. And not to me.

"But I never said—" he said to Caliope. He broke off and swallowed. "I never said that I—" He stopped again.

My forehead wrinkled. Either Caliope had been seeing him behind my back, *the hussy*, or—

Bull sighed. "Look, you came into my life—"

Oh God, I was right. He was rehearsing what he wanted to say to me!

"...and I just—I don't want to be with anyone else." He paused. Then his shoulders set as firmly as if he was about to wrestle a bronco. "Lily, what I'm trying to say is—"

I wanted to hear it so much. But I couldn't let him

say it.

"...I lo—"

SIXTY

Bull

AT THAT SECOND, there was an enormous yawn from Lily's direction. I snapped around so fast I got neck ache.

Lily was sitting up and stretching, her magnificent breasts rising under her tight t-shirt. "Good morning," she said between yawns. "Oh! You made breakfast!"

"Did you hear any of that?" I asked.

"Any of what?"

I studied her for a moment. She blinked back at me sleepily.

"Nothing." I could feel my face going red. "Coffee's ready. Let's eat."

***

The bacon was crispy, the potato hash was soft and fluffy, and the eggs had perfect, oozing yellow yolks. I'd even brewed the coffee just right. But my carefully-rehearsed speech was in tatters. She'd interrupted me right before I got to *I love you*. That had to be fate, right? Someone was trying to tell me this wasn't a good idea. Someone was trying to clue me in that Lily was going to run a mile if I said the L-word.

So we got ready to go home. We looked at the lake and both decided it was too cold for another swim. It shouldn't have been a big deal but, for some reason, it felt like one. As if I should be doing everything I could with her *now, today.*

As if this might be the last time I saw her.

Don't be stupid. We were heading back into town, not breaking up. Hell, she'd probably spend the night in my trailer, or maybe I'd actually stay in the bus for the first time ever. Nothing was going to change.

As the day drew on, the weather turned. A storm was rolling in—it wouldn't hit us for a while, I estimated, maybe not until tomorrow. But it was coming. We saddled up and did the long ride back almost in silence. Each time I looked at Lily, she was staring off into the distance, deep in thought. I knew better than to press her, but it worried me.

Goddamnit, what's happening to me? I'd always been a pretty simple guy. I'd never had to second-guess things before. If a girl got all mysterious and mopey on me, I'd just up and leave. But Lily? She had my damn heart in the palm of her hand.

When we'd stabled the horses, we walked back to her little Toyota. But instead of both of us getting in, she just stood there, hugging herself, shifting her weight nervously from foot to foot. "Um...look," she began. "I need some time."

My heart dropped right through my boots. "What?"

"It's okay," she said quickly. "Everything's going to be okay." And she smiled.

I stared at her, utterly confused. Was she breaking

up with me? She seemed to be in the weirdest mood, worried one minute, grinning the next. What the hell was going on?

"I just need some time to think," she said. "Can you give me that? Please? Just tonight. I'll call you tomorrow, I promise."

I could feel the frustration building up inside me. All the times she'd run away from me...and now, just when everything was going so well, she was doing it again. I opened my mouth to yell—

And stopped. She was looking up at me with huge, pleading eyes, begging me to give her one last chance.

With a superhuman effort, I reigned in my anger. "Okay," I said. "If that's really what you need. But I swear I don't know what's going on with you."

"I know." She suddenly hugged me tight and the feel of her against me made me forgive her everything. A week ago, it would have just been the press of her breasts that I couldn't get enough of. But now it was more than that. It was the feel of her warmth, the closeness of her—

Goddamn it, she'd turned me into a damn sissy.

She unwrapped herself from me and ran to her car.

Her little Toyota's engine coughed once before it started and then she was roaring away in a cloud of dust. "Tomorrow!" she yelled out of the window. "I'll call you first thing!"

"You better," I muttered under my breath.

Helena Newbury

SIXTY-ONE

Lily

I WAS ALMOST DANCING INSIDE, drunk on excitement. I had been ever since I'd heard Bull say it—or nearly say it. *He loves me!*

I couldn't let him say it. Not then. As soon as I'd realized what he was going to say, I'd known it in my heart.

I loved him, too.

But I couldn't let him say it. Not when I was lying to him about everything in my past—who I was, what I was scared of. It wasn't right.

I realized now that I'd been stalling all along. Now I had to make a decision. I owed him that. I had to end this thing now...or tell him everything and risk the consequences.

Back at the bus, I went down to the bathroom, ran a deep, hot bath, and slowly sank into it.

Bull was the best thing that had ever happened to me. He'd pursued me even when I'd pushed him away. He'd battled through even when I was *hard work,* as he'd put it. And the things he did to my body reduced me to a hot ball of goo every single time. He was exactly what I needed: solid as a rock, when my whole life was a paper-thin mess of lies and fakery.

He'd given so much of himself. Now it was time to give something back in return.

I lay back, submerging everything except my nose.

If I really wanted him, if I wanted this thing to be *real* the way he was real, I had to be totally honest with him.

I thought about it for a long time. And then, underwater, I gave a nervous smile.

I was going to tell him the truth.

I sat up and climbed out of the bath. The hell with tomorrow. Now that I'd made my decision, I was bursting with excitement. I'd get dressed, dry my hair, and call Bull. And, if he was in, I'd head over there and tell him right now.

SIXTY-TWO

Bull

BACK AT MY PLACE, I used the door frame of my trailer to lever the cap off a beer and then drank it sitting on the step. There was a pretty good sunset, but I couldn't appreciate it...because *she* wasn't with me.

What the hell's going on with her?

It was the first time I'd ever been in any sort of relationship crisis. Hell, it was the first time I'd ever been in a *relationship*. All that whining Kirsten and her friends did when I didn't call them started to make a little more sense.

A cold wind was getting up. That storm was still moving in—it'd be here by morning, maybe even before that. But I was too stubborn to get up and move inside.

Headlights suddenly swept across the side of my trailer and then hit me dead-on. I threw my arm up over my face as the sedan pulled up and a guy got out.

I stood up, still unable to see. "You want to kill the goddamn lights?" I growled.

The guy leaned through the window and flicked a switch. The lights died but I was still left with burning purple spots in my eyes. "You Bull?" he asked.

New York accent. Not so different to Lily's.

"Who's asking?"

He stepped forward. I hadn't even been inside my trailer to turn on the lights yet and the gathering clouds were blocking the moonlight, so I had to scrunch up my eyes to see. A big guy in a suit. Dark hair. "Antonio," he said. And stuck out his hand. "I'm out here looking for my cousin. I think you know her?"

I blinked. "Lily?"

For just a second, he hesitated, as if he didn't recognize the name. Then he smiled. "Yeah. That's right. Lily." He peered around me at the darkened trailer. "She in there?"

"No." My brain was still racing to catch up. "You're her cousin?"

"That's right. So, Lily found herself a cowboy, huh? You two...together?"

I straightened up. "Something like that."

"You know where I can find her?"

I hesitated. She *had* said she missed her family. And the guy looked kind of Italian-American, like her. But.... "I don't know you. How do I know you're her cousin?"

He gave me a look. "I've known that girl since she was a tiny little thing. I used to take her to fucking band practice. Hell, she's allergic to radishes. How about that?"

I relaxed. Okay, fine, he really did know her. "I'm glad you're here," I told him. "She's got some shit going on with the law."

His face tightened. "Oh really?"

I nodded. "There's an FBI guy hanging around. It's okay, though. She cut some sort of a deal with him."

He went white, then red. "Where can I find her?"

I hesitated. And then I told him where he could find her bus. I watched him drive away and then wandered inside to get another beer. *Damn. Should I have offered him one?* The guy was family, after all.

I was just opening the next beer when my phone rang. Lily. I snatched it up. "Hi!"

"Hi." She hesitated. "I need to talk to you."

I stood up straight, my breath catching in my chest. Every muscle in my body had gone tense. "Lily," I croaked. "Are you breaking up with me?"

"*No!* God, no! The opposite. I need to tell you some stuff. Stuff I should have told you a long time ago."

Relief sluiced through me. I sat down on my trailer's step. "Well, Jesus, girl, you had me going."

"No," she said. "It's okay. Everything's going to be okay now. Can I come over?"

My heart lifted. I let out a long breath. "Yes! Hell, yes!"

"Okay," Then she paused and I heard the puzzlement in her voice. "Wait—there's someone here. A car's pulling up."

I'd almost forgotten about him. "Relax," I told her. "It's your cousin. Antonio, from New York."

There was utter silence. Then an ear-splitting crash. I realized she'd dropped the phone.

Oh Jesus Christ—what have I done? "Lily?!"

Running footsteps. I could hear her panting in fear and my stomach twisted.

The sound of breaking glass. And then the line went dead.

SIXTY-THREE

Bull

MY PICKUP ISN'T THE FASTEST THING, but I know every back road and shortcut in town. I floored the gas the whole way, screeching around bends and nearly rolling the damn thing over twice.

When I skidded to a stop outside the bus, there was no sign of Antonio's sedan. Lily's Toyota was still there.

The door of the bus was open. *Fuck*.

I crept inside, fists ready. "Lily?"

The lights were on, but there was no sign of anyone. A cupboard had been torn off the wall and jagged chunks of plates and mugs covered the floor. A drawer was open, half of its contents scattered around. The whole place was eerily still.

Then I saw the blood. A whole spray of little red drops low down on the refrigerator door. *He'd got her down on the floor and....* In my mind, I saw his fist connect with her face and I wanted to throw up.

And then I saw the pool on the floor. Watery, but

too yellow to be water.

She'd peed herself. The bastard had scared her or hurt her so badly she'd peed herself.

I'd been angry plenty of times in my life. But the rage that took hold at that moment wasn't like anything I'd ever felt. All of the shit I'd gotten worked up about before just seemed so unimportant, now.

I tried dialing her phone but got the same unavailable signal I'd gotten the whole way over there. And then I saw the bits of broken plastic and circuitry on the floor. Someone had stamped it underfoot.

I stormed out of the bus and into my pick up...and then realized I had no idea where to go. They could be anywhere.

I sent him to her. I sent him right fucking to her.

Panic clawed at my mind. Should I go to the police? That would take hours of explanation. I didn't even know who the hell Antonio was or what he wanted.

There was only one person who might be able to help.

SIXTY-FOUR

Bull

AT THE STALLION INN, I marched right up to the desk and told the clerk to give me Agent Calahan's room number. He gave me a whole load of horseshit about privacy laws, so I picked him up by the shirt and pressed his back against the ceiling. He got a lot more cooperative after that.

I didn't mean to bust the lock on Calahan's door. I just twisted the handle and pushed and the damn thing broke in my hand. Shitty cheap motel locks.

Calahan was sitting on the bed, stripped to the waist. Damn city boy wasn't as big as me, but he was *ripped*. He looked like a damn underwear model. He dived for his holster when the door broke and, an instant later, I was staring down the barrel of a handgun.

Then he saw it was me and lowered the gun. I was a little offended.

"I'm not trying to take your girlfriend," Calahan growled. "Cute as she is. So if this is some jealous rage thing you can kiss—"

I stepped into the room. "Some guy took her. Antonio. Said he was her cousin, but—"

"*Took* her?!"

"He went over to her place and they had a fight and—there's blood. And she's gone. And so's his car."

"*Fuck!* I fucking knew it. I knew they'd find her." He grabbed his cell phone and started dialing.

"Who? Who is he?"

He gave me a disbelieving look. I shook my head firmly, my anger building. *Yeah, I'm really that dumb,* I thought. *Just tell me.*

His call connected so I had to wait again. *Agent Samuel Calahan, FBI,* he said, and then he spat out instructions to the local police in rapid-fire jargon. Then he did the same thing with the state police and the FBI. I gave him the best description of the car that I could.

When he finally put the phone down, I said, "*So?* Who is this guy? Who's got Lily?"

He looked at me tiredly. "Jesus. She really didn't tell you?"

The frustration was scalding hot inside me, now. I advanced on him. "*No!* So for the love of God will you *please* give me a straight fucking answer?"

Calahan gave a long sigh. "Your girlfriend's real name is Tessa. And she's the niece of Erico Fiorentini, a mob boss in New York. She ran away two years ago. That guy's taking her back to him."

My head spun as if I'd downed a whole bottle of whisky. *Tessa? This* is what she'd been hiding? "You're not here to arrest her?" I asked.

"*Arrest* her? I was here to try to get her to testify against her uncle." Calahan frowned. "What the hell would I be arresting her for?"

Shit. He had no idea about the passports. "Doesn't matter," I said. I grabbed his wrist and hauled him off the bed. "Come on. We gotta go."

"Go *where?* I want to find her as much as you do, but—"

"There's only one damn road to the highway. You got one of those red flashing lights on your car?"

***

We'd almost given up hope when we got a call from the state police. A motorcycle cop had pulled over a car matching my description just a few miles ahead. Calahan told him to wait.

When we pulled up behind them at the side of the road, I was out almost before the car had stopped moving. The rage was swelling inside me now like a slow-motion explosion, filling every muscle and making it hard and ready. As I strode towards the car, I was panting with it, snorting like a—

"Bull—" said Calahan behind me.

I ignored him.

Antonio was alone in the car. Wrenching open the driver's door, I hauled him out. He was a big guy but I was bigger and plenty angrier. I lifted him off his feet and slammed him down on the car's roof.

Calahan and the motorcycle cop grabbed me from behind, one on each shoulder. I shook them off like flies, got a fresh grip on the guy, and slammed him down on the roof again, so hard his teeth rattled.

"BULL!" yelled Calahan.

"Fuck off," I growled. The anger was throbbing through my veins, red hot and insidious. Anger at him for what he'd done to her. Anger at her for lying to me.

Anger at myself for sending him over to her place. *This is all my fault.*

I lifted the guy off the roof and drew back my fist.

There was a metallic click. When I glanced around, Calahan was pointing his gun at me. This time, he looked serious. "*Back off,*" he told me.

I backed off about an inch. "Where is she?" I growled at Antonio. "The trunk?" I glanced at Calahan. "Check the trunk."

Calahan lowered the gun a little and tried the trunk. "It's locked."

"*Open the damn trunk!*" I roared in the guy's face. I threw him towards the rear of the car.

He sprawled on the ground, rolled and staggered to his feet. "I want a lawyer," he panted.

I growled.

"You don't open that trunk in the next few seconds," Calahan told him, "that guy's going to tear you apart. And I'm not inclined to stop him."

I started to warm to Calahan a little.

Hands shaking, Antonio unlocked the trunk. Calahan shone a flashlight into the depths. My stomach knotted as I remembered the blood and piss at the bus. Was she tied up? Alive? *Dead?*

I stepped forward to look.

The trunk was empty.

SIXTY-FIVE

Lily

One hour earlier

I HAD A PLAN, OF COURSE. All neatly worked out and scientific. But when I saw Antonio walking towards the glass door of the bus, it fluttered right out of my brain. Suddenly, I was back in New York, watching him help to kill Annette.

I heard the phone hit the floor and realized it had slipped out of my numb fingers. Antonio was almost at the door, now, but I still couldn't move.

"*Lily?*"

Bull's voice saved me. I came back to life and slammed my hand against the *close* button just as Antonio hit the *open* button outside. The pneumatics hissed angrily as the door fought itself...but it stayed closed. I thumbed the switch to lock it.

Antonio glared at me through the glass.

I ran for the driver's seat. Plan A—get the whole bus the hell out of there. I went to fire up the engine—

And stopped. Antonio had parked his sedan right

in front of the bus. By accident or design, he'd blocked me in. There was a tree behind me, so I couldn't back up. *Shit!*

Plan B—escaping in my Toyota—was out, too. Even if I could make it out through an emergency exit, there was no way I could get to my car before Antonio caught me.

That left plan C: fight.

I heard the glass door crunch and then start to shatter. Antonio was using a tire iron on it. All he had to do was make a big enough hole to get his hand through and flip the lock....

I sprinted to my bed, stuck my hand under it, and pulled my gun from its holster.

I heard the door opening and then the crunch of breaking plastic. Antonio must have stepped on my phone.

I checked my gun was loaded.

Time seemed to slow down as I heard him climb the steps up from the door to the aisle. He took his time. Why the hell wouldn't he? He thought he knew me. He thought I was the same scared kid he'd known in New York, the one he'd ferried to swimming practice and to her high school prom.

I'd been dreading this day for two years, praying it would never happen. But that didn't mean I hadn't prepared for it. And I *was* scared. But I wasn't going to let Annette have died for nothing.

Antonio's voice was world-weary, like an adult telling off a child. "Now," he said as he stepped into the aisle. "We can do this the easy way or—"

I raised the gun, pointing it straight at him.

He stopped and we both stared at each other. His face had been so deeply burned into my memories, surfacing again and again in my nightmares, that it was a jolt to see it in reality.

"You're going to shoot me? Really?" he asked.

I couldn't speak. I nodded instead.

He took a tentative step towards me.

I raised my gun a little more, my hands shaking. "Don't," I warned.

"Don't what? Don't come any closer?" He took another step, more confident, now. "I gotta. Your uncle sent me all the way out here to bring you home." Another step. And this time he wasn't scared at all.

"I'll shoot you," I panted. I tried to stop the gun shaking but I couldn't. "I'll fucking shoot you." I centered the sights on the middle of his chest. My finger tightened on the trigger but it felt as if it was made out of lead, welded in place, and secured by girders.

I couldn't do it. I couldn't take his life as easily as he'd helped to take Annette's. And that failure screamed in my ears in her voice.

Antonio took a final step towards me and then knocked the gun aside. And then he drew his arm back and cracked his hand across my face as hard as he could.

My head whipped to the side and I stumbled, cracking my head on a cupboard and bouncing back the other way. Pain hit me from both sides at once, my cheek and lip exploding into white fire, my head throbbing so hard I wanted to throw up just to release the pressure. I slumped down to my knees.

"I've been waiting a long time to do that," said Antonio with great satisfaction.

I started to get to my feet, the whole room spinning.

Antonio put his expensive leather loafer on my shoulder and pushed, tumbling me backwards. I fell awkwardly against the bed and cried out in pain. Tears were in my eyes now, the pain in my head getting worse. The fight went out of me.

He reached down and grabbed my wrist in an iron grip. "C'mon," he said tiredly. "Let's get you in the car."

And he turned towards the front of the bus and started walking. My arm took up the slack and then I was being dragged on my knees and ass down the aisle. I grabbed with my other hand, trying to find something to hang onto, but only found the handle of my purse on the bed. It came along with me, bouncing along the floor as he dragged me.

The tears were flooding my eyes now. Worse than the pain in my head and lip was the knowledge that I'd failed. All those years building a business, building a *life*—and he'd taken it away from me in a handful of seconds.

I was utterly broken. *I'm going back to New York. I'm never going to see Bull again.*

Antonio was ignoring me, now, looking around at the bus. "What the fuck have you been doing here, anyway? Selling yourself to cowboys? Is this where you *entertain* them?"

That got to me, cutting deep even through all the other pain. He and my uncle—they still didn't even conceive of the notion that I could be strong, that I could do anything for myself.

"I tell you," said Antonio, "once we get this trial over with, your uncle's going to marry you off to the first eligible fuck he can find. Some guy who knows how to keep you in line." He shook his head. "The first time you say one wrong word to that guy, Tessa, *one wrong fucking word,* he'll beat the shit out of you. And I really hope I'm around when that day comes."

I saw my new life stretching out ahead of me, a twisted, mirror-world version of my idyllic fantasy. A life in the city, with air conditioning and limos, far away from nature, with a husband I hated.

And the fight that had abandoned me came back.

I hauled my purse up my body and shoved my hand inside. I found what I needed, but it was no good to me while he was holding my wrist.

We were moving through the kitchen area, now. Another few seconds and it would be too late.

I searched the bag, going by feel because I was blinded by tears. Lipstick. Tissues. Pen.

Pen.

I pulled as hard as I could on the hand that was holding me, opening my legs at the same time, and wedging my feet against each side of the aisle. We came to an abrupt stop.

Antonio turned to me and glared. "Cut that out! You're fucking heavy enough already!"

I lunged up and stabbed the pen as hard as I could into his wrist. It didn't break the skin but it was painful enough to make him cry out and then kick at me. But he didn't let go of my arm. *I need him to let go of my arm!*

I stabbed again and this time I got lucky and the pen actually drew blood. He kicked again, catching me in the shoulder, but I didn't stop. I stabbed at him a third time—

He let go of my arm and drew back his leg to kick me. His lips drew back into a smile—he had an excuse, now. He could tell my uncle he beat the hell out of me because I'd tried to escape.

I shoved my hand into my purse again. My fingers closed around smooth plastic and I pulled it out.

I hadn't been trying to escape; I'd just needed him to let go of my arm.

Both barbs of the Taser hit him square in the chest and the air crackled as 50,000 volts coursed along every nerve, like squirting a fire hose into a drinking straw. His back arched and he spasmed and danced. His suit pants darkened as his bladder let go. When the charge ran out, his legs turned to jelly and he started to fall.

"That's for Annette," I panted. "Motherfucker."

I stepped cautiously over his groaning body. When I was nearly past him, he grabbed my ankle.

"He'll find you," he croaked. He spat blood, leaving little splatters of it on the refrigerator—he must have bitten his lip while he was thrashing around. "I called him. Others are coming."

I drew back my leg and kicked him in the balls. He released my ankle and I ran down the aisle.

Outside, a rumble of thunder made me look up. It was dark—too dark. Clouds had pretty much blocked out the moon.

I looked at Antonio's car. I could go back, get the keys out of his pocket, and move it so the bus was free to move, but then what? By the time I was back in the bus, Antonio would probably be on his feet.

Plan B, then. I ran to my Toyota, checked my Go Bag was in the back seat, and started the engine.

It caught for a second and then died.

Oh no. Oh, God, please not now. I tried it again. It gave an asthmatic cough and died. A third time, and this time it didn't even turn over. *Shit!* Probably full of dust from all those trips up to the stables to see Bull.

I grabbed my bag and dived out of the car. From the bus, I heard Antonio moving about.

There was nothing else for it. I shouldered my bag and ran off into the night.

SIXTY-SIX

Lily

AT FIRST, I JUST RAN. I needed to get far enough away that I'd be out of sight when Antonio came out of the bus. Fortunately, the darkness gave me cover. I headed down the dried-up creek bed, just like in my nightmare. I didn't dare use a flashlight so I had to go by what I remembered of the terrain from my runs. Twice, I missed my footing and almost went flat on my face.

When I ran out of energy, I walked. After the first hour, I figured that Antonio wasn't coming after me—not alone, at least. He'd said others were on their way. I needed to get the hell out of town before they arrived. I followed the creek bed south for three straight hours.

And finally, when my legs gave out, I stopped. And, sitting with my back against a rock, I cried.

All of my fears, all of my paranoia—it had all been real. They'd found me, somehow, and everything I'd built had been lost.

Oh, not my work. I'd taken precautions with *that*. I

had enough money and fake identities in my Go Bag to get me out of the country. I had backups of my computer in the cloud—I could rebuild my business somewhere else. All of my careful planning had paid off, even if I'd had to resort to Plan C.

But Bull? The idyllic future I'd imagined? That was in tatters. I loved him and I was never going to get to be with him. Tonight had proven exactly what I'd feared. It seemed like Antonio had duped Bull into giving him my address. What would have happened if Bull had been staying with me in the bus, tonight, or had gotten wise to Antonio and tried to fight him? He'd probably be dead.

I loved him. That's exactly why I had to leave and never come back.

It wasn't that I thought he wouldn't go on the run with me. It was that I knew he would—he'd put himself in danger and I couldn't make that mistake again. Annette had already paid the price for my selfishness. I'd made my choice a long time ago—I couldn't face witness protection and a trial, not on my own. The only option was to be out on my own, where I could stay free without hurting anyone.

Free. Funny how it didn't feel very free, at the moment.

Mexico, I decided. I'd go to Mexico. I already had guaranteed customers there and the mob wouldn't dare invade cartel turf, even for me.

There was another roll of thunder and the rain started to fall, drops as big as silver dimes splatting into the dust all around me. I knew I needed to get a fire going. I picked up some dried-up twigs and started to try to build a campfire, like Bull had showed me. But too late, I realized I had no way to light it.

And I had changes of clothes, but nothing warm or waterproof. My Go Bag was meant for road trips and airports, not surviving out in the wild.

I didn't belong out here. I never had and never would.

I pulled out one of my burner phones and dialed Bull.

SIXTY-SEVEN

Bull

I WAS PACING the police station lobby. Calahan was in an interrogation room with Antonio, but he was refusing to talk until his lawyer got there and Calahan wouldn't let me soften him up with my fists.

My phone rang and I had it to my ear before the first ring had finished. "*Lily?*"

I heard her swallow. A pitiful little sob. "Bull?" she whispered.

I closed my eyes and felt my heart swell with relief. *She's alive!* I tried to keep my voice calm but it was thick and fractured with emotion. "Where are you?"

"I'm leaving," she said. "I'm okay. But I'm leaving. This is to tell you goodbye."

I gripped the phone so hard the casing creaked. "*No.*"

"Bull—"

"Lily—"

"No, *listen.* For once in your"—her voice cracked and she had to gasp for breath—"for once in your goddamn life, just *listen.*" She swallowed. "You're the best thing that ever happened to me. But I told you I couldn't be with anyone and I was right. I have to go away, where they can't find me again."

"I can stop them! I'm with the FBI guy—we can fix this!" I was panting with fear, now. I knew I was about to lose her forever. "I love you!"

"I love you, too," she whispered, and my heart felt like it was going to explode. "But this isn't some movie where you can ride in and save me."

I thumped the wall, leaving a dent in the plaster. "Let me try!"

"No. I made that mistake once." She was sobbing, now. "You know me, Bull. I'm not the schoolmarm who needs saving, remember? I'm the goddamn saloon girl. I'll be just fine on my own."

"No you won't," I growled.

"No I won't," she allowed. "Goodbye, Bull."

And she hung up. I called her back but she'd already turned the phone off.

Calahan stormed out into the lobby. "He's still not talking," he told me. Then he saw the phone in my hand. "Was that her? Where is she?"

I didn't answer him.

I didn't even know her—not really. Hell, I hadn't even known her real name until a few hours ago. She wanted to leave and she was begging me not to follow her.

But the idea of losing Lily scared me more than anything I'd ever known.

I had to get her back. *How?*

"Bull?" asked Calahan.

I've never been much of a thinker. My whole life has been about the physical: fucking, drinking, getting thrown around on a horse. But, ever since Lily came along, all that stuff felt less important. The way she made me feel...that was the only thing that mattered. So maybe it was time to start using my head.

Where would she go? *Think!*

It came to me instantly. *Mexico.* Close enough to run to but out of easy reach of the mob and the FBI. And out of reach of me. She'd hidden from the authorities for years. What chance would I have?

If she went to the nearest border crossing, maybe I could intercept her in time. But my pick up was still at Calahan's motel.

Calahan's sedan, though, was sitting right outside the police station. And it was plenty fast.

"Sorry," I muttered to Calahan.

He frowned. "About what?"

I slugged him right on the jaw. He went down hard on his ass. "Oh, you *motherfucker,"* he croaked.

I was already rifling through his pockets. I grabbed his car keys and ran for the door.

SIXTY-EIGHT

Lily

IT TOOK ME SEVERAL HOURS, two hitched rides, and God knows how many miles walking in the pouring rain to reach the border. By this point, I was so wet that there was no sense in trying to keep dry. I just trudged down the street with the rain soaking me to the bone, wondering if I'd ever feel warm again. The rain was really pounding, now, hitting the sidewalk and bouncing straight back up again to hit my legs. It was so heavy that it was difficult to see.

I knew that the best thing to do would be to get into Mexico and keep right on going, to put as much distance between myself and Gold Lake as I could. But the sun was coming up and I was so dog tired, I wasn't going to make it further than the first hotel on the Mexican side.

"I don't even care if it has roaches," I said to myself. "I just want a roof." I'd gotten so used to the drumming of cold rain on my scalp that it was difficult to remember life without it.

At this time in the morning, there was only a short line of cars waiting to cross into Mexico and the foot traffic entrance was completely clear. I could walk straight up to the border guards, show one of my fake passports and I'd be—

"Buenos fucking Dias," said a voice as low as thunder.

I spun around, squinting through the rain. Bull was leaning against a wall, as wet as I was. The water was spilling down off the rim of his hat in a thousand little waterfalls. His shirt was plastered to his skin.

He looked amazing. He looked so good, so welcome, that my chest ached. But I shook my head and backed towards the border.

He took a threatening step towards me. "Don't make me chase you, Lily," he growled. "You know what happens when I catch you."

I took one quick breath...and broke and ran, sprinting for the border post. Hot tears were prickling my eyes, mixing with the rain. If I could just get across, I could avoid all the pain. I could avoid saying goodbye. I could avoid—

A huge hand gripped the back of my blouse and lifted me a foot off the ground, then hauled me back. I gasped and kicked, spluttering against the rain. A second later, I was pushed up against the wall of an alley. The rain was lighter here, blocked by the alley's narrow walls, and I could see properly again. I gasped and panted and looked up into Bull's face.

"Now don't you fucking move," he told me.

I didn't fucking move.

"I got a few things to say," he growled.

I swallowed and nodded. I didn't have much choice. I was sandwiched between his massive, hard body and the rough brick wall. I looked up into those clear blue eyes and saw that they were full of anger...and something else that made my heart skip beats.

I waited...but he stayed silent.

"Give me a damn minute," he grunted. "I ain't fucking rehearsed it."

I nodded again.

"Okay," he said. "*Look.* I love you."

The way he said it made me suck in a little gasp of freezing air. I'd never heard anyone be so certain of anything my entire life.

"You should have told me who you were. But now that I know, I want to be there with you."

I shook my head. The tears were winding their way down my cheeks in silent, hot rivers. "I can't let you do that."

He slammed his hand into the wall beside my head. "Goddamn it, you selfish bitch! You don't get to decide that!"

I blinked at him. *Selfish?* That's what I'd been trying to avoid!

"You let me fall for you and then you decide *for me* I'm not allowed to be involved? I don't fucking think so!"

I shook my head. "Bull, we'd have no life. Look at how I was, before you found me. Living in fear. Looking over my shoulder. Too scared to have friends in case my uncle catches up to me. We both could have died tonight! It's no way to live."

He nodded. "You're right," he said. "That's why you've got to take Calahan's deal. Testify against that bastard."

My heart sank. It was exactly what I'd known he'd

say. "Bull, that would mean going into witness protection. I'd never see you again."

"You would if I went in with you."

It took me a few seconds to process what he'd said. When it finally clicked, I just stared at him in amazement.

He nodded.

It couldn't be true; I had to check. "You'd come with me?" I asked. "Bull, they'd move us away. They'd change our names. You have friends here and family. You'd never see them again—*ever*."

He looked into my eyes and nodded again.

"I...can't let you," I whispered. In some ways, it would be even worse than letting him put himself in danger. It was totally—

I squeaked as he lifted me off the ground, his warm hands around my waist. He pinned me to the wall again with my feet kicking in the air. "Where do you get this idea," he asked, "that you *let* me do anything?"

I stared down at him and slowly stopped kicking.

"I'm Bull," he told me. "And I do what I want. And what I want is to be with you so either accept me or shoot me 'cause I'm not going away."

I gaped down at him...and then flung my arms around him. It felt as if my whole soul was glowing, lit up by a blinding white light in my heart. We twisted all the way around until his back was against the wall, our soaking bodies pressed hard together. My lips searched for his and then found them, kissing the rain off them, and then our tongues were dancing together.

I ran my hands over his cheeks, feeling the rasp of his wet stubble. I was panting in the scent of him, snuggling my crotch against his—*God, I missed him so much!* Our kisses became open-mouthed and desperate as we ate each other up.

"I don't think I can walk anymore," I gasped when we stopped for air.

"It's okay. I have my car. Well, Calahan's car."

I put a hand on his chest, marveling at the valley of his pecs, the way my hand could nestle between them. "*Or,*" I said, feeling like a shameless slut, "we could stop in at a hotel. Just while I get my energy back."

He was panting too. His arms tightened around me. "A hotel?"

"Yep."

"Just while you get your energy back?"

"Exactly that."

I could feel his cock hardening against me through his jeans. "Good idea."

SIXTY-NINE

Lily

HE DIDN'T EVEN BOTHER to put me down. He walked with me still wrapped around him towards the nearest hotel. He didn't lower me to talk to the desk clerk or to sign the guest register. Nor even when we walked up two flights of stairs because the elevator was out.

Only when we got inside our room did he set me gently down on my feet. The room was tiny—made even smaller by Bull's huge size—and basic as hell, just a bed, a TV, and a bathroom. It was made for backpackers, not amorous couples. But it was safe and warm and dry and he was there, and that was all that mattered.

He pulled me into the bathroom, wrapped his arms around my soaking body from behind, and said, "Shower or tub?"

He was right—my body was numb with cold and even his big, warm form was chilled. "Tub," I said decisively. I twisted gently out of his grip and cranked the hot water on full, then dumped in the whole little bottle of bath foam. As the tub filled with steaming water and suds, I started to peel off my clothes, wincing as I pulled the cold, clinging fabric from my skin. Behind me, I heard Bull doing the same. But I didn't turn around to watch. I wanted to get the full effect.

Only when my panties hit the floor and I was completely naked did I turn around, shivering and wrapping my arms around myself for warmth. Bull was standing there, the top of his hat close to brushing the ceiling, his body damp and hard and perfect.

I glanced down at myself. It was the first time I'd been naked in front of him since the skinny dipping. And for the first time, I wasn't self-conscious. I didn't have to wonder if he liked my body. I *knew*. And, if I needed any confirmation, I saw his cock swell and steadily rise until the tip of it brushed my thigh. A deep, smoldering heat started to throb through me. I towed him over to the tub.

I was so cold that the water felt scalding on my toes. But I bravely stuck my whole foot in and then, wincing, I lowered in my ass and then the rest of me. As I hunkered down, the water closed over my shoulders, I groaned with relief, feeling the heat soak into me and my shivers start to die down.

I allowed myself a few seconds of shameless indulgence with my whole body immersed before I scooched forward and allowed Bull to climb in behind me. He would have stood there waiting for me all morning if I'd wanted him to, too tough to complain about the cold. But when he climbed in and warmed his chilled limbs, he gave the same groan of relief I had.

Bull wrapped his arms around me and slid my ass

back along the tub towards him, until my back was against his chest. He scooped up handfuls of water and used them to warm the parts of me that were out of the water, including my hair. Those huge palms smoothed over my chilled scalp again and again, until my brain was drunk on the feel of him, until I had to tear myself from his grip, twist around like an eel on his chest, and kiss him hard.

That started something. My wet breasts were against his pecs, nipples hardening against the firm muscle. My legs were between his powerful thighs and I could feel the hard length of his cock against my stomach. He chewed lightly on my lower lip and I groaned, my hands tracing the shape of his biceps.

He lifted me up his body a little. The shaft of his cock slid down my stomach, leaving a trail of fire in its wake. Then it slipped between my thighs.

He pushed me back *down* his body and I felt the silken head kiss the lips of my sex. I stiffened, looking up at him with huge eyes. "Not here," I said my voice tight with need. "On the bed."

He growled in frustration but then nodded. If we tried it in the bath, with Bull's size and strength, we'd likely break the tub. Or make it fall through the ceiling to land in the lobby.

We climbed out and almost ran to the bed. I hurled a few towels down just before we got there, because I'm practical that way. Then we were diving onto the bed, our wet bodies leaving damp imprints on the towels, me giggling and him panting with need as he rolled me over onto my back.

He buried his head in the side of my neck, nuzzling and kissing and tickling me there all at the same time and I descended into giggles again. Then it changed as he moved lower, his mouth following the shape of my breasts, his lips closing hard on my nipples until I arched and moaned under him.

He used his hands to squeeze my breasts together and pushed his face between them, licking the soft valley, his thumbs working over my hardened nipples. Then he worked his way lower: down over my stomach, down through the little curls of dark hair, down to—

I grasped the sheets with both hands, gathering them and twisting them as he kissed me there. He nudged my thighs apart and ran the very tip of his tongue along the dark line where my lips met. He went slow, my whole body became still as I focused entirely on his movements. I had to breathe in time with his licks, it was so intense. *I thought I'd never see him again!*

I closed my eyes and gave myself up to it. The heat of his breath on my moistened flesh. The touch and then press and then entry of his tongue. The way his lips brushed and then captured my super-sensitive clit. The size of him, hulking between my thighs, only made his gentleness more intense.

And then it became not gentle. As I started to writhe and thrash under him, he used his arms to lock me down to the bed, forcing me to accept the pleasure. His lips and tongue moved faster, working up to a rhythm I couldn't hope to fight. I threw back my head, eyes closed and mouth open, panting out my ecstasy as he fucked me with his mouth, stroking my throbbing bud again and again and—

I came, arching my back so hard that all my weight was on my shoulders and feet, my groin pressed hard against his mouth. Waves of pleasure rippled down me as I rocked against him. When my legs started to tremble and give way, he shoved his hands under my ass and held me there, licking and teasing me through a second peak and a third.

When I collapsed on the bed I was as weak and limp as a newborn foal. He brushed the hair from my damp forehead and smiled down at me. It was some seconds before I could get enough air into my lungs to kiss him. But when I did, it was sweet and wonderful, without any of the fear and tension that had been in the background before. We were going to be together forever. Nothing could part us, now.

It was only when I'd recovered that I became aware of the hot press of his cock against my inner thigh. A new throb of heat started up. I slowly opened my legs for him....

But he shook his head. "Turn over," he growled, a wicked look in his eye.

SEVENTY

Lily

I GAZED UP AT HIM. I wasn't entirely sure what he wanted, but all of the possibilities sent dark tendrils of heat twisting up to my brain.

I turned over. My breathing, which had been slowing down, started to speed up again.

He got between my legs, put his hands on my waist, and lifted me onto my hands and knees. His hands moved up to my shoulders and then ran all the way down my back to my ass, tracing its shape. I drew in a long, shuddering breath and squeezed my thighs together for a second, circling them unconsciously at the building heat within. I could feel his eyes watching my ass sway and move. "Now that's a beautiful sight," he said in a voice thick with lust.

I heard the bed creak as he leaned forward and planted a kiss in the center of each cheek. Then his hand wrapped around the crease of my thigh, his fingers brushing my clit, and the thumb of his other hand was stroking down the length of my lips. He worked me like that for long minutes, deftly but agonizingly slowly, as I got steadily hotter and hotter. My hips began to churn and buck as my pleasure rose and rose.

My breasts started to swing and bob beneath me. My ass was thrust right back towards him. I've never felt more aware of the shape of my body—or prouder of it. Because as he continued, he started to whisper in my ear.

"I am going to fuck you," he growled, the vibrations echoing out to every part of me. "I am going to fuck you until these beautiful breasts slap against my hands. I am going to fuck you until the gorgeous soft ass feels like it's getting a spanking. I am going to fuck you until you cry out my name and then carry on until you forget yours."

The heat was throbbing out from somewhere deep inside me now, as if the whole center of me was full of molten rock, lighting me up from the inside. I nodded weakly.

"But I'm not gonna do any of that..." he said.

Why not?! My addled brain was slow to catch on.

"...until you ask for it."

The heat took on a new dimension. I twisted my hips again, rocking back towards him, but his fingers and thumb didn't change their maddening pace. I nodded again.

"Not good enough." He removed his thumb and then I felt it—the warm, throbbing press of what could only be his cock, naked against me. He teased it against my lips, brushing up and down but not quite entering me. "Say it."

My face flared, but the heat only added to what was going on inside me. We were in a cheap border hotel and this felt right, somehow. He was behind me, huge and powerful, his knees spreading my thighs, and I was going to beg him to—

I swallowed. "F—Fuck me," I said.

His cock advanced a delicious few millimeters, then stopped. "How do you want it?" He leaned over me and planted a kiss on my shoulder, making me twist and gasp. "Soft and delicate?"

The blood was rushing in my ears. No. I didn't want it soft and delicate. I shook my head.

He leaned over me again and licked my back. I could feel his body pressing against the inside of my legs, against my ass, against my back. The muscled hugeness of him was mind-blowing.

He slid into me, filling me, and my lids fluttered closed again at how good it felt. He went slow but deep, until I felt the press of his hips against my ass and gasped at the hardness of him right up inside me.

His hands moved to my ass and he began to move—long, slow strokes, at first, getting me used to how deeply he could go in this position. There was no pain, just the glorious sensation of us being completely connected and the hot thrill of being so filled.

Then he started to speed up and the heat began to twist and thrash inside me like a living thing. I could see the two of us in my mind's eye—the tanned, muscled man kneeling on the bed, his body huge and hard, towering over the paler, softer woman before him. Taking her. Mounting her. The image lit a fuse in my brain, burning and sparking along a trail that led all the way down to my groin. Just as Bull sped up again, the pleasure exploded in my groin and I groaned, throwing my head back.

He started to really pound me, each hard thrust

making my hanging breasts sway. He put his hands under me, not cupping them but letting them slap lightly against his palms with each swing, releasing bursts of silver, sparking pleasure with each contact. He wrapped himself against me for a second, licking the back of my neck where my hair had slid away to reveal a sensitive spot. Then he knelt up again and took me even harder.

The silken stroke of him inside me, so big and powerful, was sending cascades of little explosions rippling through my body, chain reactions that were building towards something bigger and bigger. My arms couldn't support me any longer. I sank down onto my forearms and then my shoulders, turning my face to the side so that I could breathe.

That presented my ass to him even more completely and I groaned as he found a new, even better angle. His hips were slapping against me hard, now, brutally—just what I wanted. My ass began to throb deliciously from the slaps, the heat radiating out and adding to the pleasure.

His hands scooped underneath me and he palmed my breasts, his thumbs rubbing my nipples. Then he caught each one between thumb and forefinger and squeezed. "Bull," I gasped. "*Bull!*"

He kept going, just as he'd promised, his thrusts building to fever pitch. The pleasure was throbbing so hot inside that the bed and the room and the whole hotel seemed to melt away, until it was just us in the darkness of my closed lids, my body flexing and writhing and pushing lewdly back against my lover as he thrust into me again and again. I could feel him hot and hard, *naked* and the thought of it made the pleasure fold back on itself, twisting and growing—

I was Lily. I remembered that much. But Tessa, that girl who'd always filled my mind with fear and suspicion? I forgot her and let her go forever.

I cried out and pushed *back* just as he pressed *forward* and then we were both groaning, locked as tight together as two people can be. The pleasure contracted and then exploded, washing every other sensation away except for the hot rush of him inside me.

We rocked like that, grinding against each other as we rode out our climaxes, and then collapsed onto our sides with him spooning me from behind.

Both of us had been awake all night. I'd walked for miles and Bull had been frantically driving around with Calahan. I nestled back against his chest...and slept.

***

It was nearly noon when we woke, but there was just time to catch the hotel breakfast. Both of us ordered creaking platefuls of bacon, eggs and toast, washed down with orange juice and coffee. The food made me feel a hell of a lot better...but as we got ready to drive back to Gold Lake, the scale of what we were about to do began to sink in.

"We need to say our goodbyes," I said. "Once the FBI takes us off somewhere, there's no going back." I looked at him seriously over the rim of my coffee cup. "You know that, right? No going back *ever*."

"I know."

I heard the edge of panic in my voice. "It's easier for me, I don't have family. But you're going to have to—"

He put a hand on mine. "I know."

Our eyes met and my chest contracted with the enormity of it. God, he was willing to give up his whole life for me, even after knowing me such a short time. Even though I'd lied to him. My eyes teared up. "What did I—I don't know what I did to deserve someone—"

He put one huge hand on my cheek and wiped away the first tear with his thumb, catching it just as it started to fall. "I don't know what *I* did," he told me, "to deserve *you.*"

"What are you even going to do for work? We don't know where they'll send us! It could be...Detroit or Miami or Illinois." The panic was taking hold, now. *"There are no horses in Illinois!"*

"We'll figure something out," he said. And he said it so firmly I couldn't help but believe him.

"And what about me? I'll have to get a proper job. I've never had a proper job. I can't keep doing what I'm doing, with the government looking over my shoulder!"

Bull grinned. "I can see you in an office."

I gave him an incredulous look.

"In one of those skirts like they used to wear in the sixties, all tight on your ass. And a tight blouse with lots of buttons undone."

I kicked him under the table. His jokey, I-don't-take-anything-seriously attitude was infuriating...and exactly what I needed.

"And maybe we could get you some of them glasses with the little horns—the big black ones?" He made a noise that was halfway between *mmm* and a growl. "And you could put your hair up in a bun—"

I crossed my arms. "Oh, you've really thought

about this, haven't you?"

"And stockings and heels. Big heels. And you can introduce me to all the city folk you work with."

"And how am I going to explain a cowboy?"

"I won't be a cowboy, by then. I'll be something else."

"What?"

"I don't know. Something physical. Construction, maybe? A construction worker."

I imagined him in a hard hat and—what did construction workers wear? I couldn't picture the clothes, so I just imagined him stripped to the waist. *Mmm.* I took a deep breath, feeling a little calmer. "Thank you."

He stared right back at me and squeezed my hand. "You're welcome."

***

It was mid-afternoon by the time we arrived back at Gold Lake and pulled up outside Calahan's motel, *The Stallion Inn*. His car was plastered with road dust. "He's going to be pissed," muttered Bull as we got out.

On the other hand, getting me as a witness would be a coup for Calahan. If it meant my uncle went to jail, that was the sort of thing careers were made of. I figured he'd forgive the borrowing of his car. We strolled inside. There was a white horse in the field next to the parking lot—presumably, the stallion they'd named the place after. It ambled over as we passed by it. I stopped to let it nuzzle my palm. Funny, how I'd gotten to like horses.

When we got to Calahan's room, the door was ajar. That set off a warning bell in my mind, but my whole body was feeling warm and slack with happiness. I'd lost my edge.

Bull pushed the door wide and walked right in. I walked in behind him and almost collided with him when he suddenly stopped. It was at about that point that I wondered why the door was open, but by then it was far too late.

Calahan was in the corner of the room, tied to a chair with duct tape over his mouth. Three men were standing around him, pointing guns at us. I recognized all of them—my uncle's men.

"Hello, Tessa," said one of them.. "Time to go home."

SEVENTY-ONE

Lily

THEY WAVED BULL over to a chair that was back-to-back with Calahan's. When he resisted, they put a gun to his head.

"Please, Bull," I said, feeling sick. "Just do it."

"Yeah," said one of the guys, a young one with close-cropped dark hair. "Listen to her and you'll get out of this alive."

Bull looked as if he didn't believe that for a second and neither did I. But we didn't have any choice. He sat down and they tied him to the chair. He and Calahan had matching, murderous glares.

I was doing my best to stay strong, but I knew it was over. I was glad they'd tied Bull to a chair because he had no chance against three armed guys. They'd kill anyone who got in their way.

"You're fucking lucky you're the boss's niece," said the eldest, who seemed to be the leader. "Because if you weren't, we'd be beating the hell out of you for what you did to Antonio. As it is, I'll settle for you playing nice all the way back to New York. You got that straight? Now we're going to walk out of here and get in the car." He nodded towards the remaining man, who had a shock of blond curls. "And Georgio here will stay with these two and fucking execute them if you try and run. Got that?"

I didn't miss the look he exchanged with Georgio. Bull and Calahan were dead the second I was safely in the car. But there was nothing I could do except pray I was wrong. "Okay," I croaked. I eyed the door to the bathroom. "Can I, uh, *go* before we go?" *Maybe there's a window.* Or I still had my gun in my backpack. I could go in there and come out shooting and—

The eldest one snatched my backpack from me. "You think I'm fucking stupid? You can piss yourself for all I care. Get in the car."

The eldest one and the dark haired one started to hustle me out the door while the blond one strolled towards Bull and Calahan. I looked over my shoulder at Bull, my eyes filling with tears. I knew this was the last time I'd ever see him. He was sitting there stoically, staring right back at me, telling me silently that it was going to be okay.

And then the door closed and he was gone.

SEVENTY-TWO

Bull

THE BLOND-HAIRED ASSHOLE started screwing a silencer onto his gun as soon as the door was closed. I'd figured they were going to execute us both but I wasn't overjoyed to be proven right. "You damn idiot," I muttered to Calahan over my shoulder. "You just let them walk in here and take you? Where was your gun?"

"*Mmn mny arr,*" mumbled Calahan through the duct tape. He sounded pissed.

"What?"

The blond-haired asshole helpfully ripped the duct tape off Calahan's mouth.

"*In my car,*" Calahan snarled. "My gun was *in my car.*"

"Oh," I said, a little abashed.

"You two got any preference?" asked the asshole, cocking the gun.

"Him first," we both said at the same time.

The asshole shook his head tiredly. "You," he said to me, and used the silencer to knock my hat off my head. Then he pressed the end of the silencer into my forehead. I tried to think up a plan, but nothing came to mind.

The asshole's finger tightened on the trigger. *Think, Bull!*

But I've never been much of a thinker. So I decided to just be myself.

"Hey," I said. "You know why they *really* call me Bull?"

The asshole rolled his eyes and leaned in to listen. I lunged forward and head butted him as hard as I could. He crumpled to the floor.

"'Cause my mama said I got a head made of nothing but bone," I told his unconscious body. I started trying to get out of the ropes. Behind me, Calahan was doing the same. After a few seconds of straining, I lost my patience. *They're getting away!* "Don't you have a fucking FBI special-issue knife or something for shit like this?" I snarled.

"They're ropes, cowboy, aren't you meant to be good with ropes?"

I felt myself getting angrier...which was just what I needed. We both heaved and growled and finally yelled. Calahan's ropes snapped and he gave a shout of victory. A split-second later, my chair tore apart into chunks of wood, which quieted him down. We stood there panting and, for a second, grinning. Then we remembered ourselves.

"Pretty boy asshole," I spat as I pulled the remaining ropes off me.

"Dumb hick," he spat in return.

I grabbed my hat off the floor and shoved it on my head. "Call for backup," I told him and ran for the door.

Outside, I headed for Calahan's car. They were well ahead of me, but there was only one road they could take and—

Shit. They'd slashed the tires on Calahan's car, just to be sure.

I looked desperately around the parking lot, my chest tightening in fear. And then my eyes fell upon the field next door.

SEVENTY-THREE

Lily

THEY'D PUT ME IN THE BACK with the dark-haired one. The older one was driving. We had to go through the center of town to reach the highway and traffic was heavy so we'd slowed almost to a crawl. The driver slapped the wheel in frustration.

I stared out of the window at the town I'd never gotten to know. Just as I was finally starting to fit in. Just as I'd found someone. Was Bull even alive, or had they already killed him?

The guy driving pulled out his phone and dialed. I knew immediately who he was calling. "We got her," he told my uncle. He listened for a second. "He wants to talk to you."

He passed the phone back to the dark-haired guy, who passed it to me. I braced myself for a voice I hadn't heard in two years.

"Tessa," it said with honeyed venom.

I wasn't sure whether he was going to have me killed, when I got back to New York, or keep me imprisoned in the house and force me to testify in his defense. I wasn't sure which would be worse.

"Fuck you," I said instinctively. Tears were flooding my eyes. I threw the phone back at the dark-haired guy and stared out of the window. I didn't want them to see me crying. I stared at the street, at passing cars, at the driver-side mirror—

And saw something unbelievable.

Coming down the street behind us, riding between the lines of cars, was Bull on a white horse.

"You guys are in so much trouble," I told them.

They followed my gaze and then twisted around to look out of the rear window. The dark-haired guy pulled out his gun, glanced around at the hundreds of witnesses and nervously holstered it again. The driver honked his horn, but there was nowhere for the traffic in front of us to go.

"He's just one guy," the driver said. "He doesn't stand a chance."

"Yeah," I told them. "But he doesn't know that."

That was what was so great about Bull. Sure, he was arrogant and pushy, with an ego the size of Mars. But that meant he never let anything get in his way. He simply couldn't conceive of an obstacle big enough to stop him...and so nothing could.

And sometimes, that's exactly what you need.

The horse grew closer. Close enough that we could see the snarl on Bull's face.

The dark-haired guy bailed, grabbing my wrist and pulling me with him. Out of the car and across the street, into the first store we came to.

SEVENTY-FOUR

Bull

I SLID DOWN off the horse, gave it a pat and stalked into the store. *Betty's Fine China Emporium,* said the sign.

Inside, narrow aisles threaded between shelves. The shelves groaned under the weight of plates and teacups in a million different patterns.

I saw the dark-haired asshole halfway down an aisle, dragging a protesting Lily behind him.

I saw red.

I bellowed and charged down the aisle. The shelves shook under my footsteps, setting up a clattering vibration. The aisle narrowed and my shoulders were too wide for it.

Fortunately, the shelves weren't attached to the floor. I just smashed them out of the way, jolting and sometimes tipping them. Piles of china slid and crashed all around me, drowning out everything else. When the Mafia guy turned to glance over his shoulder, I had to settle for seeing his lips move. "*Shit,*" he mouthed.

He pulled his gun and fired once, twice. A teapot and a stack of side plates exploded. The third bullet grazed the top of my shoulder. And then he ran out of time.

I'd lowered my head to avoid the shots and wound up hitting him in the legs like I was sacking a quarterback. He slammed backwards into another shelf of crockery and the gun fell from his hand. He slumped, limp and groaning.

Suddenly, the store was very quiet aside from the occasional plate sliding off a pile and breaking. Outside, I heard sirens. Probably Calahan and the local police catching up with the driver.

Lily was standing with her back up against a shelf, panting. "You crazy fool," she told me. "You could have been killed!" Then, in her next breath, "Thank you."

I rubbed my head and figured that was probably the right time to kiss her, so I did.

EPILOGUE

Lily

WITH ANTONIO and the other thugs who'd come to Gold Lake in custody, Calahan allowed us a day to say our goodbyes.

Meeting your boyfriend's parents is always hard. Meeting them and telling them what *we* had to tell them...that was on a whole different level.

I cleaned myself up as best I could, put on a blouse and jeans that I prayed made me look respectable and we drove to Dallas: Bull, me and an FBI agent.

The house was a huge white mansion. The driveway alone must have been a mile long, with white fences the whole way and horses grazing in the fields on either side. By the time we pulled up, Bull's mom and dad were already waiting for us on the doorstep.

His mom was a petite little thing with a cloud of frizzy blonde hair that had been brought firmly under control with about a thousand pins. His dad was in his sixties—a towering man with a thick white mustache.

"Mom," said Bull. "Dad. This is Lily."

We'd decided I was going to keep the name, for now. *Tessa* felt like someone else.

His parents hugged me and told me how pleased they were to meet me. His mom bustled off to get drinks and his dad started to show me around and it was only when they saw our worried faces that things...stopped. We'd hoped to get them sitting down but in the end we blurted out most of our story standing in the hallway.

"No," said Bull's mom. "No. No, there must be some other way."

"There isn't," said Bull. "Even if Lily's uncle goes to jail, the rest of the mob will be looking for us. We have to disappear. New names. A new town. We don't even know where we'll be going."

His mom had tears in her eyes, now. *"No!"* she insisted. "Your sister's not home! Your brother's in North Dakota, of all places! They need to see you, they need to say goodbye!"

His dad stepped forward and put his arms around her, but she shook him off and grabbed Bull, pulling him into a tearful embrace. I made myself scarce.

Outside, I leaned against the fence, tears welling up in my eyes. How could I ask him to leave all this behind, and with zero notice? I'd never known a real family. I couldn't even conceive of how difficult it must be for Bull.

His dad quietly leaned against the fence next to me. We both stood staring at the horses.

"Hell of a thing," said Bull's dad. "*Hell* of a thing."

I nodded sadly.

"His brother can maybe get here," he said. "I just made the call. But his sister I can't get hold of. You can't even stay a day or two?"

I shook my head. "There are people who want to kill us," I told him. "They're *desperate* for this trial to fail. It's not just my uncle. If *he* goes down, there are other bosses who are worried he'll turn *them* in. Too many people have a stake in seeing him walk." I turned to him. "It's not too late, for Bull. If I go on from here on my own and he stays in Texas..."

"Is that what *he* wants to do?" asked Bull's dad.

"No, but—"

"Is this the *same Bull* we're talking about?"

We exchanged looks and, despite everything, we both smiled.

"All I know is," he said, "I saw the way he looked at you when he introduced you. My boy's no stranger to women, but I never saw him look at one the way he looks at you." He put his hand on my shoulder. "I'm sorry I won't get a chance to get to know you, Lily. But I'm glad you're with my son."

***

Bull's brother flew in that night—the benefits of having a private jet at your disposal. Bull hadn't been kidding about him being rich. He was very different to Bull, less hulking muscle, more of a lean panther. But he shared Bull's good looks. When he heard what was going on, he pulled Bull into a man hug that lasted for long minutes.

Bull's sister, though, we only managed to reach at the last minute and she couldn't be there until the next morning. We begged the FBI agent but his orders were clear. And we knew that by staying there, we could be putting the whole family at risk. When we drove away, Bull's mom tried to hold it together—but at the last minute she broke down and ran after the car, sobbing.

"Keep going," said Bull in a broken voice. It was the only time I'd ever seen him with tears in his eyes.

I knew we were doing the right thing. That didn't stop it feeling wrong.

***

We spent three months in a temporary home in Illinois (where, as I'd thought, there were no horses) while the pretrial work was completed. We had to stay out of sight so we went quietly stir crazy. I read a lot. Bull, who wasn't much for reading, probably would have lost it completely if it hadn't been for sex. Fortunately, with both of us at home all day, there was plenty of that.

We debated what to do with the bus. I hated the idea of it going to a junkyard, after all my hard work on it. But we couldn't take it with us—it was far too recognizable. Eventually, we donated it to charity and it wound up as a mobile, drop-in health center for the homeless.

***

On the first day of the trial, I held Bull's hand and waited for them to appear. I hadn't been able to eat breakfast that morning. I'd been fearing this day for so long...

Antonio appeared first, his jaw set and his whole body tense with brooding, vicious anger. His eyes searched the courtroom...and then found me.

I squeezed Bull's hand so hard that any other man

would have gasped in pain.

Then my uncle, looking as calm and refined as ever. *He doesn't believe he can lose,* I realized. As I watched him walk across the courtroom, every memory of my childhood came spinning back to me. I felt as if I was falling backwards through time.

And then he turned and saw me and his gaze pinned me to my seat. *You're still mine,* it said. *You still belong to this family.*

I dropped my eyes, overwhelmed. When I dared to look again, there was a look of victory in his eyes.

I grabbed Bull's hand in both of mine and felt his warmth and strength pump into me.

I looked back to my uncle...and this time, I met his gaze and held it.

***

There was a whole raft of charges to work through, from racketeering to drug trafficking, but the key to the trial was Annette's murder. Bull and I sat side-by-side in the courtroom day after day as the case unfolded.

We received death threats—some subtle, some hollered on the courtroom steps. Calahan and his team probably stopped many more of them before they reached us. Each time, I gripped Bull's hand and carried on.

When it was my turn in the witness stand, I recounted everything that had happened to Annette. When my uncle's stare got too much for me and I broke down and sobbed, I looked over to Bull for a moment and let those blue eyes fill me with their calm. And then I carried on.

I testified about all the things I'd seen and heard, growing up—contract killings and protection rackets, bribes to politicians and the police. I left the jury in absolutely no doubt as to the sort of man my uncle was.

I testified against Antonio, too, for his part in the killing and for his attempted kidnapping on the bus. At first, he glared contemptuously at me from his seat. As the hours passed, though, his expression started to falter. He was beginning to realize he'd underestimated me.

The trial stretched on for weeks. But when it came time for the jury to deliberate, they took less than a day. They found my uncle guilty on all charges and Antonio guilty of conspiracy to commit murder, attempted kidnapping and assault.

My uncle and Antonio both looked at me as the verdict was read out. And for the first time, it was them who looked scared. I let out a breath I hadn't realized I'd been holding...and then I felt Bull's strong arms around me, lifting me up out of my seat and pulling me close.

The trial was over...and our new life could begin.

***

We could pick any names we liked, as long as they weren't our own. I couldn't be Lily *or* Tessa, so I chose Mary. After teasing me with *Cletus* for a while, Bull chose Luke.

"Mary and Luke," I noted. "Very Old Testament."

Bull shrugged. "They're good names. *Honest* names."

We weren't given a choice as to our destination,

but I pleaded with the FBI for somewhere in the country. It was a huge relief when they told us we were going to Montana.

Within a few days, Bull's comment about honest names made sense: he enrolled with the sheriff's department as a trainee.

It took a while longer for me to figure out what to do with my life. I couldn't go back to faking passports and driver's licenses—it felt like that was tempting fate. I boxed all of that stuff up...but couldn't quite bring myself to throw it away. Those skills had helped me escape my uncle—without them, I'd never have met Bull.

So I stashed the boxes under our bed and told all my clients I was retiring. I pulled back from all the underground forums I was on and kept just one email address alive, for emergencies. Because, you know. You never know.

A month after we arrived in Montana, I went back to college...but nothing to do with computers, this time. I started training to be a teacher.

"You turned out to be a schoolmarm after all," said Bull, coming up behind me. I was standing on the porch, looking out over our land. We'd bought a cozy little place on the edge of town with a couple of acres of land. There were trees and a river and we were even talking about getting a couple of horses. It was simple. It was everything we needed.

"Don't forget, though," I said, turning around. "I'm a former saloon girl." And, after checking that no one was in sight, I hooked one shoulder strap of my summer dress off, then the other, and let the whole thing fall to the floor.

Underneath, I was wearing a scarlet bra and

panties set. Bull took a step back so that he could fully appreciate the view. He gave a long, low growl of approval. "Woman," he said, "I hope there ain't nothing you need to be doing for the next few hours."

I yelped in delight as he scooped me up into his arms and carried me towards the bedroom. It was exactly the reaction I'd been hoping for.

And if red underwear had that effect...well, wait until he found out that what I'd done just before we left Gold Lake for the final time. I'd contacted the photographer from the fair and bought the saloon girl outfit.

One Year Later

Bull

"Are you sure about this?" I asked. "We're taking a risk."

"If you try to control everything," said Lily wisely, "you won't have any fun."

I stared at my fake passport for the seventeenth time. *"Cletus?"* I asked. "You couldn't resist, huh?" I scratched at my stuck-on beard. "This itches like all hell." I ran a hand through my newly-blond hair. "And I think the bleach has done something to my scalp..."

"Quit complaining," said Lily. She tossed her long, auburn hair. "Do you see me complaining?"

I forgot my gripes and just stared at her. She did look *very, very good* as a redhead.

"You sure it's okay?" I asked. "I don't want to put them in danger. That rule about no contact—it's there for a reason."

"Most witnesses don't have access to *me*," she said. "They can't make whole new identities like I can. As long as we're discreet and it's only once a year and we use different identities each time...I think it's okay."

I nodded. "Okay," I said. "Let's do this." And I knocked on the door.

When my mom opened it a few seconds later, Christmas music spilled out around her. In the background, I could see my dad, brother and sister dressing the tree.

My mom stared blankly at the two strangers in her doorway. And then she took a second look.

Lily and I leaned our head together. "Surprise!"

Lily

"Wait, really?" I asked. Bull's mom kept ladling out more of the Christmas punch and I was already tipsy, but this revelation had me suddenly alert. "Bull's real name is *Bull?*"

She nodded at me happily. I don't think she'd stopped grinning since we walked through the door. She looked across at her son. "It just always seemed appropriate. Stubborn, strong and impossible to control."

I stood up, walked over to my cowboy, and slid my arm around his waist. Then I leaned in and laid my cheek against his chest. Bull reached down and stroked my hair. Behind me, out of sight of his folks, he slid his other hand down to my ass and gave it a squeeze through my jeans. I tilted my head up and gave him a *stop* look. Then a *don't stop* look. And then he kissed me.

Stubborn, strong and impossible to control. It was true.

And it was exactly the way I liked him.

<<<<>>>>

Thank you for reading! If you enjoyed this book, please leave a review :)

Get my newsletter and I'll let you know when a new book comes out, so you can grab the ebook at the launch price of 99c instead of paying full price. I'll also send you *Brothers,* a full length ebook novel and *Losing My Balance,* an ebook novella. Both are exclusive to my newsletter readers.

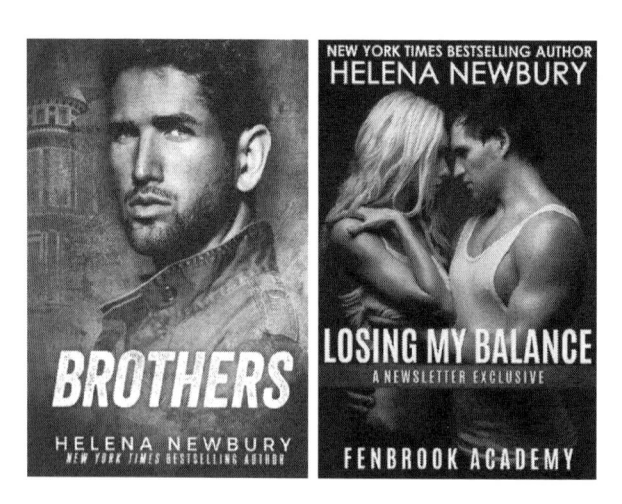

http://list.helenanewbury.com

CONTACT ME

If you have a question or just want to chat, you can find me at:

Email: helena@helenanewbury.com

Blog: http://helenanewbury.com

Twitter: http://twitter.com/HelenaAuthor

Facebook:
http://www.facebook.com/HelenaNewburyAuthor

Goodreads:
http://www.goodreads.com/helenanewburyauthor

Pinterest: http://pinterest.com/helenanewbury/

Amazon Author Page
http://www.amazon.com/author/helenanewbury

Printed in Great Britain
by Amazon